PRAISE FOR *THE LINE THAT HELD US*

"With *The Line That Held Us*, an outstanding Southern Gothic . . . Joy is on the verge of cementing himself as one of the finest purveyors of gritty literature in this country." —*LA Review of Books*

"Unflinching . . . Joy writes about rough-hewn men and women eking out a living in an economically depressed area, trying to avoid—but often affected by—violence and drugs that permeate the region. Their lives are tied to the land, its history and their families who established lives there decades ago." —Associated Press

"Straight up Southern gothic, and it is as horrifying and delicious as that label suggests. . . . Despite its brutality, *The Line That Held Us* is, at its core, about fraternal love and loyalty, and just how far a man is willing to go for his friend or brother. . . . Joy's story gains momentum and gallops to its gripping conclusion." —*Atlanta Journal-Constitution*

"Exquisitely written, heart-wrenching . . . Joy's descriptions are lyrical and lingering, his characters clinging to their humanity." —*Milwaukee Journal Sentinel*

"[A] raw, unpredictable inhale-it-in-one-sitting read . . . [Joy is] a gifted storyteller who raises plausible questions about love and circumstance." —*The Missourian*

"David Joy's novel brought me to my knees. Exquisitely written and heart-wrenching, it reminded me of Faulkner in its dark depiction of family loyalty—that 'old fierce pull of blood.' . . . Joy's descriptions are lyrical and lingering. . . . In the end, the line that holds Joy's characters may be fraught and frayed, but its pull is fierce." —Minneapolis *Star Tribune*

PRAISE FOR *THE WEIGHT OF THIS WORLD*

"Bleakly beautiful. . . . [A] gorgeously written but pitiless novel about a region blessed by nature but reduced to desolation and despair."   —Marilyn Stasio, *The New York Times Book Review*

"Darkly stunning Appalachian noir."   —*Huffington Post*

"Scenes unfold at a furious pace, yet contain such rich description that readers will do well to read slowly, savoring Joy's prose. . . . Joy's work perfectly aligns with the author's self-described 'Appalachian noir' genre, as a sticky film of desperation and tragedy cloaks everything his characters touch. April, Aiden and Thad are hopelessly conflicted, dripping with history and heartache, yet they cling to unique dreams about what life could look like if they carried a bit less weight of the world upon their shoulders."   —Associated Press

"Joy is a remarkably gifted storyteller. The life he fuels into his characters is so high-test that if they are not lying face down in a pool of blood by novel's end, they keep rambling through the mind. . . . How these characters deal with their demons gives redemption a new dimension."   —*The Charlotte Observer*

"Reeks of authenticity; this world is grisly and bleak. . . . [Joy] tells a hell of a story."   —*Shelf Awareness*

"Joy kicks the doors wide open with *The Weight of This World*, a rollicking, methamphetamine fueled drug-deal-gone-bad odyssey through the backwoods and back roads of Western North Carolina. It's that line between what is right under the eyes of God and what is rightfully your—perhaps—one and only chance for something more. . . . [Joy is] one of the bright flames of this next generation of southern noir novelists."   —*Smoky Mountain News*

"Appalachia provides the evocative setting for this tale of a brutal world filled with violence and drugs. . . . Lyrical prose, realistic dialogue, and a story that illuminates the humanity of each character make this a standout." —*Publishers Weekly* (starred review)

"Joy neither condescends to his characters nor excuses them but simply depicts them amid the crushing poverty and natural beauty of their environment. With prose as lyrical as it is hard-edged, he captures men still pining for childhood and stunned to find themselves as grownups with blood on their hands. Joy is one to watch— and read." —*Booklist*

"Readers of Southern grit lit will enjoy Joy's excellent sophomore outing, which is both dark and violent. Ron Rash aficionados will appreciate Joy's strong sense of place in his vivid depiction of rural Appalachia." —*Library Journal* (starred review)

"Not a single word is wasted in *The Weight of This World*, a dark and violent literary page-turner that burns with a white hot intensity rarely found in fiction today. A perfectly executed novel, this is a book that will endure." —Donald Ray Pollock

"David Joy's *The Weight of This World* is a tale of exquisite grit. A fearless writer, Joy is willing to go to all the dark places, but his voice and his heart serve as such strong beacons that we'll follow him and take our chances. Those chances pay off in a story that is as tense and harrowing as it is achingly tender. Don't miss this book." —Megan Abbott

PRAISE FOR *WHERE ALL LIGHT TENDS TO GO*

"[A] remarkable first novel . . . This isn't your ordinary coming-of-age novel, but with his bone-cutting insights into these men and the region that bred them, Joy makes it an extraordinarily intimate experience."　　　　　—Marilyn Stasio, *The New York Times Book Review*

"A savagely moving novel that will likely become an important addition to the great body of Southern literature."　　　—*Huffington Post*

"[An] accomplished debut . . . [A] beautiful, brutal book."
　　　　　　　　　　　　　　　　　—Minneapolis *Star Tribune*

"Bound to draw comparisons to Daniel Woodrell's *Winter's Bone* . . . [Joy's] moments of poetic cognizance are the stuff of fine fiction, lyrical sweets that will keep readers turning pages. . . . *Where All Light Tends to Go* is a book that discloses itself gradually, like a sunrise peeking over a distant mountain range. . . . If [Joy's next] novel is anything like his first, it'll be worth the wait."
　　　　　　　　　　　　　　　—*Atlanta Journal-Constitution*

"This beautiful brutal book begins with despair but ends in defiance."　　　　　　　　　　　—*Milwaukee Journal Sentinel*

"Joy's grim but satisfying story of the McNeely family faithfully echoes the language and atmosphere of this largely lawless mountain culture. . . . A story skillfully written."
　　　　　　　　　　　　　　—*Shelf Awareness* (starred review)

ALSO BY DAVID JOY

The Weight of This World

Where All Light Tends to Go

G. P. PUTNAM'S SONS

NEW YORK

THE LINE THAT HELD US

DAVID JOY

PUTNAM
— EST. 1838 —

G. P. PUTNAM'S SONS
Publishers Since 1838
An imprint of Penguin Random House LLC
penguinrandomhouse.com

Copyright © 2018 by David Joy

The Library of Congress has catalogued the G. P. Putnam's Sons hardcover edition as follows:

Names: Joy, David, author.
Title: The line that held us / David Joy.
Description: New York : G. P. Putnam's Sons, 2018
Identifiers: LCCN 2017033793 | ISBN 9780399574221 (hardcover) | ISBN 9780399574238 (epub)
Classification: LCC PS3610.O947 L56 2018 | DDC 813/.6—dc23
LC record available at https://lccn.loc.gov/2017033793
p.   cm.

First G. P. Putnam's Sons hardcover edition / August 2018
First G. P. Putnam's Sons trade paperback edition / July 2019
G. P. Putnam's Sons trade paperback ISBN: 9780425280287

Printed in the United States of America
1   3   5   7   9   10   8   6   4   2

BOOK DESIGN BY MEIGHAN CAVANAUGH

For my father, who walked the worn path

There is a pleasure, sure,
in being mad, which none but madmen know!

—JOHN DRYDEN

THE LINE THAT HELD US

ONE

DARL MOODY DIDN'T GIVE A WET SACK OF SHIT WHAT THE
state considered poaching. Way he figured, anybody who'd whittle
a rifle season down to two weeks and not allot for a single doe day
didn't care whether a man starved to death. Meat in the freezer was
meat that didn't have to be bought and paid for, and that came to
mean a lot when the work petered off each winter. So even though
it was almost two months early, he was going hunting.

The buck Darl'd seen crossing from the Buchanan farm into
Coon Coward's woods for the past two years had a rocking chair
on his head and a neck thick as a tree trunk. Coon wouldn't let a
man set foot on his land on account of the ginseng hidden there,
but Coon was out of town. The old man had gone to the flatland to
bury his sister and wouldn't be back for a week.

The cove was full of sign: rubs that stripped bark off cedars and
saplings, scrapes all over the ground where button bucks scratched

soil with something instinctual telling them to do so but lacking any rhyme or reason. A mature buck knew exactly what he was doing when he ripped at the ground like he was hoeing a line with his hooves, but the young ones ran around wild. They'd scrape all over the place, trying to add to a conversation they were too inexperienced to understand.

Darl locked his stand around a blackjack oak that grew twenty feet high before the first limbs sprung off. He climbed to a strong vantage and surveyed a saddle of land where early autumn cast patches of the mountains gold in afternoon light. An unseasonable cold snap following one of the driest summers the county had ever seen brought on fall a month ahead of schedule. It was the last week of September, but the ridgelines were already bare. Down in the valley, the trees were in full color with reds and oranges afire like embers, the acorns falling like raindrops. The nights were starting to frost and within a few weeks the first few breaths of winter would strip the mountains to their gray bones.

Darl sipped a pint of whiskey he had stashed in the cargo pocket of his camouflage pants, took off his ball cap and slicked the sweat from his forehead back through a widow's peak of thinning hair shaved close. He scratched at the thick beard on his chin and listened closely for any sign of movement, though just like the past two evenings, he'd yet to see or hear a thing but squirrels. Soon as the sun sank behind the western face, the woods dropped into shadow and it wouldn't be long for nightfall. Still, he would stay because there was no telling when that buck might show, and in full dark, he would find his way out by headlamp.

Somewhere up the hillside, a stick cracked beneath a footstep, and that sound came through his body like current. His heart raced and his palms grew sweaty, his eyes wide and white. Dried leaves rustled underfoot, and behind the scraggly limbs of a dead hemlock he could see a slight shift of movement, but from such distance and in such little light, what moved was impossible to discern. Through the riflescope, he spotted something on four legs, something gray-bodied and low to the ground. The 3-9x50mm CenterPoint was useless in low light, but it was all Darl could afford and so that was what he had.

Sighting the scope out as far as it would extend, he played the shot out in his mind. At two hundred yards, the animal filled a little less than a quarter of the sight picture. He rolled the bolt and pulled back only enough to check that a round was chambered, then locked the bolt back and thumbed away the safety.

A boar hog rooted around the hillside for a meal. Each year those pigs moved farther and farther north out of South Carolina, first coming up from Walhalla ten years back and now overrunning farms all across Jackson County. There was open season on hogs statewide due to the damage they caused. A father and son out of Caswell County were hunting private land between Brevard and Toxaway earlier that year when the son spooked a whole passel of hogs out of a laurel thicket, and the father drew down on a seven-hundred-pound boar. That was right over the ridgeline into Transylvania County. That pig weighed 580 pounds gutted, and they took home more than 150 pounds of sausage alone. Do the math on that at the grocery store.

All his life there'd been a thoughtlessness that came on before the kill. It was something hard to explain to anyone else, but that feeling was on him now as he braced the rifle against the trunk of the oak and tried to steady his aim, a mind whittled back to instinct. A tangle of brush obstructed his view, but he knew the Core-Lokt would tear through that just fine. He tried to get the picture to open by sliding his cheek along the buttstock, but the cheap scope offered little play. When the view was wide, he toyed with the power ring to get the picture as clear as possible, nothing ever coming fully into focus as he drew the crosshairs over the front shoulders. He centered on his pulse then. *Breathe slowly. Count the breaths. Squeeze between heartbeats. On five, pull the trigger.* The sight wavered as he counted down. *Three. Two. Squeeze.*

The rifle punched against his shoulder and the report hammered back in waves touching everything between here and there and returning in fragments as it bounced around the mountains. He checked downrange and the animal was felled.

"I got him," Darl said. His body tingled and his head was swimming. Adrenaline coursed through him and left him breathless. He was in disbelief. "I fucking got him."

Darl sucked down the last of the whiskey in one slug, slung his rifle over his shoulder, and climbed his way down with his treestand. In less than an hour, the light would be gone. He knew he had to hurry. There'd barely be enough time to field dress the pig and get it out of the woods before dark. Maybe Calvin Hooper would help him dress out the hog. Cal had a nice hoist for dressing deer, and that sure beat the hell out of the makeshift gambreling stick Darl had at the house. Whether you were scraping hair or skinning him out, a pig was a whole lot easier with two sets of hands working than one. Cal wouldn't want anything for the trouble. Never had. As soon as Darl got that pig back to the truck, he'd head to Calvin's. "I fucking got him," he said.

A small branch of water ran at the bottom of the draw, and through a thicket of laurel, the hillside steepened. Darl staggered through the copse of trees and slowly climbed until he was near the ledge where the pig had fallen. He tripped on a fishing line strung between two dogwoods, a pair of tin cans with rocks inside clanking loud in the limbs above him. Darl froze and looked around. As his eyes focused, he saw rusted fishhooks hung eye level from the trees, trotlines meant for poachers, and he brushed them back one by one as if he were clawing his way through spiderwebs. That's when he saw him. Not a pig but a man, flat on his stomach. A brush-patterned shirt was darkened almost black with blood, his pants the same grayish camouflage as his shirt.

Darl stepped closer, knelt by the man's legs, and placed his hand on the man's left calf. His body was warm, but there was no movement, no sound of breath. In absolute shock, Darl crawled forward and saw where the bullet had entered the man's rib cage. He'd been quartered away, the lead core mushrooming as it cut through him and exited behind his right shoulder, blowing the top of his arm ragged. The man's left arm hung by his side, his hand open, palm up, and Darl could see a few shriveled red berries balanced at the tip of his fingers. He realized then that he was kneeling in a thick patch of ginseng, mostly young, two-prong plants, but some much, much older. The man had an open book bag on the ground beside him with a tangle of thick, banded roots stuffed inside, the thin runners off the main ginseng shoots snarled like a muss of hair.

Darl knew the man shouldn't have been there the same as him. This was Coward land, and they were both trespassing; two poachers who shouldn't have been there, but right there they were. There they were, one of them gone from this world, and the other facing it in its enormity. While he crouched there on hands and knees, dumbstruck as a child, his mind washed between astonishment and terror.

The man's face was turned and angled into the ground. His neck was sunburned red and dotted with dark orange freckles, the back of his hair thick and curled, a yellow blond the color of hay. Darl stepped across the body, being careful not to get his boots in the blood around him. The man wore a camouflage hat with hunter orange lining the edge of the bill, the words CANEY FORK GENERAL STORE stitched across the front. The hat was knocked crooked on his head and Darl grabbed the bill to try and turn the man's face out of the dirt.

As soon as he saw the dark purple birthmark covering the right side of the man's face, Darl knew him. Carol Brewer, who everyone called Sissy, lay stone-cold dead on the bracken-laced ground. Darl had known Carol all his miserable life, a half-wit born to a family that Jesus Christ couldn't have saved. Some people believed Carol's daddy, Red, might've been the devil himself. There was a meanness that coursed through him, a meanness that was as close to pure evil as any God-fearing man had ever known. Carol was the runt of the family and, by most accounts, the only one who ever had a chance. Some thought if he'd been able to get out from under the wings of his father and older brother, Dwayne, he might've been all right, but things didn't work out that way, and Carol wound up being as much trouble as the lot of them.

Darl let go of the cap bill and Carol's head came to rest on the ground. His eyes were closed with his mouth slightly opened. A yellow jacket buzzed by Darl's ear and landed on Carol's lips. The wasp started to crawl into his mouth but Darl swatted the bug away, his fingers brushing Carol's face. He stomped the bee where it hovered above the ground, then looked to the west to gauge what light remained. Darl knew it wouldn't be long, though nightfall didn't matter like it had minutes before. His thoughts were wild with what would come, but he knew the darkness was a gift now and he welcomed it. His mind raced as the night slowly closed around him like cupped hands. He had until dawn to dig a grave.

TWO

DWAYNE BREWER GOOSE-STEPPED DOWN THE BEER AISLE
of the Franklin Walmart wearing a latex chimp mask he'd found
on the floor by the Halloween decorations. The mask was hot and
his breathing was loud. The inside smelled of cheap molded rubber
and he slicked the nylon hair back through his fingers while he
chuckled at a woman who sneered.

She wore pastel-colored scrubs and white tennis shoes, her highlighted hair pulled back in a ponytail. Through the eye slits of the
mask, he saw a little girl, maybe six years old, with one of her fingers hooked in the corner of her mouth, standing beside the woman.
Dwayne scratched under his armpit with one hand and clawed at
the back of his head with the other, hopping around bowlegged like
a monkey, and the child laughed. He pulled the mask off and tossed
it into the open cooler, his skin cold with sweat as he ran his hand

over his face and reached for a case of Bud heavy. Tearing a ragged hole in the cardboard, he fished out a beer and cracked the top.

"Have a blessed day," he said with a wide smile, tilting the open can toward the woman and nodding. She eyed him like the fiend he was, her little girl hiding behind her leg, spellbound with curiosity as the giant man before her swallowed half the can in one tremendous gulp.

The thing about Walmart was that even a man like Dwayne Brewer could go unnoticed. People pushed their buggies with dead-eyed stares, everything sliding by in the periphery. Consumerism scaled this large had a way of camouflaging class.

At the end of the aisle, he squeezed past a beefy gal in tiny shorts who had a baby on each hip and three children running circles around her. One of the kids reached out as he made his next lap and knocked an endcap of Cool Ranch Doritos onto the floor. The woman was in the middle of a conversation with someone she knew, an older woman who had a toddler with her finger up her nose riding in the buggy. The beefy gal kept saying over and over, "Lord no this ain't mine," shaking the child on her left hip, "Me and Clyde stopped after this one," shaking the one on her right, "This here's Sara's. You remember Sara, don't you? This is Sara's little girl, Tammy. She's my niece."

Buggies were banging and lights were flashing and cash registers were beeping and kids were wrestling a Halloween blow-up ghost decoration that was meant to stand in a front yard and the sheer madness of it was enough to send any sane person into a seizure, but Dwayne didn't have a care in this world. He strutted right through the middle of the chaos, smiling because it was Friday and he had a wad of cash in his pocket from pawning five stolen chainsaws and a flat-screen TV.

Black teddies and bloodred lingerie were rolled back to $9.87. He finished that first beer standing by the floor rack running satin through his fingers with his eyes closed, daydreaming about the last woman he'd slept with. When he was finished, he crumpled the can in his fist, balanced it in the cup of a beige-colored bra, and opened another.

From where he stood, he could see straight down the shoe aisle where a kid sat on a bench. The boy reminded Dwayne of his brother. Shaggy, strawberry-blond hair covered his ears, and his red skin was dotted with freckles. Aside from a thick pair of Coke-bottle glasses, black military frames, he could've been a spitting image of Sissy at thirteen or fourteen years old. The kid wore a shabby shirt and grass-stained jeans that were muddied at the knees. He was trying on a pair of gray-colored tennis shoes, some off-brand jobs with Velcro straps. Out of nowhere two boys came around the corner and loomed over him. A boy in tight jeans, with hair that sliced at an angle across his eyes, snatched one of the shoes out of the boy's hands, looked it over, shook his head, and crowed.

At that distance, Dwayne couldn't hear what was said, but he understood. He could read it on that poor boy's beaten face. He'd heard it all his life, about the house he grew up in and the car his daddy drove, that his shoes weren't any good and neither were his clothes. He heard it about his drunk grandfather who stood on the bridge in town and cussed at the river when he was old and lost his mind. He heard it about having a funny haircut and for smelling musty after gym class, heard it for getting free lunches, heard it because someone saw him standing outside the laundromat, heard it because his mama worked the register at Roses. He'd heard that word *trash* all his life and, over the course of thirty-six years, he'd heard about enough.

There were two ways to cope, but Dwayne had only ever known the one. He'd haul off and open a boy's head to the white meat in the blink of an eye and that'd be that. *They don't talk so much with blood in their mouth,* he thought, and it was true. But he'd seen the other way of coping in his brother, the way bitterness and anger, sadness and sorrow meld into a vacant stoicism.

Bury it inside. Keep your eyes forward.

The boy stared straight ahead, expressionless and empty.

The kid with tight jeans jerked his head to the side to flip his hair out of his eyes. He fit his hand inside the shoe and pressed the sole against the boy's face. The boy didn't move or say a word. He kept his eyes on the boxes of shoes in front of him while the other boys taunted him. The longhaired boy shoved him hard in the side of the head then and Dwayne's blood rose up into his eyes. He could feel his fists clenching tight and he took a long slug of cool Budweiser to try and ease that feeling. The bully hesitated for a second, testing the water. When he saw the kid wasn't going to react, he shoved him again, harder this time, so that he fell onto the floor. They stood there chuckling and the kid climbed back onto the bench and gazed straight ahead until they walked away with wide-set smiles, their eyes aglow with arrogance and pride.

Dwayne watched the boy on the bench for a long time. The boy didn't cry. He didn't lash out in anger. He went right back to what he was doing, trying on a pair of kicks, like nothing had happened at all. Dwayne wanted to go over to him and tell him that things didn't have to be that way, tell him he needed to stand up for himself and bash that little motherfucker's head in next time, that then they'd learn, but he didn't. He wandered on back toward the sporting goods, hoping they might have a brick or two of Winchester white box.

He finished his third beer at self-checkout while the attendant verified his ID and plugged his birth date into the computer. At first she seemed like she wanted to say something about him drinking in the store, but in the end she shook her head and stamped away because it's hard to give a shit for $7.25 an hour. He fed a twenty-dollar bill into the machine and waited for it to spit out his change.

There was a commotion by the entrance, and when Dwayne looked up he saw those same two boys strutting along, the one with long hair hobbling pigeon-toed with his hand limp at his chest, making a face like he had some sort of mental defect. Dwayne looked behind him and that's when he saw the woman the boy was mocking, a handicapped greeter with a bowl cut and tinted glasses staring on like she was witnessing a miracle. The longhaired boy tossed a set of keys to his buddy and turned into the bathroom as his buddy headed for the far exit.

Dwayne set the suitcase of beer by the opened men's room and stuck his head inside long enough to make sure the kid was alone. The boy was facing the ceiling with his eyes closed at the urinal, and Dwayne knelt down to make sure there weren't any feet in the stalls. There was no one in the bathroom but the two of them. A CLEANING IN PROGRESS sign was stashed behind the door and Dwayne barred it across the jamb to stop anyone from interrupting. He walked inside and stood directly behind him, the boy not having a clue he was there until he turned.

Dwayne Brewer was a giant of a man, six-foot-five and two hundred sixty if he weighed an ounce. When the boy turned around, there he stood, and the boy jumped back like he'd walked onto a snake. "Shit, mister, you scared the hell out of me."

Dwayne didn't say anything. He stood there for a moment, silently studying him.

The boy had on a black T-shirt that read YOUNG & RECKLESS. A pair of mint-green jeans painted his legs. He had long hair that cut down his face and he kept flipping it out of his eyes like some sort of nervous tick.

"How old are you, boy?"

He looked at Dwayne funny. "Sixteen," he said.

Dwayne scrubbed at the back of his head with his knuckles, squinted his eyes like he was weighing a tremendous decision. "That's old enough," he said. He pulled a 1911 pistol from the back of his waistline and aimed it square at the boy's forehead.

The boy's face immediately fell and his arms came up instinctively, hands raised as if by strings.

"You scream and I'll blow your little pea-headed brains out. You understand?"

The boy's mouth sagged open and he nodded.

"What's your name?"

"Brett," he said.

"Brett what?"

"Starkey."

"Starkey? I don't believe I know anybody named Starkey."

"I live up Clarks Chapel."

"Where up Clarks Chapel?"

"Sunset Mountain Estates."

"Your family from around here?"

"What?"

"I said is your family from around here?"

"My mom and dad are from Saint Pete."

Dwayne pinched the bridge of his nose between his fingers and closed his eyes for a second, then nodded his head. He looked down at the boy's clean pair of high-tops. He wore the shoes loosely with the laces untied and stuffed inside, the tongues pulled over the bottoms of his jeans. "How much them shoes cost?"

"I don't know," he said.

"What do you mean you don't know?"

"I mean, I don't, I don't know," the boy stuttered. He had one of those faces that turned beet red when he was about to cry. His eyes were almost crossed as he stared down the gun.

"You mean you don't know because you don't remember, or you don't know because your mama and daddy paid for them?"

The boy gaped dumb and speechless.

"Which is it?"

"My mom bought them."

Dwayne grunted and nodded his head. "Well, I'm going to need you to go ahead and take them shoes off."

The boy didn't move.

"This is the last time I'm going to say it, boy. Take them shoes off your feet."

Toe to heel, the boy slid his shoes off and stood on the wet floor in bleach-white socks.

"Now, pick them up," Dwayne said.

The boy did as he was told.

Dwayne nodded toward the beige metal partition sectioning off the stalls. "I want you to go over there to that first stall and open the door."

The boy walked over and pushed the door open with his elbow.

Dwayne followed and stood with his back against the tile wall by the sinks, the gun still raised and steady. He peered around the boy and saw what he expected: a commode backed up with toilet paper and tinged water. "Go ahead and put your shoes on in there."

The boy looked at him in disbelief. Tears glassed his eyes. He hovered over the commode and set his shoes down gently.

"Don't just float them on top. I want you to put them down in there."

The boy pushed them slightly so that water lapped at the soles.

"I said push them down in there!" Dwayne growled through clenched teeth. He lurched forward until the gun was less than a foot from the boy's face, and the boy dunked his shoes underwater, his arms wet above his wrists.

He cried hard now. His cheeks were slicked with tears and his breath sputtered from his lips.

"Don't go getting soft now," Dwayne said. "You were a tough guy a few minutes ago with that boy, wasn't you? I saw how you were shoving him around. You was tough with him, so be tough now."

The boy's eyes were squeezed shut and he looked like he was going to be sick. He had his head turned away from the toilet and his face shone like a moon lit by the yellow light above the stall.

"That's good," Dwayne said. "Now put them on."

"What?"

"I said put them on."

Setting his shoes on the floor, he slid his feet inside like he was putting on a pair of bed slippers. A puddle widened around him and his feet squished inside.

"Go on and tie them now," Dwayne said. "We wouldn't want them falling off your feet, or you tripping over the laces. That's no way to walk."

Again, the boy did exactly as he was told. Dwayne found himself thinking that the kid might've been all right if it had been a gun to his head every second of his life. The boy hovered there like he was trying not to put all his weight down. He looked like it was the first time in his life he'd ever been put in his place, and that made Dwayne proud. *Everyone needs to be broken,* he thought. Empathy's not standing over a hole looking down and saying you understand. Empathy is having been in that hole yourself.

"I want you to remember this," Dwayne said. "All your life, I want you to remember this day. What could've been and what was."

The boy stared at him, confused.

"The two of us, we crossed paths for a reason. It was fate that brought me here. You understand?" He tucked his pistol in his waistband at the small of his back and flipped his white T-shirt over the grip to conceal what he carried. Checking himself in the mirror, he strolled toward the door and took down the sign, heading out the way he'd come and picking up his beer as he passed. Outside, things were the same as they were a few minutes before, but inside, inside felt different.

One man could not even the hands of Justice, but he could tip the scales for a moment, pin down the privileged at least long enough to smile. The sun was going down and Sissy had said he'd be home by seven.

Dwayne couldn't wait to tell his brother the story.

THREE

TEMPERATURES WERE DROPPING AS FALL CAME ON, AND by the middle of next week the weatherman expected the mountains would see heavy frosts. Calvin Hooper thought it was about damn time. He hated summer as much as anybody with half a brain who worked outside for a living. The den where he sat flashed bright as the nightly newscast cut to commercial, only the television for light, and Calvin reached for what was left of a Jack and ice, the whiskey watered down but cold.

He swirled his drink around the bottom of a faceted jelly jar, threw what was left down the back of his throat, and walked into the kitchen to pour another. It was almost midnight, but he wasn't tired. Truth was, he never slept worth a shit anymore. About ten o'clock every night he reached a point where he was more awake than any other time of the day. If he lay down when his girlfriend,

Angie, went to bed, he'd toss and turn four or five hours before he finally dozed off. Most nights his feet would get to killing him and he'd have to get up and take a couple Advil to find any rest at all. His mama told him to rub witch hazel on his legs and believe it or not that helped, but when his feet quit hurting his brain ran wide open and either way he didn't sleep a wink.

The little light in the freezer shone white against his bare chest while he filled the jar to the brim with ice. The whiskey bottle sat nearly full on a Formica countertop and he poured himself another drink in the half-light offered from the other room. When he'd capped the bottle, he rattled his glass, the ice tinkling against the sides. Aside from tying one on maybe once a month, he never drank to get drunk. Most nights he didn't even catch a good buzz. The two glasses he drank those last two hours of a night brought a dreamless sleep so that he could catch enough shut-eye to get up and do it again.

The phone rang in the living room and Calvin walked back toward the couch with one hand down his sweatpants, the other holding his drink against the center of his chest. No one ever called this late. The cell phone lay faceup on the side table by the couch and he glanced down to check the caller ID. The screen read DARL, and Calvin considered letting it go to voicemail, figuring Darl was probably drunk and would talk his ear off about God knows what with Calvin having to be up at six to work another Saturday. In the end, guilt got the better of him. Darl was Calvin's best friend, always had been, so the thought that he might actually need something outweighed anything else.

Calvin pulled the power cord from the cell phone so as not to be tethered to the wall when he answered. "Hello."

"You asleep?" Darl asked. There was something strange in his voice, his breath heavy in the phone as if he was winded.

"I'm sitting here watching the news." Calvin sat down on the couch and dug a pack of cigarettes from between the dark vinyl cushions. He lit a smoke and moved a small glass ashtray from the coffee table to the arm of the couch, tapped the first bits of ash over a pile of stubbed-out butts. "What you doing?"

"Your trackhoe at the house?"

"That old eighties model's down there in the back pasture. All the big machines are up at a jobsite, why?"

"I was going to see if you might ride over to the house and dig me a horse grave in that back pasture."

"'A horse grave'?" Calvin chuckled. It was just like Darl Moody to call somebody at midnight wanting help to dig a hole for a dead horse. "What the hell's wrong with the bucket on your tractor?"

"Boom's busted."

"Well, yeah, I can help you. I got to meet with some folks down there at the Coffee Shop tomorrow morning about eight, but I can swing by on my way back through."

"No, I need it done now."

"Now? It's almost midnight you son of a bitch. I ain't digging no horse grave in the middle of the night." Calvin laughed and took a long drag off his cigarette. He blew the smoke toward the popcorn ceiling above. "I'll be by there in the morning."

"It can't wait till morning."

"What the hell you worried about? Coyotes? Hell, Darl, if the damned coyotes get after that horse it'll be less to bury." He took a sip of whiskey and brushed the thigh of his sweatpants where the condensation on the outside of the jar had left a ring.

"Look, I ain't worried about no damn coyotes, okay? But this can't wait till morning. So can you go over there and do that for me or not?"

"No, Darl. It's midnight. Angie's in there asleep and I got to be up at six. I'm going to finish this drink and hit the hay."

"It won't take you an hour."

"An hour my ass. It'll take me an hour to get loaded up. I ain't piling up and going to dig a hole in a field for a goddamn horse. What's wrong with you?"

"Then let me come over there and borrow your trackhoe. I'll have it back before you wake up." Darl's voice was frantic. Calvin knew something was wrong by the tone, the way you recognize those things in the voices of the people closest to you.

"This ain't about no horse."

"Don't worry about what this is about. All I need to know right now is whether you can come dig me a hole in that back pasture?"

"I ain't doing anything unless you tell me what's going on."

"I can't do that, Cal."

"Then I'm not coming." Calvin took a final drag off his cigarette, the last of the tobacco burning down into the filter, and mashed the cherry out into the glass.

"Goddamn it," Darl said. "Goddamn it."

"What the hell's going on?"

"Can you get over to Coon Coward's place?"

"Coon Coward's?"

"Can you get over here or not?"

Calvin thought about Angie asleep in the back. He hated to wake her up and try to explain where he was going, hated even more for her to open her eyes and him be gone, but she slept like a rock. *Probably won't even wake up,* he thought. He didn't know what was going on, but he knew Darl needed him, that he wouldn't ask if he didn't, and he knew Darl would do the same for him if the time ever came.

Family didn't ask questions. Family offered hands. And that's how their friendship had always been, like family.

"Yeah," Calvin finally said.

"How long?"

"Just let me put some clothes on. Twenty minutes."

"All right, then," Darl said.

"All right," Calvin said.

When Darl was gone, Calvin reached for his pack of cigarettes and lit another smoke before he stood. He stared at the television, though he didn't see or hear what was being said, his head full of questions as he reached for his whiskey and drained it to ice.

THE PICKUP RATTLED over a washed-out section of Coon Coward's driveway, and as the truck crept up a small incline, the headlights climbed from Darl's feet to his chest, on up to the top of his hat. His head was bowed and, as he looked up, the light made a moon out of his face, his eyes aglow like an animal's.

Calvin cut the headlights, killed the engine, and stepped out into the night. There was a chill to the air and he flipped the hood of his black sweatshirt over his head and fit his thumbs into the pockets of his jeans. The last cries of summer crickets chimed from dew-covered grass, but their calls were overshadowed by the crunch of gravel underfoot.

"Where the hell's Coon?" Calvin asked as he came to the back of Darl's truck where Darl sat on the tailgate, his feet swinging free of the ground.

Darl grabbed a plastic soda bottle from beside him, unscrewed the cap, and spit a line of tobacco inside. "He's out of town," Darl said. "His sister died."

"Oh," Calvin mumbled. "Well, what in the world you doing out here?"

Darl rested his hand on the walnut stock of a Savage 110 that lay across the truck bed. A climbing stand was loaded under the truck box. Camouflage pants rose on the necks of his logging boots, his T-shirt a different brush pattern from his trousers. "Hunting," he said.

"Poaching," Calvin corrected him.

Darl nodded and scratched at the corner of his eye with the side of his hand. He had a steep brow that cast his eyes in shadow, an underbite that jutted his chin, pushing the thick wave of his beard even with his nose.

"Well, what's going on?"

"I don't want to get you involved with this," Darl said.

"I'm here, ain't I?"

"Yeah, but you ain't got to be."

"You know, in all these years, every time I needed something, you was right there, now wasn't you?"

"I guess so."

"And every time you've ever needed me, right there I've been, ain't I?"

"Yeah," Darl said.

"Then get on with it."

Darl stood from the tailgate and the nightglow was bright around them. A full moon rose—a *supermoon* the news had called it—and there was a lunar eclipse that cast its face a dim orange, the color of farm eggs. Darl was a head taller than Calvin. They were only a few feet apart, and he met Calvin's eyes for a second or two, though he didn't hold them and glanced down to his feet. "Come on, then," he said as he turned.

Calvin followed Darl to the edge of the woods and they headed into the thicket, the thin brush raking them up to their waists as they melted into the trees. Darl wore a headlamp over his cap, but he did not turn it on. The moon was up and provided enough light to wander. Through the woods, an old Plymouth coupe rusted down into nothing next to a small, trembling finger of creek. They climbed a small knoll and the land opened into a field of broomstraw where a derelict barn rotted into jagged timbers.

Crossing the field, they entered the trees again, and Calvin knew this place, having been here dozens of times as a child with his father and grandfather to coax speckled trout from the stream. Those times on the creek during summers that seemed as if they'd stretch on forever were about as good as life had ever been. Calvin's father would bait their hooks with pearls of Silver Queen corn or red wrigglers depending on the color of the water, and they'd slip those speckled trout into the mouth of a jug until they had a mess of fish for supper. His grandfather fried the fish with ramps and wild potatoes, those trout so sweet and delicate they'd eat them heads and all. The stars had seemed brighter then and, as Calvin looked up into the spangled heavens at this moment, he believed that maybe they were. Maybe there're only one or two moments like that in a man's whole life and maybe man is just too dumb a creature to recognize that moment's the one until everything's long gone.

Darl held back a whip of laurel for Calvin to pass. When he was through, Darl turned on his headlamp and shined into the woods. They were too deep into the forest now for anyone driving by to see them from the road.

"Let me go first," Darl said, as they climbed farther up the hill-side. All of a sudden, Darl jerked back as if something had taken a swipe at him and Calvin tripped over the homemade alarm, the cans jingling in the trees above them.

Calvin was tangled in the line, and as he stepped to get loose, he saw Darl's light shining on the rusted fishhooks that dangled at their faces. "What the hell is this?"

"The old man's ginseng patch," Darl said. "He's got the place booby-trapped."

They crept along, patting at the air in front of them so as not to get snagged, and in a few more steps Darl stopped with his light shining down on the body. Calvin's eyes settled first on the treads of the man's boot soles, his legs twisted, and torso bent with one arm by his side, the other outstretched above. Calvin Hooper stood there in disbelief, not sure what to say or ask or do, stilled and silenced by what lay before him.

"Who is that?" Calvin finally said, those three words filling his mouth.

Darl stepped around the body and knelt by the dead man's shoulders. He reached down and pinched the bill of the man's ball cap, lifted his head and shined the light onto his face. At first Calvin thought his cheek was bloodied, but then he realized it wasn't blood. The mark was too purple, too flat in hue. His eyes were clouded over but that birthmark made him unmistakable.

"Jesus Christ, is that Sissy?"

"Yeah," Darl said. "That's Carol fucking Brewer."

"What the hell happened?"

"I told you I was out here hunting."

"Yeah, but how did this happen?"

"I was up in a treestand down there in that cove and I heard something rustling around in the leaves up here and when I looked through the scope I thought it was a hog. Hell, he was rooting around on all fours. Looked like a goddamned pig."

"Fuck, Darl." Calvin's mind cracked. "Why didn't you call somebody?"

"He was dead as soon as I got to him. There wasn't anything I could do. There wasn't shit anybody could do." Darl looked up and his headlamp was blinding. "Calling wasn't going to do him any good."

"We got to call somebody," Calvin said. "We've got to get somebody out here."

"I ain't calling anybody, Calvin."

Calvin couldn't see Darl's face, but the light shook back and forth with his answer. "What do you mean you're not calling somebody? You've got to call somebody, Darl. You've fucking killed somebody."

"I know that! Don't you think I know that?" Darl's voice was loud and stern now.

"You said it yourself. It was an accident. You might get lawed for poaching, Darl, but it ain't murder. Not right now, it ain't. But if you go and do something crazy it might be. You can't do something like that."

"And what then, Cal? What you think's going to happen after that? That's Carol Brewer, Carol fucking Brewer! *Brewer* by God!" Darl said that name loud. "You think his brother Dwayne is going to let that go? You think Dwayne Brewer's just going to say, 'Hey, man, I know you killed my brother and all, but you didn't mean to. No hard feelings.' You think that's what he's going to say?"

Calvin didn't answer.

"I'd be lucky if all he did was come after *me*," Darl said. "But knowing him, knowing everything he's done, you and me both know it wouldn't end there. I bet he'd come after my mama and my little sister and my niece and nephews and anybody else he could get his hands on. That son of a bitch is crazy enough to dig up my daddy's bones just to set him on fire."

"You're talking crazy, Darl."

"Am I?" Darl looked down at the body and the light lit Carol Brewer's face. Where the bullet had exited from his shoulder the wound was crusted with fragments of broken leaves and pine needles.

"So what the hell are you going to do?"

"I'm going to bury him. I'm going to bury him and ain't nobody ever going to know anything about it."

"You've lost your mind, Darl. You've lost your fucking mind."

"Look, if you want to go, say so. I told you I didn't want to get you involved. Now if you want to leave, turn around right now and you forget everything and I'll do what I've got to do."

"Then why the fuck did you call?"

"Because I needed a favor, Cal, and you're the only one I got."

Calvin looked over at the body that lay stretched between them. A bluish-purple hue, nearly the same color of the birthmark, had settled into the undersides of Carol's arms like a bruise. Calvin knelt beside him and put his hand on Carol Brewer's forearm. His skin was cool and his muscles stiff, but there was no smell to him. Not yet. None of that horror in dying had reached him in these few hours.

Calvin stood and looked around, the trees towering overhead so that they blacked out the starlight. All of a sudden he felt surrounded. He slowly turned a circle, looking at the darkened woods, the cries of the last few katydids now deafening in their mourning the turn of season. In that moment, he knew that he was standing in the midst of something that would never be forgotten, something he'd carry from this place and bear the rest of his life. There was no turning back.

That single certainty consumed him.

FOUR

AT THE TOP OF ALLENS BRANCH, SISSY SHARED A WHITE-washed shotgun shack with a mischief of wharf rats and field mice and one chalk-white possum he called Milkjug. The possum slept all day in the crawl space and Sissy got to where he loved putting leftovers on a plate and setting the food on the back steps to watch that possum scarf down anything from cathead biscuits to cream corn each evening. The small run-down house was where Red Brewer had been raised, and after his folks died, he handed the keys to his sons.

For years, Dwayne and Carol split a bedroom, small kitchen, living area, and a dirt-floor bathroom addition until their folks died five years back. After Red drove him and his wife off the side of Cabbage Curve, Dwayne headed back down the road to their childhood home, leaving his brother to fend for himself.

Dwayne had been sitting on Carol's couch twiddling his thumbs since eight o'clock. His brother told him that morning he'd be back from digging ginseng by seven, but it was closing in on midnight and Dwayne hadn't seen hide or hair. The springs were busted in the sofa so he was sunk down into the musty yellow cushions as if crouched in a foxhole. An amber glass lamp across the room lit the walls warm with false firelight, while a fifty-inch flat-screen blared the froggy voice of some nighttime salesman peddling pocket-knives. Dwayne looked at the set of samurai swords being show-cased on the television screen as he reached for a pizza box that sat at the edge of a white wicker table by his knees. He flipped back the cardboard top and found a slice half eaten by a rodent, ripped away the chewed section, and swallowed what was left whole like a snake.

For the past hour, he'd been timing himself fieldstripping and reassembling his Colt 1911 as fast as he could with his eyes closed. His fastest time yet was a fuzz over two minutes, but he was sure he could shave another ten seconds off if he focused. A full maga-zine was loaded, a round chambered as always, when he reached for the gun on the arm of the couch. He placed the pistol on his right thigh, his hand flat overtop, then hit start on his cell phone's stopwatch with his free hand, instantly closing his eyes and going to work.

Dwayne thumbed the mag release, the magazine falling into his lap, then yanked back on the slide to eject the chambered round. He heard the *tink* of brass as the cartridge was ejected onto the couch beside him, and immediately eased the slide back and turned the emptied gun toward himself. Bracing the pistol between his thighs, he mashed the recoil spring plug with his right thumb then turned the barrel bushing clockwise, the spring and plug now free to slide out beneath the barrel. The next step was the hardest without peeking as he pulled back the slide and tried to align the end of the slide lever with a small half-moon notch on the left side. Lined up, he pushed the slide lever free, then flipped the gun upside down, pulled the slide from the frame, then removed the guide rod and barrel. The gun was fieldstripped, the parts placed neatly on the cushion to his left; and now he tore off in reverse. When the gun was back together, he slapped the magazine in, yanked the slide, and opened his eyes. The stopwatch continued past 2:16.

"Come on now, Dwayne," he mumbled to himself disappointedly, flicking the safety up to lock the hammer. He dropped the magazine and reloaded the ejected cartridge from the cushion to his right before setting the pistol back on the arm of the couch. When he was done, he reached for a can of Budweiser on the wicker table, wiped the condensation from the sides, and took a long slug of lukewarm beer, *America* scribbled down the side of the can in cursive.

Something in his periphery by the door caught Dwayne's attention and he cut his eyes to see. A wharf rat picked about the corner of the room and Dwayne slowly stretched for the pistol. With the gun in his hand, he thumbed down the safety and drew his aim, lining the three-dot sights over the rat's body. The rat studied him and bunched into a ball, appearing unsure whether it was hidden or exposed. But there was no time for such questions. The hammer came down and the shot flashed the walls, the sound deafening in that tiny slapdash room. Dwayne's head rang and he lowered the gun to look. The .45 hollowpoint had shred the animal's body clean in two. The back half of the rat kicked at the floor, the front half still conscious as it spun itself around on nothing but those front legs, crawled to its flapping back half, and latched on as if that mean living thing must've been what did this.

Dwayne Brewer laughed at this sight, as if it was the funniest thing he'd ever seen in his life. He was almost in tears as he set the pistol back beside him on the couch and looked at where the blood had splattered against the wall, the meat a reddish-purple like venison. His eyes wandered up the wall to where a picture of his great-grandmother hung in an ornate, golden-scrolled frame the same as it had ever since he was a child. Her hair was in a bun, a white ruffled collar tight against her thick neck, a dark woolen dress beneath. The glass came out from the frame so that it had always appeared as if she was coming into the room, something that had frightened Dwayne as a kid. He stood and crossed the floor to the picture, wiped a speck of blood from the glass with his thumb and smeared it down his pants leg.

The woman in the picture did not smile. She peered blankly, her face like his grandmother's, rounded features that had carried down to his brother. He wondered where the hell Carol was. Dwayne glanced down at the dead rat between his boots, shook his head, and smiled, thinking, *Sissy's going to get a kick out of this*. He nudged at the rat with the toe of his boot and it was surely dead. Dwayne gathered his things and headed out the door. He'd grown sick of waiting.

THE '78 DEUCE AND A QUARTER that Dwayne Brewer had inherited from his grandparents still rode like a dream. There was some rust around the wheel wells, and the undercarriage was nearly eaten in two from three decades of winter roads covered in salt and snow. But the burgundy paint still held its shine in spots, and the white vinyl over the back half of the cab wasn't entirely gone. More than sheer beauty, that old two-door Electra floated down rutted-out dirt roads like a goddamn drift boat.

Dwayne was fiddling with the radio dial trying to pick up the sermon of some dime-store preacher when he swung wide onto Caney Fork and forced an oncoming driver into the ditch. The road wound and rose before dropping back down into farmland where some years they grew corn and some years they grew strawberries and every year they watched whitetail come out of the hedge each evening to graze the field as the last bit of light glowed yellow and gone.

He swung onto Moses Creek headed toward Coon Coward's in hopes of finding his brother. A muddy cut shot off to the right, two red-dirt tracks swerving back into the woods where tractor tires left the ground bare and field grass rose knee-high in the space between. A hundred yards back, the taillights of Carol Brewer's Grand Prix shone red in Dwayne's approach. He parked behind his brother and took a can of beer from the open cardboard suitcase in the passenger seat, cracked the top, and stepped outside.

Dwayne took a long swallow of beer, set the can on the roof of his brother's car, and opened the door thinking the asshole might've passed out behind the wheel. The car was empty and he reached across for a crumpled soft pack of Doral 100s, took a cigarette out and lit it from a lighter stashed in the console. Through the woods, he thought he spotted a flashlight, but as he took a step forward and started to yell for his brother, the light vanished and he figured it was ghostlight or a figment of his drunken mind. *I bet that son of a bitch has stumbled onto a gold mine,* Dwayne thought, knowing that if his brother had found one of Coon Coward's ginseng patches, he might wind up digging all night.

He chased a sip of beer with a drag from his brother's Doral, strutted to the back of the car, and wrote *Sissy's A Puss* in the dust on the back glass. He stared up the tractor trail he knew led to an old field where farmers used to graze their cattle out of the heat in summers. Fall was in the air, though the last of summer sound still filled the woods, and he shut his eyes and felt the world close in around him.

Back in his car, he cranked the Buick and drove in reverse down the cut, the car jumping about as it hit the state road. He headed out the way he'd come, taking a right out of Caney Fork onto Highway 107, with the pedal mashed to the floor. As he rounded a bend, the sky glowed a pale brown behind the mountains, a fogged sky dirtied with light pollution from the college. The silhouette of the ridgeline was black against it, lights from houses dotting that blackness so that it seemed as if the world had been turned on its end, the ground suddenly sky speckled with starlight, what used to be clouds now earthen in hue.

When he passed the university, he'd made up his mind how he'd spend the rest of the night. He'd ride by O'Malley's and No Name, maybe swing by the new brewery, to see which bar had the biggest crowd. The college kids had a place on the backside of campus called Tucks, but there were always university police keeping an eye out. Dwayne was used to places where bartenders were scared to serve drinks in glass, places where nights ended in the parking lot with knives and sirens, places that weren't around anymore, like the Rusty Lizard. *God those nights at the good ol' Crusty Rusty*, he thought. The world had turned so goddamned soft.

In the old days, getting in a bar fight was as simple as stepping on somebody's boots. Now, he had to egg it on all night for someone to shove him. Dwayne wanted to find a group of cologne-soaked frat boys with parted hair and dress shirts and he wanted to break one of those pretty-boy faces simply to see him bleed. If he was lucky, they'd jump on him like a pack of dogs and he'd have the time of his life till the blue lights came and the bodies scattered. He hoped someone might draw a knife so that he could draw his own. It was Friday night, after all, and a man deserved some fun.

FIVE

DARL AND CALVIN DRAGGED CAROL BREWER OUT OF THE woods in an old tarp Darl kept behind the seat of his truck, and loaded the body into the bed of his ragged Tacoma. Calvin tailed him to the house, at times following so closely that his headlights disappeared from Darl's rearview. Though Darl hadn't meant to pull Calvin into this, he was knee-deep now and would soon be up to his neck. Despite Darl's plan, Calvin had insisted they bury the body at the back of his family's farm.

A group of mailboxes stood at the end of the road, different-colored tin with different numbers all sharing the same name. Since before this county was ever a county at all, this land belonged to Hoopers. There were nine of Calvin's kin signed to the petition on December 10, 1850, for a new county to be formed from Haywood and Macon. One of those signatures was so shoddy that the first name couldn't be made out, but it didn't matter because that surname read Hooper just the same. This land belonged to them then just as it belonged to them now. Here there was blood tied to place the same as there were names tied to mountains and rivers and coves and hollers and trees and flowers and anything else that ever seemed worth naming. People and place were some insepara- ble thing knotted together so long ago that no amount of time had allowed for an answer of how to untie them.

Darl sat in his truck on the dusty pull-off by the mailboxes, his headlights shining on a cattle gate where Calvin was working a chain loose from the fence. When the gate was open, Darl pulled up with his window down and his arm resting on the door. The night was misty below that bright blood moon, so the whole world seemed to reside within a hazy rust-colored glow. Calvin stood there by the window and glanced into the bed of Darl's truck.

"When you get back to that middle field, cut your lights so you don't shine up there toward the house."

"All right," Darl said.

"Head into that back pasture and you'll see where I've been dig- ging stumps out. I'll be back there in a couple minutes. This diesel's too loud to cross that field without it echoing up there to the house." Calvin nodded back to his truck.

Darl headed into the field and Calvin shut the gate behind him. As Darl drove across the pasture, his headlights lit the eyes of Angus and Hereford cows standing motionless in the oat grass. Calvin's family once had nearly a hundred head, but was now down to twenty or thirty. A red fox stopped for a moment in its tracks and studied with eyes aglow before lifting its nose to the air and trotting after the scent of something gone before.

The pasture was mostly flat but rose toward the back before dropping into the middle field. Darl killed the lights as he approached the fence line. The air was damp on his arms when he stepped out to open the gate. There was plenty of light to see as he crossed that second pasture, the grass there eaten down to ragged stubble. The field bottomed out beside a small creek where he and Calvin had caught spring lizards together as children and coaxed crawfish from under lichen-covered stones with torn bits of hotdog baited on fishhooks. The last pasture ran long rather than wide, and at its back, mounds of red dirt rose beside a small '80s-model Cat excavator. Darl pulled in beside the trackhoe and cut the engine.

From his truck, he watched the land in his rearview and waited for Calvin to come over the hill. He thought about how many generations this land had belonged to Hoopers, and he wondered how far into the future it would remain that way. *Names are a funny thing,* he thought. Names were tied to place and occupation and condition, something that brought folks to ask things like "So are you a Little Canada McCall or a Glenville McCall," to which you might say, "Yeah, I'm from Little Canada," or "Yeah, I'm from Glenville," or "Naw, my family come from Balsam Grove." Some families were farmers and some families built houses, some ran equipment and some ran stores, some were lawmen and others were outlaws. Somewhere far enough back most names tied together, but names had history that might bring someone to say something like "Yeah, that's the Franks coming out in her" when Leigh Ann Rice got mean at the Ingles deli, so that names became things that even if you married out of them had a way of sticking with you. Darl thought about who lay in the back of his pickup. *Brewer* was a name that demanded things be done this way.

A silhouette rose from the hill as if what came had clawed its way out of the ground. As the figure came closer, Darl could hear the brush of steps through waist-high sedge, and in a few moments Calvin was there beside him. Darl stepped out of the truck and they stood by the back tire, neither saying a word, expressionless as they considered what lay before them. Calvin walked over to the track-hoe and cranked the engine. The diesel sputtered loud, but this far back into the field the sound was contained, the woods and the land providing a barrier of secrecy.

It did not take long to dig the grave, and when it was done they rolled the body out of the tarp. Darl refused to look in to see how Carol lay in the bottom. Calvin pushed dirt into the hole as if they were covering a mended waterline, and when the grave was filled, he packed the dirt with the weight of the machine balanced beneath its bucket. The night was all but gone by then, and they rode back through the field with a faint breath of light growing behind the eastern ridge.

They were sitting at the kitchen table drinking coffee with a haze of cigarette smoke shifting overhead when Angie Moss came from the bedroom. She was wearing one of Calvin's T-shirts, a ratty Guy Harvey shirt with a pair of puppy drum on the back. The sleeves ran to her elbows and the bottom cut her mid-thigh where a pair of striped boxer shorts ended, so that it looked as if the shirt might've been all she wore. Angie stopped in the doorway and stood there scratching at the back of her head, her eyes peering half asleep.

A very strange awareness came over Darl as he sat there, to have come from where they returned and now be back in a room so commonplace, a room where he'd sat a thousand times over the course of his life. Nothing seemed real just yet. They were not men accustomed to such darkness. They were ordinary men—work-hard, weekend-warrior, get-up-and-go-to-church kind of men—and what they'd just seen, where they'd come from affected them so. Numbness and disbelief hollowed his insides, a fire trapped in his flesh with the truth of what they carried.

"What in the world you doing here?" Angie asked.

No one said anything. Calvin had a look like he and Darl had been caught in the middle of something. Angie looked back and forth between them trying to figure out if there was a joke she wasn't in on, something she didn't get.

"Good to see you, too," Darl finally said. He forced himself to grin, thinking, *Act normal. Just smile.*

Angie walked over to the coffeepot and Darl watched her, studied the curves of her legs, how her breasts swayed beneath her shirt as she came back to the table. She sat down in a ladder-back chair and blew steam off her cup, tried to take a sip then set it down to cool. Even having rolled out of bed, she was so stunning it was hard not to gawk. Her blond hair held natural waves, eyes green as mill marbles. Freckles crossed her nose and dotted her cheeks like specks of mud. She ran her hair through her fists till it was all pulled over her right shoulder.

Calvin had lit another cigarette and she reached to take it from his fingers. He slid an open pack across the table, a lighter rested on top of the box.

"I don't want a whole one," she said. "I'm trying to quit."

He handed her his smoke and she took a long drag, holding it in for what seemed forever before blowing the smoke out the corner of her mouth. Her legs were crossed and she was rocking her foot, that single motion shaking her whole body. She started to give Calvin his cigarette, but took one more quick puff before she passed it.

"Really, Darl, what in the world you doing here so early?"

"Came to see Calvin about some work." Darl glanced across the table at Calvin, who cut his eyes down to the ashtray and tapped a fingernail of ash into the glass.

"Why in the world you covered in mud?"

Darl looked down to where his camo jeans and boots were caked with red clay. "Some of us ain't got somebody to wash our clothes for us."

"That might be part of your problem, chief. You're running around looking for a woman to cook and clean *and* have to look at that face of yours." Angie grinned and cradled her cup with both hands in front of her mouth. "That's a hard sale."

Calvin finished the rest of his coffee, then stood and walked over to the refrigerator. He opened the door and peered inside, not finding anything that suited him, and walked over to pour what was left of the pot.

"What time you have to be at class today?" Calvin asked when he came back to the table.

Angie was in school at the community college, studying to be an RN. She was eight years younger than Calvin and Darl, but had a good head on her shoulders, had grown up here like they had, her family coming off Bradley Branch over in Whittier.

She looked at Calvin, confused. "It's Saturday," she said.

"Oh, yeah," Calvin said. "What you got planned?"

"Thought I'd ride over to Uncle Bill's Flea Market and see if I couldn't find some curtains." Angie nodded toward the den. "There's a lady there that used to have all kinds of linens and curtains. She has one of those electrolarynx."

"An electro what?"

Angie held her fist to her throat and mimicked the electronic sound. "That'll be ten dollars and fifteen cents," she grunted.

Neither Darl's nor Calvin's expression altered.

"What the hell's wrong with the two of you?"

They didn't answer.

"Well, I'm going to go by there and see if I can't find some curtains and then I'm going to run by and see Mama, see if she needs me to do anything for her. She's been sick as a dog the past week and a half. I bet Daddy's starved to death."

They sat there for a few minutes and didn't say anything, each sipping their coffee, eyes forward. There was a dreamlike glow about the room as the morning grew outside and filtered in through thin white curtains and old crown-glass windowpanes. Darl sat there in a trance, the room around him, Calvin and Angie sitting there beside him, all of it feeling like make-believe.

"You know, I don't think bear season opens up for a few more weeks, Darl," Angie said. Her words came out of nowhere and caught him off guard.

Darl looked at her, confused. "What are you talking about?"

"I said I don't think bear season opens up for another week or two, does it, Cal?" She glanced over at Calvin then cut her eyes back to Darl. "Deer season don't open till Thanksgiving. So if you can't run bear and you can't hunt deer, what exactly are you all dressed up for? Getting ready for Halloween?"

Darl didn't answer. He looked down at the camouflage clothes he wore and no words came to mind. It scared him that he didn't have an answer.

"Geez Louise! Talking to the two of you's like talking to a couple stiffs this morning," Angie said. "I'm just giving you a hard time. I don't care if you poach deer all year as long as you bring me some."

Angie stood and walked over to the counter. She folded a checkered dish towel back on a wooden bowl filled with fresh eggs.

Opening a cabinet, she grabbed a milk-glass bowl, started cracking different-colored eggs and whisking them with a fork.

"You know, one time my daddy killed a doe somewhere back in Whiteside Cove and it was the night before a doe day and he figured he'd leave it in the woods overnight till he could come back and get it." Angie's story mixed with the sound of the fork beating against the side of the bowl. "So he field dressed that deer and he sunk it down in a beaver pond to keep it from spoiling, then he came back that next morning and pulled it out. Well, when he took it down to Burt Hogsed that next day, Daddy said Burt opened that deer up and there were crawfish crawling inside it. He said Burt looked up at him and said, 'Where'd this deer come from? There's a bunch of crawfish in here.' Daddy said he told him, 'Deer'll eat about anything when they're hungry.'" Angie shook her head and laughed and turned back to the table.

Darl met her eyes and he shook his head and forced a smile. "I better be getting on," he said.

"Why don't you stay for breakfast? I'm going to scramble some eggs and I think there's some sausage in there that needs to be cooked. I'm making it anyways."

"No, I better get on," Darl said. He stood from the table and stretched his arms at his sides.

"Well, at least take some eggs with you." Angie grabbed the wooden bowl filled with fresh eggs and offered it toward him. There was a mix of brown and cream-colored eggs, a few green and a few pale blue Easter eggers. "There's some egg crates stacked over there on the washing machine. We've got eggs coming out of our ears."

"I'm okay," Darl said. "Really."

Angie came over and stood on her tiptoes to kiss him on his cheek. He felt her lips wet and cool against his skin. His face was on fire.

Outside, there wasn't a cloud in the sky and the sun had barely broken over the mountainside to burn the fog from the fields. A mixed brood of Araucana and Rhode Island Red chickens scratched around the side of the house, pecking grubs and grain from the grass. Calvin followed Darl out to the driveway and they stood by the front bumper of Darl's pickup. The white farmhouse looked the same as it always had. The tin roof was newer, but everything else was as it had always been: a small, white-sided one-story with black shutters; a porch centered the front of the house with decorative black cast-iron columns with vines and leaves like used to be on all Southern homes. Darl looked at Calvin and could see the same boy he'd known his whole life right behind the man's face, same green eyes and boxy jaw. Folks had always thought they looked like brothers, but Calvin was short and stocky while Darl was long and lean.

"She must not have woken up when I left last night," Calvin finally said. He faced the house with his back leaning against the grill, while Darl hovered over the hood of the truck and faced the road.

"Must not have."

Calvin turned and leaned his elbows on the rough, worn paint of the hood. "Well, what now?"

"What do you mean?"

"I mean what do we do?"

"We don't do anything. We go on to work and get right back to what we've always done."

"And what if something happens?"

"Ain't nothing going to happen," Darl said, though saying it seemed almost like a curse, and he looked around for a piece of wood to knock for luck but found nothing within reach.

"But what if it does?" Calvin said. There was fear in his voice.

"Then it'll be me."

Calvin looked at Darl with a look of guilt and worry.

"I'll take all of it, Calvin. You have my word. You don't worry about anything."

Calvin didn't speak again, though he stood there for another minute or two as the morning grew around them. Neither said goodbye when Calvin walked back to the house. Darl waited there at the front of his pickup until Calvin was inside.

When he was gone, Darl climbed into his truck and sat there with the engine running for a minute more, watching the house vacantly. Nothing had settled in his mind just yet, that night and what they'd done as unreal and dreamlike right then as if he'd imagined it. Not enough time had passed to know whether this was something a man could live with, or if it would gnaw him in two. They were still too close to what had happened to see it with any sort of perspective.

He grabbed a can of Skoal wintergreen from the seat, loaded a thick plug of tobacco against his gums, and put the truck in reverse. By the mailboxes, he sat with his mind blank and dumb, unsure whether to turn right or left. He knew his way home, but things that had always been simple would never be that way again.

SIX

BY THE THIRD DAY, THE GUILT HAD NEARLY GNAWED DARL Moody in two. He snapped awake from a dream, the sheets soaked with sweat, unable to shake the image of Carol Brewer's blood-soaked clothes.

Sitting on the church pew beside his mother the morning before, he'd listened to the preacher tell the story of Joseph and his brothers, how Joseph had received a message from God and how his brothers, filled with jealousy, had plotted to kill him, then faked his death and sold him into slavery. It was the image of Joseph's coat—the fabric sopped with animal's blood, the brothers taking it to their father to prove to him Joseph was dead—that must've triggered the dream. Darl saw crimson stains spotting heavy weave like rose petals, a dark puddle spread wide and so black in the middle that it seemed endless, bottomless; as if, had he slipped and fallen into that black, he would fall on forever.

There was something in the back of his mind that just kept saying, *Confess,* and the more he thought about it, the more he started to believe that going to the sheriff might be the only way to clear his conscience. Right and wrong was easy. The hard part was handing your life away, it was being brave enough to look around at everything you had and say, *Yeah, I'll give it all up just to make things square.* As he lay in bed that Monday morning, his mind awash with the consequence of it all, he decided to give it a week. Holding off might've been selfish, but if he was going all in, he needed to know what all he was pushing into the pot. He needed to have a proper accounting.

That morning, he drove to his sister, Marla's. She and her husband lived in a trailer park a quarter mile south of Jimmy's Mini Mart in Tuckasegee with their three sons and a baby girl. Early morning blushed a stand of poplar yellow with fall. The reflection brought warm, golden light through linen curtains, but in a home with a two-year-old such things weren't noticed.

Smoke filled the kitchen and the fire alarm wailed and Marla waved a dirty dish towel to clear the air while her husband, Rusty, ran out the front door with a heavy cast-iron pan. Their two-year-old, Ruth, screamed from her high chair at the table, her tiny fingers sticky with applesauce. She was fighting off a hand, foot, and mouth infection that covered her in a rash and turned her into a twenty-five-pound weapon-grade siren. The boys, who were each a head taller than the one before so that side by side they rose like a set of steps, were fighting over crumbs. Darl watched the chaos in that tiny kitchen and he thought about how much he'd miss it.

The haze drifted in the room, but the alarm stopped and Rusty topped off his coffee before sitting back down at the table. The kitchen smelled of burned bacon and eggs. Marla wore a ratty bathrobe and her hair was pulled back in a greasy ponytail. Her bare feet made a sound like a dog smacking its chops as she crossed the sticky linoleum from the stove and slid a plate across the table. A charred pile of scrambled eggs sat beside four strips of bacon black as railroad ties. Rusty looked so tired he didn't even notice. He merely reached for the salt and pepper, seasoned rashly, and swallowed it down without so much as a word.

Darl watched Rusty eat his breakfast bit by broken bit and he wondered how much longer the man could last, how much longer they all could last. Ten years back Rusty had owned a shiny black Peterbilt covered in chrome with a jake-brake that sounded like a machine gun firing down the mountain. He had been working for himself, gone three weeks, home one, making more than they knew what to do with, raking in money hand over fist. Then one day, he had a seizure. A few days later, he had another. They came on him out of nowhere and stole everything that he had. The state took his CDLs, even took his regular driver's license. He couldn't run equipment like he'd done most his life. He couldn't even drive a car. A fellow who worked at the County garage gave Rusty a ride each morning to the Justice Center, where he scrubbed toilets and washed windows and emptied trash and brought home barely enough to sink slowly.

Rusty scraped at his plate with his fork and swallowed the last of what he had. He checked the time on the microwave, snatched his lunch from the counter, kissed his wife and tousled the hair of his youngest boy, nodded at Darl, and out the door he went, too tired and beaten for words.

Now it was Darl, Marla, and the kids. Ruth was still screaming at the top of her lungs and Marla was working her way through the dishes as the boys licked their plates clean and dropped them into soapy water. A horn blew outside and the boys raced for their book bags, their footsteps shaking that tiny singlewide like thunder, and out the door they tore to beat out the other kids in the park for window seats on the school bus. When they were gone, Marla wiped her hands down her bathrobe, came over to the table, and scooped Ruth into her arms. The child was crying and Marla rocked her against her shoulder, patting her back, and shushing softly in her daughter's ear, a sound about as calm and peaceful as any sound Darl had ever heard in his life.

Looking at his sister was like looking in the mirror, both carrying the same sharp nose and heavy chin of their mother. Their old man had kicked the bucket early and for Darl that meant the burden was on his shoulders. A man was put on this earth to provide for his own and for Darl that meant watching after his mother and making sure his sister and her family never went hungry. Marla and the kids were part of the reason he stayed in the woods. He could catch limits of trout every month but March, shoot deer come fall, drop dove and rabbit in winter, call turkeys in spring, and keep the freezers full year-round. Thinking about that right then, he wondered how in the world they'd survive without him. Who'd make sure his mama didn't want for nothing? Who'd put food in the pot when the money ran dry? Confessing what he'd done wasn't just a matter of giving away his own life, it was bigger than that. It was sacrificing everyone he loved.

"What was it you wanted to talk about?" Marla asked when the baby finally quit crying long enough for her to speak.

"Can I hold her?" Darl asked.

"Of course you can," Marla said.

Darl held that little girl against his chest, her body hot against him, and he touched the tip of his nose against the top of her head.

There was this indescribably sweet smell that was faded like a vase of flowers carrying from a room across the house. It was so soft, so faint, but there was no missing a smell like that, and he inhaled as deeply as he could, as if he couldn't breathe without it, like that smell was oxygen.

"What was it you wanted to talk about?" Marla asked again.

The smell of that little girl filled his lungs and coursed through his body like a drug. "Nothing," he whispered, that word only a breath against that little girl's scalp. "Nothing at all."

SEVEN

THE GRAND PRIX HAD NOT MOVED FROM WHERE IT WAS parked along the tractor path. Over the past few days, a tulip poplar had begun to shed its leaves, a storm the night before blowing the treetop bare. Yellow leaves stuck to the windshield and driver's-side glass, the turquoise paint slapped here and there with goldenrod shots of color. Dwayne Brewer had driven here every day to check on his brother's car. He was certain now that his brother wasn't coming out of those woods.

The old man sat at his kitchen table eating a bowl of oatmeal. His gray beard hung from his chin like Spanish moss, the wires of it caked with bits of food that fell from his spoon and caught. His hair had thinned to a deep widow's peak, and what remained was slicked back with a comb. Dwayne could see him through the screen door, the entrance opening into a small den, the kitchen off to the left. He rapped with his knuckle against the wooden door-frame where crackled white paint now chipped away.

The old man glanced up from his bowl, flicked his eyes upward as he blew steam off his next bite. He stared for a few seconds, and even from such distance Dwayne could see sunlight through a kitchen window showing his eyes pale blue. "Whatever it is you're selling, I ain't buying," Coon Coward hollered across the room.

"I need to talk to you."

Coon now rested his spoon in the bowl and set his palms on the table. "Well, if you've come to try and get me to go to one of your newfangled churches with TVs and guitars, I don't want no part of that neither. Been a member of Moses Creek all my life and don't have much of a mind to change now."

"Open the fucking door, old man!"

Coon Coward stood and disappeared to a place in the kitchen that Dwayne could not see from the porch. When he came around the corner, he was shoving a small revolver into the side pocket of his overalls. The old man walked with a long gait, his right leg following behind as if it were tied to him with a leash. He came onto the porch and where he stopped his boots made a right angle on the weathered planks, his right foot never coming straight.

"What's this about?" Coon asked.

"My brother," Dwayne said. He stared at the old man's eyes, and in the hollows around them was the reason for his name. Tillmon Coward had almost drowned in Bear Lake as a child and the blood vessels had ruptured around his eyes, the skin darkening around them like he'd been in a fistfight. For one reason or another, the darkness never left, deep purple sockets that made his pale blue eyes look almost white against them.

"My God, you're Red Brewer's boy, ain't you?"

Dwayne didn't answer.

"Shame what happened," Coon said. "How long's that been now?"

"Five years," Dwayne said. He thought back on what had happened to his parents and he knew it wasn't anything at all like folks thought. His daddy was drunk and drove right off the side of a mountain, but it was neither an accident nor a shame.

The old man grunted and shook his head. "A shame," he said. "Your daddy worked for me up there at the plastics plant that used to be in Cashiers. I had to fire him for peeping in the women's locker room. Hated to do it really, but my hands were tied."

"Ah," Dwayne grunted, wishing the old man would stop reminiscing and get on with it.

"Now what's this about your brother?" Coon asked. His head tilted to the side. He wore a look of confusion.

"My brother was back in there on your property this past weekend, and I ain't heard a peep out of him since."

"What was your brother doing on my property?"

"You know as well as I do what he was doing."

"No, I can't say that I do."

"I ain't here to play grab ass, old man, so cut the shit," Dwayne yelled. "Ginseng!" His voice was deep as if the words were bellowed from a cave.

Coon's eyes squinted and his brow lowered. "Well, if your brother was back in there stealing my ginseng, I don't rightly know what happened to him."

"Either you saw him or you didn't."

"I ain't seen a soul, son." Coon strolled past Dwayne like he wasn't there, then hobbled down the front steps and crossed the yard to his car. He pulled the revolver from his pocket and placed it on the roof of the Oldsmobile, then fished a set of keys from his overalls and hit a button on the key chain. The trunk popped and he shoved the keys and the wheelgun back into his pocket. He pulled a navy-colored vinyl suitcase from the trunk, set it on the gravel drive, and slammed the lid. "I been out of town attending to my sister's funeral the past week and a half," Coon said. "Ain't been home an hour."

He came back onto the porch, dropped his luggage by the door, and sat nonchalantly in a rocking chair as if he were going to pass the last of the day whittling a stick with his pocketknife.

"I don't know where you come from, old man, and I don't much give a shit, but I'm telling you my brother was back in there and ain't been out since. His goddamn car is sitting right down there on that road that goes up to your back field where he left it."

"I don't know what to tell you, son, aside from he ain't have no business being here in the first place."

"I'm telling you something's happened to my brother." Dwayne's fists clenched by his sides. He stepped forward and hovered over the old man. "And if I find out it has anything to do with you I'm going to tie you up and drag you behind my car till there ain't a lick of meat left on your dried-up bones."

Coon Coward leaned onto his hip and pulled the revolver from his pocket. He held his finger on the trigger and rested the .38 against his thigh as if he didn't have a care in this world. Dwayne almost found humor in how the old man didn't seem to give one single shit what he was telling him. Maybe it was age, maybe it was knowing he was nearing the end anyways that made him that way, or maybe that old man was stone-cold crazy. Coon Coward sucked at his back teeth and watched Dwayne out of the corner of his eye.

"Well, if there was anybody back in there on my property while I was gone, there ought to be an easy way to find out."

"How's that?" Dwayne asked.

"I got a game camera in there on the main trail. If anybody was back in there while I was gone I probably got a picture of him. Unless they come in some other way, but I doubt it," Coon said. "If a man was smart, he'd cut his own way in, but they ain't ever smart. They're lazy. People don't want to have to work for nothing so they walk that same path like a bunch of doe-eyed children." Coon Coward shook his head, slapped his hands against the worn thighs of his overalls, his right still clenching the revolver, and stood from his chair. He limped to the edge of the porch and spit out into the yard. "Let's get on with it," he said, shooting Dwayne a look like he couldn't quite decide who was killing whom.

Coon wandered out into the yard and never turned back, and in a moment Dwayne followed the old man's lead. They walked to where the grass met the woods and then they were in them, neither quite sure what they'd find.

THE ROOM COON COWARD used for an office was piled floor to ceiling with cardboard boxes taped shut and labeled with permanent marker. A monitor sat deep on top of a cheap laminate desk, the wood grain peeled back to particleboard. Coon grabbed a pair of reading glasses from behind the keyboard and balanced them on the tip of his crooked nose, and when the computer was running, he stuck the memory card they'd pulled from the game camera into a small drive by the mouse pad.

"I cleared this card right before I left for my sister's, so anything on here came while I was gone." Coon sat in a creaky swivel chair. Dwayne pushed a stack of boxes out of the way with his boot and knelt beside the old man so he could see.

The computer screen offered the only light in the room and Dwayne watched the old man's face, the way he kept his head tilted up to see through his glasses, how he stroked his beard down his chest. The only sounds in the room were that of the old man's coarse hair running through his fist and the hum of the computer's fan. There was a startling juxtaposition of time in these mountains, in the way a man might still plow his field with horse and harrow as if it were a hundred years before, then turn right around and pull a brand-new iPhone from his pocket to tell his wife he'd be late for supper. Dwayne didn't think of it with that sort of complexity, but it seemed queer to see that old man fiddling with a computer.

When the photos were downloaded, a program opened and Coon double-clicked the first file. He tapped his way through the pictures with the arrow keys, the first ten or so only nighttime animals: a skinny black bear with tall shoulders strolled through the trees, picking about for what acorns littered the ground; there were three or four photos of a mother raccoon leading her litter of kits along the trail, her eyes fluorescent as fireflies in the green light of the camera's hidden flash; four or five does crossed in front of the tree each morning, but the large buck Coon called Solomon only showed in one frame, following fifteen minutes behind the girls one foggy morning with his nose to the ground, his tail straight as a pointer's. Finally, there was a photo of a man in camouflage with a rifle cradled in his arms and a treestand on his back slipping down the trail.

"Bingo," Coon said as he drew a marquee around the man on the screen. Zoomed in, the photo was too blurry to make out. The tres-passer's back was turned to the camera. But in the very next shot, Coon could see him clear as day as the man made his way back out of the woods the same way he'd come in a few hours earlier. "I be damned," Coon said. "That's Sharon Moody's boy, sure as the world. Darl Moody. That sneaky little son of a bitch."

Dwayne knelt quietly and glared at the screen, studying the pic-ture as he committed the name to memory. He knew Darl Moody from growing up. Darl was three or four years younger, some-where around the same age as Sissy, but Dwayne hadn't ever known him to be much. In the days that followed, there were photos of Darl Moody going past the camera around the same time every evening, making his way to the stand sometime around five-thirty and leaving at dusk.

"I bet that little son of a bitch knew I was out of town," Coon said. "Me and his mama in the same Sunday school class. The nerve of that little shit."

"I don't give a fuck about this, old man. I couldn't care less if he shoots every deer in here. Get on to Friday and see if you got any pictures of my brother."

Coon x-ed out of the photo and double-clicked a file further down in the folder. Once again, Darl Moody made his way into the woods around suppertime and a little more than two hours later he was on his way out, though it looked like he was running. "Some-thing's got him spooked," Coon said. In the next photo, it was pitch-black, the backs of two men, one in full camo, the other in jeans and a dark hooded sweatshirt, were lit green by the camera's flash. "That looks like Darl again."

"Who's that with him?"

"Beats me," Coon said. He clicked forward and what came next left them both confused. Darl Moody walked with his hands behind his back pulling a tarp, the person with him following behind with the other end so that the tarp swung between them like a hammock.

Dwayne shouldered the old man out of the way and drew a marquee around the tarp in the picture. It was impossible to tell what was inside, though it looked heavy, a visible strain evident in the way both men's bodies hunched, their shoulders raised to bear the weight. Darl was easy to make out, the long face and sharp nose, a thick beard that curved in waves from his chin. But the man with him, a short, stocky fellow, was hidden in the shadow of his hood. Dwayne zoomed in hoping to see something, but it was equally dark and fuzzy up close. "What's that say on his shirt?" Dwayne asked. He tried to get as close as he could to the logo on the breast of the sweatshirt, but like the man's face, it was out of focus. "What's after that?"

Coon took the mouse and clicked through the rest of the photos, about eleven more shots of raccoons and possums wandering the nighttime woods like gypsies. When he'd reached the last of the pictures, Coon took off his reading glasses and set them on the desk. "That's it," he said. "And your brother's not in any of them pictures."

"He was here," Dwayne said. "His goddamn car's still parked right down there where he left it."

"You ever think maybe he parked his car right there in my woods and then doubled back to the road?"

"What the hell would he be doing going back to the road?"

"I don't know," Coon said.

"He came after your ginseng, old man."

"Well, I don't know what to tell you."

Dwayne stood from the floor and sneered at the back of Coon Coward's grease-slicked head. The old man's contrariness had gotten under Dwayne's skin and he looked around the room at the boxes searching for the heaviest thing he could find: a brick, a rock, anything. His fists clenched and he thought for a second about bashing in that old man's skull with his bare hands, but he knew it wouldn't change a thing. Coon Coward had said all he had to say and he had pictures right there to prove it.

Dwayne breathed deep through his nose, then turned and headed out of the room, and the old man watched him go without so much as goodbye. There were a million questions running through Dwayne Brewer's mind, buzzing around his skull like flies. *Somebody's going to give me a goddamn answer.*

EIGHT

THE SIMPLEST WAY TO KNOW FOR SURE WAS TO STOP AT Walgreens on the way to Asheville. Take a pregnancy test. Plus or minus, yes or no. Be done with it.

Angie always started on Sundays. Her cycle always lasted three days. You could set your daily planner by it. Three days late might not have meant anything for most women, but the fact it was already Wednesday had Angie thinking a million things while she waited in the restaurant booth for Calvin to meet her for supper. More than anything in particular, something just felt different. Something had felt different for the past week and a half.

Colima Mexican Restaurant was slammed for a Wednesday. The waiter had rushed by twice to check on her and she'd ordered a frozen margarita, though as soon as he brought the drink, she knew she wouldn't take so much as a sip. A couple in their early sixties was eating with two little girls, probably granddaughters, in a booth across the room. Angie watched the younger of the two girls pour four sugars into her soda, the grandmother finally stopping her when she reached for a fifth.

Even if Angie was knocked up, she wasn't going to run off and get married just to save face. Nine times out of ten, those marriages fell apart. So many girls she'd gone to high school with got pregnant soon as they graduated and married before they were nineteen. Nowadays, most of them were divorced, splitting custody of six-year-olds, and meeting at gas stations and grocery stores every other weekend to swap off, barely a word left to say to the men they'd sworn to spend the rest of their lives with.

Truth was, she wasn't in any sort of hurry to have kids. After this fall, she needed thirteen credit hours, mostly clinicals, before she could take the National Council Licensure Examination to become a registered nurse. Lately, she'd been thinking about going to the university when she finished her associate's. Western had an RN to BSN program that'd set her up for grad school, go on to be a family nurse practitioner. All told, she was looking at another four or five years to finish, and at twenty-four that seemed like forever.

Through the doorway leading into the front dining room she spotted him stopping to talk to a pair of state troopers eating with two town cops. In a place like Jackson County, most everyone knew one another, and if they didn't outright know you, they probably went to church with your kin. Commonality could typically be reached within a name or two or by asking what cove you came from. If you couldn't make heads or tails of someone by then, odds are they weren't from around here.

As Calvin wandered into the room, the older man at the table she'd been watching stood and grabbed ahold of his hand, shook with one and patted him hard on the shoulder with the other. The two little girls examined him while the man's wife smiled as if sitting on a church pew. They spoke for a minute back and forth, but Angie couldn't hear what was said over the soccer game playing on the television in the corner of the room.

The restaurant kept salsa in syrup dispensers, and she poured some into a black bowl and took a chip from a basket in the center of the table. Salsa ran down her chin as Calvin scooted into the booth, and Angie cupped her hand to catch what spilled, grabbed a napkin, and laughed.

"How ladylike," she joked.

"You been here long?"

"Maybe ten minutes."

A tall waiter with a kind smile squeezed Calvin on the shoulder. "Amigo," he said. The restaurant was family owned, all the waiters looking almost identical except for facial hair and haircuts. "You know what you want to drink?" the man asked.

"I think I'll have a Dos Equis," Calvin said.

"Grande?" The waiter raised his eyebrows and stretched his hands to show the height of the mug.

"Sure," Calvin said, and the waiter nodded his approval before walking away.

When his beer came, Calvin squeezed a lime wedge and sprinkled a dab of salt into it. Angie ordered shrimp fajitas and Calvin asked for two chicken burritos with nacho cheese and red sauce, the same as he had every time they'd ever come. Staring through the window onto the shopping center parking lot, Angie saw a group of college kids sneaking nips from a metal flask as they strutted toward the Quin Theater ticket box.

"You know, that's the first place you ever took me," Angie said.

"Where's that?"

"To the movies," she said, nodding through the glass toward the theater across the parking lot. "You took me out to eat Robbie's Char-Burger and then we went and watched a movie. I can't remember what we saw."

"*World War Z*," Calvin said.

"You know you're lucky I ever went out with you again." Angie traced some of the salt from the rim of her margarita glass and licked it off the tip of her finger.

"Why's that?"

"You took me to the Char-Burger, Calvin. Had grease all over your shirt."

"So why'd you go?" Calvin raised his eyebrows.

"I don't know," Angie said. "I guess I felt sorry for you."

"Sorry for me?"

"Yeah." She smiled. "You were just pitiful."

Calvin grabbed his beer, leaned back in the booth, and took a long draft. He shook his head and peered out the window. There was something about the way he always looked at her. They'd been together two and a half years and she'd loved every minute. They were always picking at each other and laughing, and sure, that was part of it. But the reason Angie knew she wanted to spend the rest of her life with him was that there was comfort even in silence. They didn't have to say anything.

Angie thought about how she'd hesitated to tell Calvin about wanting to go back to school. They'd only been together six months at that point, and while the mountains were changing, there were still plenty who bought into that old-fashioned idea that women were wives and mothers. To her surprise, though, he was encouraging.

He told her to get out of her lease and move in with him so she could save some money and focus on her schoolwork. If that's what she wanted, he said he'd do anything he could to help her.

Remembering that right then, she still didn't know how he'd take the news of a baby, if there was a baby, but she knew she could tell him anything.

In a few minutes, the waiter brought the food, a cast-iron pan sizzling with shrimp and peppers and onions, the rest of the plates circling a tray he balanced on his outstretched arm. He slid the pan onto the table, warning, "Hot plate," as he emptied the tray and asked if they needed anything else.

"I think we're good," Calvin said.

Angie was starving, having skipped lunch to make it to micro-biology lab. Wednesdays were her hardest days of the week: de-velopmental psychology, health system concepts, and lab before one; three hours of clinicals from two to five. She loaded one of the warm flour tortillas and shoveled half a fajita into her mouth, scarfing it down, never shy about eating.

Calvin chewed a small bite of food forever, finally choking it down as if it pained him to swallow as he picked about his plate. Over the past three or four days he hadn't eaten much of anything that she'd seen. Wasn't sleeping, either, though that wasn't all that strange. He dropped his fork and it clanked against the plate as he kneaded his eyes with the heels of his hands. He stretched his eyes and pinched the bridge of his nose, turning in his seat and appear-ing to look back at that table where the troopers sat.

"Why you so squirrelly?"

"I'm not."

"You not going to eat?"

"I'm not very hungry."

"You getting sick or something?"

"I don't think so."

Angie shoveled shrimp and peppers onto another tortilla. She was headed out of town for a few days to visit one of her girlfriends in Asheville. "You sure you don't want to go with me? We can go out to some of the breweries. I know how much you *love* Asheville," Angie said sarcastically.

"I can't," Calvin said. "Not in the middle of the week. We're already behind and Dad ain't going to be there to make sure anything gets done."

Angie wondered if work was wearing him down. As long as she'd known him, he'd been busting his ass six days a week, and he was too stubborn to listen when she told him to slow down. That's the way he was, working himself to death, and in a complicated way that was one of the things she loved most because no one carried that old-time work ethic anymore. That drive reminded her of her father and grandfather, salt-of-the-earth men who worked head down with callused hands.

The older gentleman from across the room wandered over to their table, hobbling bowlegged ahead of his family like he'd climbed off a horse. He rubbed his stomach with one hand and held a styrofoam to-go box in the other. A thick mustache crossed his lip. His hair was thinning and he had a pumpkin for a gut.

"Tell your dad I asked how he was doing, all right?"

"I will," Calvin said.

"I don't believe we've met." The man's wife shuffled in front of her husband and held her hand out to Angie. Angie covered her mouth until she'd had a chance to swallow. The woman wore a loose-fitting T-shirt and a long denim skirt, her hair permed and dyed. "I'm Dottie Mathis," she said. Her voice was high-pitched and nasal. "Our boys grew up with Calvin. Played ball together."

"I'm Angie." She shook Dottie's hand and smiled.

"You're a Moss, aren't you?" Dottie said.

"Yes, ma'am."

"I think I know your mother."

Angie nodded.

"She work down there at Freeman's?"

"She does."

"I thought so," Dottie said.

"And who are these little cuties?" Angie turned her attention to the girls.

"These are our granddaughters," Dottie said. "Amber and Tiffany." The older girl, maybe fourth grade, stood proud with her hair in a frizzy ponytail and black-framed glasses; while the younger girl, about five years old, tried to look tough hiding shyly behind her grandfather's leg. "They belong to our oldest, Mark. The two of y'all ought to be having some kids of your own pretty soon. Y'all tied the knot?"

"No," Angie said. Her face blushed as she thought, *Who the hell asks that?*

"You not asked her yet, Calvin?"

Angie turned to Calvin, who clenched his fork in his hand. He looked like he wanted to stand up and ram it right in her ear. "No," he said. "Not yet."

"You're living together, aren't you?"

"Yes, ma'am," he said.

Who the hell is this woman?

There was an abrupt pause in the conversation, everyone smiling awkwardly.

"Well, let's let them get back to eating," the man said, and he gathered his wife and grandchildren, putting his arms behind them to lead them toward the cash register.

"It was good seeing you," Calvin said.

"Nice meeting you," Angie said.

"And it was nice meeting you," Dottie added.

"Tell your dad I said hello," the man said, and then they were gone.

Angie waited until they'd left the room. "They seemed nice."

"They are," Calvin said.

"Then why you say it like that?"

"Nosey old bat." Calvin pinched his nose. "You're living together, aren't you?" he mocked. Angie shook her head and snorted.

Reaching across the table, she scooped a chip through his refried beans and raised her eyebrows with her mouth full. "Well?"

"Well what?"

"What's stopping you?"

"Stopping me from what?"

"From asking." She beamed, having put him to the fire.

Calvin looked at her, and the last of daylight came through the window and shone in his eyes like lake water. "You not going to drink your margarita?"

NINE

THAT FIRST WEEK WORK KEPT DARL MOODY BUSY SUNUP to sundown and that was his savior. They were building a rock wall along the front of a piece of property owned by folks who summered in the mountains. The last week had been spent digging and pouring a footer, but now that the concrete was dry, he got to do what he did best—and while his hands worked, his mind was thoughtless.

Now, in theory, with enough time and practice, any man could learn how to lay block. But the truth of the matter is that anyone who's spent time trying knows good and well that what looks simple enough simply ain't simple at all. There's an art to it. There's muscle memory to throwing mud and there's a God-given eye for level. Some of that can't be learned, but Darl Moody was a natural.

Early that first summer out of high school, he went to work and it was clear as day he'd been born with a gift. From the way things normally operated, even an outsider could look on at a crew and tell the pecking order. There were usually four men, and the youngest mixed mud and moved block. If the youngest was smart, he kept his mouth shut and stayed out of the way and watched the older men work and tried his damnedest to learn something in how they moved. Then there was an older one who could prep block and lay it well enough to make quick work of sidewalls, which was easy enough because there were line blocks and mason string to keep things running true. The boss man usually spent most of his time staring through a transit, moving that transit all around the jobsite to make sure everything was plumb. But the man who mattered, the most experienced mason, was the one who built the corners, because all of it, the whole wall, tied back to how those corners were laid.

What took most folks years took Darl Moody about a month. He had a natural eye for balance so that what he put down left little need to check for level. He laid block like a savant, cocking his head to the side, shifting things a hair, so that when his hands let go, it was plumb. Every time. Like clockwork. He didn't have to think much about it to do it. The truth of it was that when his hands were moving he never thought about anything at all. And that's how he worked.

The sun came up and the frost burned off and the day warmed the men's backs so that by lunchtime the others were beat, but Darl kept working. He turned, grabbed block, threw mud, and went on until the day was gone and there was no more light to see.

Visiting his sister had complicated things in a way he hadn't expected. Though guilt was eating him alive, he'd started to think that maybe that was punishment enough. Having to live with those feelings. Having to hold on to that secret. If he confessed, it wouldn't just be him who'd pay. His conscience would be clear, but all of that weight would shift onto the people he loved most. So him carrying it started to seem like the more honorable thing to do. Sacrifice the one for the many.

After work, Darl stopped in town, grabbed four junior bacon cheeseburgers from Wendy's, and scarfed the first three down before he was a mile up the road. He'd save the fourth for breakfast and get started early. *Best to stay busy,* he thought. *Best to just work yourself dog-tired, drink yourself to sleep, and hope you don't dream.* Dreaming was the worst of it anymore. Within that space a man had no choice whether or not he ventured into the shadow of memory.

He shook a can of Skoal to check if there was any left, then threw the empty tin on the floorboard and reached for a new can out of a roll he kept behind the seat. He ran his fingernail around the edge to rip the paper seal and loaded his lip with wintergreen, the tobacco stinging his tongue as he licked his fingers clean.

Darl lived in a doublewide tucked in a grove of scrub pine by the hay barn on the last of his family's land. His father had rented out the trailer all Darl's life, but after the old man died of a heart attack not long after his son finished high school, Darl shacked up in the trailer so that he could stay close to home and keep an eye on his mother. At one point in time, the Moodys had owned somewhere close to two hundred acres at the end of Moses Creek. But through the years, bills came due and folks lost jobs and times came where the family couldn't even afford the taxes, so now they were down to a final twenty-acre plot that didn't amount to much more than a few thousand dollars each fall when Darl cut the fields for hay.

It was almost nine o'clock when he pulled down the gravel

alongside the barn and made his way to the house. A car was in the drive and Darl didn't know who in the hell the beat-up Buick belonged to or what they were doing at his house. He reached under the seat for his pistol only to realize he'd left it by the bed that morning. As he pulled alongside the car and parked, he could see the shadow of someone sitting in a white plastic chair on the porch. Darl stepped out of the truck, raked the tobacco from along his gums, and tossed the plug of snuff into the pine-needle yard.

"Can I help you?" Darl asked.

"Wouldn't be here if you couldn't," a voice grumbled from the porch.

When he got to the front steps, Darl could see him in the yellow porch light. Dwayne Brewer sat low in the chair, his back bent awkwardly with little posture at all. He wore a pair of dark canvas carpenter's pants and a white T-shirt that climbed high on his arms. Dark black hair covered him from his shoulders to the backs of his hands. Dwayne stood when Darl came onto the porch. He was a good three or four inches taller than Darl and built like a concrete pillar. His hair was shaved low and he wore no beard, though stubble grew from the base of his neck to his eyes.

"I'm Dwayne Brewer," he said.

"Yeah, I know," Darl answered. He fiddled in his pocket for his keys. "What you doing here?" Darl asked, as he stuck his key in the dead bolt and opened the door.

"I got a few things I need to ask you." Dwayne stood behind Darl as if he were going to follow him inside.

"Well, to be honest with you, I'm beat," Darl said. "I ain't much in the mood for company, and I don't know a thing in this world me and you would have to talk about."

"It won't take long," Dwayne said, a certainty in his voice that ensured he would not leave until he got what he'd come for.

"All right," Darl said. "Let me just run take a leak right fast."

"I'll come inside." Dwayne waltzed into the house without waiting for a response.

Darl hit the lights in the living room. Clean laundry he hadn't folded was heaped on the couch. He tossed his keys on a side table and walked toward a darkened hallway. "Make yourself at home," he said. "I'll be out in a minute."

A small bathroom opened to the left before Darl's bedroom, but he headed for the gun. Darl flicked a lamp by the bed and found the M&P Shield where he'd left it and he shoved the pistol down the back of his pants, the grip hanging on the ridge of his belt. In the bathroom, he panicked. He turned on the faucet and stared at his reflection in the mirror over the bathroom sink. The water ran into his hands and he cupped it to his face, droplets catching in the curve of his beard. He tried to tell himself that it was all right, that things were going to be okay, but the feeling in the pit of his stomach said different. Darl flushed the toilet nervously in case Dwayne was listening, then made his way back to the front of the house.

Dwayne Brewer sat at the head of the dining room table, picking at his teeth with his finger while he stared at a picture hung on the wood panel wall.

"Is that your daddy?" he asked, nodding his head toward a picture of Darl's father sitting on a red Massey Ferguson with Darl as a baby on his lap.

"It is," Darl said. The front of the doublewide was a living room, dining room, and kitchen all bunched together. Darl walked into the kitchen, opened the fridge, and grabbed a beer. He offered one to Dwayne, but Dwayne shook his head, and so Darl took one for himself then came back to the table and sat. He could feel the gun at the base of his spine and that was the only thing at all that kept him from falling apart. *If he comes at me, I'll shoot him*, Darl thought. *If the son of a bitch moves, shoot him.*

"Come to think of it, I think I will have a beer," Dwayne said. He reached across the table and took the can from in front of Darl, popped the top, and sucked the foam through his teeth as it rose over the lid. Swishing the beer around in his mouth for a second or two, he swallowed hard and sighed. Darl didn't stand to get another.

"What's this about?"

"I got a few things I'm going to ask you, and after that I'll be on my way."

Now Darl went to the refrigerator to get himself another beer and to put enough space between them so that he didn't have to look Dwayne in the eyes while he spoke. He cracked the can and swallowed about half a Budweiser down in two gulps, the sides of the can crumpling in his fist. "Go on and ask," he said as he leaned against the side of the cabinets at the edge of the kitchen, Dwayne having to turn to face him. "I've done told you, I'm tired."

"All right," Dwayne started. "I'll come right out with it. Somebody told me you was back in there hunting on Coon Coward's land this past weekend and I want to know what you saw."

"Well, I don't know who you been talking to, but I wasn't back on nobody's land. Hell, it ain't even hunting season." Darl sipped his beer.

Dwayne stood and opened his arms like he was hung on a cross. He turned and sidled over until he and Darl weren't more than a foot apart. Darl looked up into his eyes, dark hollows as if Darl were staring down the pipes of a side-by-side shotgun.

"There's a problem with that," Dwayne said. "I know for a fact that you were. I seen it." He split two fingers like a peace sign and tapped at the bags under his own eyes.

"I don't know what you're talking about," Darl said.

"There you go again." He came closer until Darl could feel Dwayne's breath steaming against his forehead. "You're going to need to get real honest real fast or this ain't going to end well. Not for you, and not for anybody else, so why don't you go back over there to that table, sit down, and start over."

Darl went back to the table and Dwayne waited until he was seated to join him. A cheap brass chandelier suspended above them cast yellow streaks of light against their faces. Darl ground his teeth and studied the top of his beer can while he twisted it between his hands in circles against the tabletop's veneer.

"Thing is, I know you spent every evening last week going in and out of Coon Coward's property like you owned the place. I know that every evening after you got off work, you threw on your hunting clothes, grabbed your rifle, and waltzed in there like Elmer fucking Fudd. I know it like I know my name, because I seen you. I seen you with my own two eyes. You see, you didn't know it, but that old man has him a game camera in there and it was snapping pictures of you every time you went in and every time you come out and he showed them to me." Dwayne raised his eyebrows and waited for Darl to speak.

Darl could feel the sweat blistering his forehead and he was edging closer and closer to a moment when he'd snatch that gun loose from the back of his pants and shoot Dwayne Brewer with every bullet he had. *It'd be self-defense,* he thought. *He's in my house.*

"I ain't hear you," Dwayne said.

Darl still didn't speak.

"The way this all come about is that my brother went down in there after one of that old man's ginseng patches. Sissy told me he was going and I was waiting on him at the house when he never showed. Now you can tell me, like that old man did, that maybe my brother wound up running off somewhere else. But the fact is, his car is sitting right down there on that tractor trail where I know he parked it. That car's still sitting right there, but he ain't. So you're going to tell me what you saw or I'm going to have to think of some other way to find out why you're lying to me."

"I ain't seen nothing," Darl said.

"Who was that went in there with you Friday night?"

"I don't know what you're talking about, Dwayne." Darl was in it thick now, and he couldn't see any way out. His vision tunneled with the thought that Dwayne knew about Calvin.

"There you go again, Darl. That's the third time now, and I ain't going to let you lie me again. Three strikes. Ain't that how it works?" Dwayne rolled his knuckles along the tabletop, tapping a four count. "The fact I'm letting that slide is about as reasonable a man as I can be. I wish you'd show me the same kindness."

Darl could see a visible rage building someplace far back in the darkness of Dwayne Brewer's eyes.

"I saw a picture of you go into the woods Friday evening then a picture of you running out of there two hours later. A little while after that, here you come again only this time you wasn't by yourself. And the next time, the two of y'all come out of the woods you was carrying something, now wasn't you?"

"Is this about the deer?" Darl saw his last chance and grabbed ahold.

"What deer?"

"About the deer I poached off Coon Coward's land. Look, if it's about the deer, I'll give it to you. All of it. You just say it."

"I've already told you. This is about my brother."

"And I told you I don't know a thing about your brother. I didn't see him in there once. Not one day."

"Where's the meat?" Dwayne asked.

The question caught Darl off guard. "At the processor," he stuttered.

"At the processor?" Dwayne smiled and cut his head to the side to look at Darl from the corners of his eyes. "You mean to tell me you took a deer, out of season no less, to the goddamned processor?"

"I told him I was hunting depredation tags off a buddy's corn-field."

"Told who?"

"The processor."

"Who's processing it for you? Burt Hogsed?"

"No, Singleton's." Darl thought fast to come up with a story that couldn't be fact-checked. Bottom line was Wilson Singleton's drunk ass always had a pile of deer hanging in his walk-in freezer, but half the time he was too sauced to make heads or tails between back strap and chicken thighs.

"Wilson Singleton?" Dwayne Brewer laughed and shook his head. "You might as well let a kindergartner whittle on that deer with a penknife. My daddy went to school with Wilson. Said one time in ninth grade they was dissecting frogs in biology class and old Wilson got caught sticking his pecker in a frog's mouth. Said they called him Tadpole."

"Never heard that."

"Think you'll get much meat out of it?"

Darl could tell Dwayne was fishing. "Ought to."

"Not gutshot or nothing? What you shoot? .308? .270?"

"Ought six."

"I like a 7-08, myself. You handload?"

"No."

"What was you shooting?"

"Core-Lokt."

"Deadliest mushroom in the woods," Dwayne said with a smile, his teeth a shiny white juxtaposition that seemed unnatural. Everyone in his family had jarringly white teeth. "Hard to beat a bullet's been around seventy years. I've switched to the Nosler Partitions. Tried shooting the ballistic tips, but they ate up a lot of meat. Glad to hear you'll get plenty out of that deer you killed."

Darl nodded.

"I think I'll ride over there and have old Wilson give me a pound or two off yours, if that's all right. My freezer's damn near empty, and I don't know if I'll be able to get in the woods this fall or not."

"Have at it," Darl said. A pound, the loins, Darl would tell that son of a bitch he could take the whole damn imaginary thing if it'd get him out of the house.

Dwayne pounded his fist against the tabletop and scowled at the table where the base of his hand hit, as if weighing his options. In a moment, he stood and strolled toward the door like he was wandering down the road picking soda bottles out of the ditch. Darl watched him and when Dwayne was almost to the door he stood from the table. Dwayne turned then and stared at Darl in a way that filled Darl Moody with as deep a fear as he'd ever felt, a feeling he'd never known as a man, something older, something he hadn't felt since he was a child.

"You never did say who that was helped you carry that deer out."

"Just a friend," Darl said.

"A friend." Dwayne grinned and nodded his head. "Friends can get a man in a lot of trouble." He raised his eyebrows as if willing Darl to speak.

But Darl had nothing to say.

"I'll be seeing you," Dwayne said as he went outside and closed the door.

Darl crossed the room and reached for the lock. His hand paused. He wanted desperately to turn the dead bolt, but he was hesitant, fearing that Dwayne might hear that latch turn and come back. He pulled his gun from his waistline and clenched the grip in his fist by his side. *You can go out there right now and end this,* he thought. *You can finish it right now.*

But he did not move. He could not move. He simply stood there facing the door.

TEN

SOME SWEAR A PREDATOR CAN SMELL FEAR, BUT WHETHER there's an actual scent or something else entirely doesn't really matter. Dwayne Brewer could sense weakness. That feeling came to him like goosebumps. That natural. That fast. And in those moments Dwayne had always known he was in complete control. Walking out of the doublewide, he knew Darl Moody was scared, but whether or not he'd seen Carol in those woods, Dwayne wasn't sure.

A waning moon shone through scraggly pines, a ring around it so that its white face was haloed. Old-timers said that meant it was going to snow, but while there was a bite in the air, Dwayne didn't believe this. He believed in all kinds of wives' tales like that eggs set on Sundays would hatch all roosters or that yellow rattlesnakes always followed black ones, but despite his superstitions he was sure it wasn't going to snow the last day of September.

He stood on the edge of the porch for a moment and slipped a soft pack of smokes from the ruler pocket along the seam of his pants. He struck a match from a book that had come from Hill's Minnow Farm, took a long drag, then blew the smoke before him so that he parted his own cloud as he went down the front steps into the yard. He was in no particular hurry. Instinct told him Darl Moody was full of shit, but then again there hadn't been any pictures of his brother on that camera so he couldn't be sure. He'd find out one way or another, though. There was always a way to backtrack what a man said, and if Darl was lying, Dwayne would return.

The Deuce and a Quarter sat crooked by a burning bush that glowed yellow even in the cold tones of night. Darl's truck was parked close, and as Dwayne reached the driver's-side door of his car, he stopped and looked in the back of Darl's pickup. A cheap, drop-in liner bowed and warped across the bed. The bottom was ridged so that water would run out the back. Pine needles and dirt filled the grooves, with half an eighty-pound bag of Sakrete and a few loose penny nails scattered over the plastic bed. On the far side something caught Dwayne's eye. Metal flashed with moonlight so that there was a dull glare from whatever lay between the ridges of the bed liner. He walked around the back of the pickup, rested one arm on the tailgate, and reached for what he'd seen.

Dwayne Brewer held a pocketknife he'd held a thousand times over the course of his life. He turned the cheap Case sodbuster over in his hands, twisting it by its ends like he was rolling a cigarette. The yellow Delrin handle was split on one side so that only half the scale remained. This had happened long ago when the knife slipped from his own pocket and cracked against a rock while he and his brother were playing in the woods as children. Red Brewer had slapped Dwayne unconscious and put a cigarette out on Sissy's arm for letting his brother steal their father's knife. Dwayne squeezed the notch and opened the carbon steel blade, holding it in the light so that he could see the waves of dark gray patina blued into the steel all these years. Swipes against whetstone had eaten the blade back so that it was now thin as a fillet knife, though it still held a razor's edge. This was the only thing Carol had wanted of their father's when he died, and Dwayne hadn't argued. At the time, he hadn't been sure whether his brother specially liked the knife or whether it was something else altogether, a sort of portal to a memory that he could hold in his hands and go back and forth between the before and after.

A rage grew in him now, something he always felt first in the center of his chest that grew upward with a fiery intensity until it pushed into his eyes. What came next was thoughtless and wild as it had always been, a body driven by emotion rather than sense. Dwayne crossed the yard onto the porch and took the front door off its hinges with his fifteen-wide logging boot. Darl was by the dining room table and he turned, stupefied with terror, and slapped around at the table before coming up with the gun. Dwayne was already on him by then, and as Darl raised the pistol, his wrist was forced upward toward the ceiling so that the shot blasted against the brass chandelier, a bulb shattering in the wake, the fixture swinging from its cheap chain and cord. Dwayne had one hand gripping Darl's arm and the other squeezing the air from his windpipe. Darl's back arched against the table and then he was on the floor, the gun being hammered from his grip, Dwayne's fists coming down like stones.

Dwayne settled in and the fire spread over him. He could feel his entire body warming as if by a shot of whiskey. His fists came down and Darl cried for help at first, blood coming out of his nose and mouth; but soon there was no other sound than the dull clap of knuckles against meat. Dwayne hammered Darl's forehead and his scalp opened and that flash of white bone that quickly filled red triggered a moment of reason in a mind that had been wiped clean and blank. Dwayne's shoulders fell loose and he settled his hands around the neck of Darl's T-shirt, letting his weight sink onto Darl's collarbones. Darl Moody was unconscious beneath him, and Dwayne sat there straddling his stilled body, unable to catch his breath.

WHEN DARL MOODY WOKE, he rolled his head from side to side looking swollen eyed around the room as if trying to make sense of where he was. His family's hay barn was filled with faint light and shadow. He stood with his back against the spiraled face of a large, round bale of hay. His arms were stretched wide, his wrists bound by nooses of half-inch cable ratcheted to a shoulder-popping tension around the bale by a come-along on the opposite side.

Dwayne sat on a flipped milk crate and dug black soil from under his fingernails with the tip of his brother's knife. He glanced up at the sound of Darl's breath quickening as he came to. A mix of blood and mucus drooled from Darl's mouth and nose. His face was pulverized, his heavy panting labored and loud. When their eyes met, Darl screamed for help but his voice stammered as his breath ran out. He sucked for air and screamed again, this time his feet stomping wildly at the ground though the weight at his back could not be moved. Darl grunted and coughed then wailed again until his body finally wilted with exhaustion.

"Are you done?" Dwayne asked calmly, his eyes barely glancing up as he swiped the grit from the knife's tip back and forth against his thigh. Darl screamed again at the top of his lungs and Dwayne shook his head with disgust, then went back to cleaning the dirt from under his nails.

When the place was quiet, Dwayne Brewer stood, pinched the knife blade between his fingers, folded the pocketknife closed, and slid it into his pocket. He crept within a few feet and stood with his legs shoulder-width apart, his hands behind his back. Darl watched him and when their eyes met this time, he dropped his chin to his chest.

"Are you ready to tell me what happened?" Dwayne asked, his voice still low and collected.

Darl started to yell again and right then Dwayne grew sick of waiting. He lurched forward until the two of them were face-to-face and screamed into Darl's eyes. Darl was shaking his head and crying, his voice falling into a whimper, but Dwayne hovered there in front of him so close that he could smell the wintergreen on Darl's breath and he wailed with all of his might and all of his air like some lonely animal howling into the sky for anything that might return his call.

The barn smelled of seasoned hay, the ground a soft dust beneath him as Dwayne spun and scanned the room. The same rusted Massey Ferguson from the picture in the house of Darl and his father sat in the center of the barn with a loader attached to the front hydraulics. Bolted onto the loader, a long, dull bale spear with its mustard paint worn from the shaft jutted from the base of the bucket. Dwayne walked over to the tractor and climbed into the seat.

The keys were in the ignition and he pedaled down the clutch with his left boot, then turned the key. The starter whined before the engine caught. The tractor rumbled drowsily, then climbed into a faster groan as Dwayne adjusted the choke to a quickened idle. He toyed with the hydraulic levers till he figured out how to raise the loader and bale spear, and when he understood the controls, he put the tractor in gear and eased forward. The spear climbed until it was aimed at Darl's chest. The tractor skulked forward, and when he was close, Dwayne dropped the tractor into neutral, cut the engine, and feathered the brake so the machine inched ahead, the spear easing into Darl's sternum as the tires rolled.

Dwayne did not wish to impale him and the tractor spear did not break skin. Instead, it pushed into Darl's chest, the hay cushioning his back, so that he now wheezed for the slightest breaths. There was no sound but that of the engine ticking as it cooled and the asthmatic moans from Darl's lips. Dwayne climbed off the tractor and kicked at the front tire with his boot. He looked at Darl then and sniffed the air, a mix of gasoline and exhaust now filling the barn.

"Now we can talk," Dwayne said.

Darl had to save up two or three shallow breaths to speak, and when he did, his words were barely more than a whisper. "Are you going to kill me?"

"Yes," Dwayne said matter-of-factly, as if giving an answer to whether or not he was hungry.

Darl started to cry, hardly any breath reaching him now so that he choked as if he were drowning. Dwayne shook his head. He was absolutely disgusted by how a man could sit there with no fight left in him, sit there crying, helpless as a fucking child. There was no room in this world for the weak. He crossed the few feet between them and turned his face close to Darl's so that he could feel each exhale from Darl's mouth against his cheek.

"You know what I've seen," Dwayne said. "You know I know

you were there and that you and somebody else carried something out of the woods that night. What I want to know is what was in that tarp?" Darl didn't speak. Dwayne pressed his finger hard into Darl's forehead and roared. "Answer me! Was that my brother?"

"Yes," Darl whimpered.

"Who was that with you?"

Again Darl Moody did not speak.

"You're going to tell me or I'm going to take them farrier pliers over there and start taking pieces off of you like a goddamned science experiment. I think you'll be surprised at how much a man can lose without dying. You'll pass out, but you'll come to. You'll wake up and I'll keep going."

Darl sobbed and blubbered something indiscernible.

"What was that?" Dwayne asked.

Darl wept harder, and with every bit of air he had, he groaned his best friend's name, "Calvin Hooper."

Dwayne nodded his head and backed away from Darl's face. He stepped toward the tractor and rested his right foot on the front tire. "Did y'all bury him or just dump him off in the woods someplace?"

"Buried," Darl said.

"And did Calvin Hooper help you bury him?"

Darl nodded his head and tried to swallow a mouth filled with spittle and blood.

That was all Dwayne needed to know. He didn't much care how it happened, whether it was an accident or on purpose. Either way, his brother was dead, and either way two men had put him in the ground. Two men were what it all boiled down to now. Two men who both knew the same thing. One was no better than the other. Either could take him to the grave. Whittling that number down would make things so much easier.

Dwayne Brewer took his brother's knife from his pocket and unfolded the blade. He checked the sharpness against his thumb, the edge shining sheer white in that tiny bit of lamplight. He came forward fast and in one clean motion ran that blade lengthwise against Darl Moody's neck, his throat opening like lips. Blood shot out in long lines, rushing down the front of him, painting his shirt and that bale spear and his pants, and spilling onto the dirt floor. Darl was choking and his feet stamped violently at the puddle he made. Despite the way movies made things look easy, there was no grace in dying. He was pissing and shitting himself, the sound of him searching for air gurgling like a clogged drain.

Dwayne stood there staring into Darl's eyes like he was watching the nighttime sky. As a child, he'd been fascinated by the fact that stars could die and there'd been so many nights he and his brother had lain in the woods behind their house, watching through gaps in the trees, waiting for the lights to burn out above them. In all those nights, they did not see one. The stars held on to their shining, all those years, all those years, but in a few short seconds Darl Moody's eyes did not.

ELEVEN

EVERY NIGHT SINCE THEY BURIED CAROL BREWER IN THAT back pasture, Calvin Hooper woke up every ten minutes from dreams that always ended the same. Sometimes he was on a track-hoe at a jobsite or he could be standing in the batter's box at a softball game or maybe looking through the kitchen window as he washed dishes, but something would catch his attention out of the corner of his eye, and as he turned to look he'd see patrol cars with deputies stepping out and he knew why they were there, and they were too close for him to run, and that certainty, that overwhelming certainty, would shake him awake and he'd choke for air, his throat dry and aching.

Once again, he couldn't sleep. He was halfway through a bottle of Pepto-Bismol, lying flat on his back above the sheets, smoking a cigarette with a glass ashtray resting on his stomach, when he heard a creak from the front porch. The bedroom window was open, and as he peered out, he saw nothing across the moonlit yard. Over the past few weeks an animal had been coming onto the porch at night to steal kibble from a bowl left out for a stray cat. Calvin figured that's what it was and he went to the front door to run off the scavenger.

Through the storm door, he couldn't see anything on the porch, and as he looked to each side the glare on the glass made it impossible to see into the darkened corners. He flicked on the porch light and stepped outside and that quick he saw someone standing to his right. He tried to turn back for the shotgun he kept by the front door, but there was already a pistol aimed between his eyes.

"Don't do that," the man said. "You go on and have a seat over there in that swing."

Calvin froze. His heart pounded and he held his breath until he was dizzy. For a split second he looked Dwayne Brewer in the eye, then focused on the end of the pistol Dwayne held, the gun high enough that Calvin could see straight down the barrel. Dwayne was a good foot taller so that Calvin had no choice but to stare upward to meet his eyes.

"I said have a seat," Dwayne repeated, motioning with the pistol to a wooden porch swing at Calvin's back.

His legs were locked and when he did not move Dwayne came forward and slapped the pistol against the side of Calvin's face, his left brow ablaze in the wake. Brass gnats swarmed his vision. With both hands cupped to his eye, Calvin stumbled back to the swing and Dwayne came closer with his aim unwavering.

"You know who I am?"

Calvin nodded. The side of his eye throbbed and when he moved his hand a trickle of blood ran beneath his beard along his jawline, dripped from his chin onto his bare thigh.

"Then you know why I'm here."

Calvin stared blankly and did not say a word. All of a sudden, he wasn't feeling sick or tired. His mind was wired like he'd snorted a line of some marvelous drug.

"I've been by Darl's and we can take a ride over there to see what came of that, or you can save us some time and take me right to where y'all buried my brother."

"What did you do to Darl?"

"I don't think you're a dumb man, Calvin."

"What happened to Darl?"

"He got what was coming to him, just as you'll find yours," Dwayne Brewer said. His voice was deep and calm, a definitiveness in his words that left little room for wonder. "An eye for an eye, a tooth for a tooth. Ain't that what they say? You know what he did and he paid what he owed."

"And what about me?"

"I ain't quite figured that out yet." There was a strange look on Dwayne's face, a slight curve at one corner of his mouth like he found amusement in what he was thinking. He stepped a bit closer, to where the porch light fastened by the door was right over his shoulder, his figure now a menacing silhouette. "An eye for an eye, Calvin. The rule don't change."

"I don't know what you're talking about."

"You're going to take me to where the two of y'all buried my brother, and you're going to give him back to me so that I can make it right."

"How?"

"How ain't none of your goddamn business. He was my *brother*," Dwayne said. He growled that word and Calvin understood what they'd taken and what that meant. "He was the last bit of family I'll ever have, and I aim to make it right."

"And what then?"

"You'll find out what happened to Darl soon enough, and you already know why it had to be that way. *It had to be that way.*" He stressed that sentence as if it were destiny. "As for you, your time will come soon enough. And until then, your burden won't be light."

Dwayne Brewer had a strange way of speaking, what he meant slowly coming to rest in Calvin's mind so that the sheer weight of it made the world spin so much faster. Calvin's vision closed in and for a second he had to clench his thighs as tight as he could to keep his head from swimming. Everyone is scared of dying, but having it held over you like some unflinching shadow, a darkness neither growing nor receding, always there, that was enough to drive a man mad.

"A man's mind is its own kind of hell," Dwayne said.

Calvin watched, vacuous and silent.

"Enough time passes and I figure you might wind up doing it yourself," Dwayne said. "Save me the trouble. If not, we'll find some other way. Now let's get on with it."

"I need to put some clothes on," Calvin said. All he wore was a pair of plaid boxer shorts.

"I think all you'll be needing are them boots right there." Dwayne nodded to a pair of muddy logging boots by the door. He stooped to grab them, never once taking the pistol off of Calvin. He tossed the boots over so that their soles clopped against the porch planks. "And a shovel."

"There's one in the back of my truck."

"All right, then," Dwayne said.

Calvin Hooper pulled the boots onto his feet, the insides cool and sticky against his skin. He tightened the leather shoestrings in their eyelets and laced them back and forth around the speed hooks, pulling them taut, and wrapping them once around his ankles before whipping each boot into a double knot. When he stood from the swing, Dwayne Brewer motioned down the stairs and Calvin walked into the yard with his head hung low. The night air was cold around him but its temperature was no longer comforting. Now it was something else altogether, something utterly lonesome. He had no words to describe what he felt inside.

THROUGH THE FIELD, Calvin Hooper walked at gunpoint, the nighttime sounds quieting around them as if silence were their passenger. Calvin's legs were slick and itchy with dew from grass that rose waist-high in the first field. The cattle followed them, expecting to be fed, then gathered at the gate into the middle field and bawled as the two men went farther into the dark.

The night smelled wet with hay and manure, a sweet, earthy tang that was so familiar Calvin barely noticed it at all. They crossed over the small hill in the middle field and dropped down to the last pasture: a long, narrow pass edged on one side by creek and cut at hard angles into the tree lines. The trackhoe was right where he and Darl had left it, its mechanical arm turned away from the scab of fresh red clay.

Dwayne Brewer had carried the shovel from the house to keep Calvin from doing anything stupid, and when Calvin stopped where the dirt crumbled into the grass Dwayne threw the shovel at his feet.

"Dig," Dwayne said.

"It'd be faster if you let me on that machine."

"Yeah, it would," Dwayne said. "And you might tear into my brother's body and I'd have to cut you up into pieces."

Calvin bent over and took the shovel from the ground. He didn't have any gloves and the wooden handle was slick with dew. He knew his callused hands would be blistered in minutes, but he stabbed the spade into the ground, pressed it deeper with his boot, then loosened and tossed the first shovelful of clay from the grave. The ground was bony with rocks and roots, but the trackhoe had broken most of that up so digging out the refilled hole was much easier than it would've been the first time.

Mud slopped his shins and calves, splotches of clay climbing to his thighs, as he worked his way around and dug a foot down, then two, then three. Muscles burned and sweat ran over him so that if he stopped digging, even for a minute, the night air froze him solid. Calvin imagined he was somewhere close to halfway when his body started to give. He speared the shovel into the ground so that it stood on its own, then sat at the edge of the hole, his boxers and hamstrings slick with dirt.

"I need a cigarette," Calvin said, without turning to look to where Dwayne hovered in shadow. He heard something pat the ground behind him and as he looked over his shoulder he saw a soft pack of Doral 100s with a book of matches shoved behind the cellophane. Calvin slipped a cigarette out of the pack and struck a match.

"Them right there belong to the man you're digging up."

Calvin stuck the matches back where he'd found them and set the pack on the ground. There was a surreal calmness over him now, his mind slowing as his body neared exhaustion. "You know it was an accident," Calvin said.

Dwayne didn't answer. The only sound was a screech owl shrieking every now and again from somewhere far in the timbers.

"Darl didn't mean to shoot your brother, Dwayne. He was out there in the woods trying to kill a deer, and he saw what he thought was a pig rooting around."

"Thought he was a pig, huh?"

Calvin wasn't sure how to answer.

"I think you ought to get back in that hole," Dwayne said.

Calvin dropped back into the grave and rolled his head in circles, lifting his shoulders to try and work the tightness from his muscles. The cigarette dangled from his lips and he ran his fingers through his hair, his palms raw and burning. There was still a good ways to go and Calvin tried to remember how Carol Brewer's body had lain at the bottom so that he could be sure not to dig into him. He hadn't wanted to look at all, but for a second he had. His mind flashed back to that image he couldn't stop seeing and in that memory his thoughts quaked with an unsettling volatility. Scared to let his mind wander, he gripped the shovel's handle, speared into the ground, and dug deeper because that was easier, and in a few minutes his mind dissolved into the work.

Carol Brewer's left boot found air first. When he saw it, Calvin rested the shovel against the side of the grave and fell to his knees. His hands were bloody and busted and he clawed the soft clay with his fingers and tossed it aside. For hours there'd been the repetitive *chomp* of the shovel biting into the ground, the soft tumble as what was dug was thrown from the hole. But now there was silence and Calvin saw a shadow grow over his shoulder.

The smell of rot mixed with that of turned soil, but it was not nearly as overwhelming as he expected. Carol Brewer's boots and legs came out of the dirt. His camouflage pants were caked red with mud. When Calvin reached Carol's waist, he saw skin darkened an unnatural hue lightened only by the color of clay. The body was still stiff, the same as it was when they buried him, the ground having preserved him in some way, slowing what would have come quickly if left aboveground. At the head, the ground was sticky with some sort of fluid, only that dark birthmark offering any proof at all that this was Sissy Brewer. Calvin stopped once the body was exposed and he gaped at the dark figure above him.

"Even a dog you'd wrap in a blanket," Dwayne said, disgusted. Calvin knew he was right, that perhaps this was the most shameful part: He and Darl hadn't even treated Carol Brewer as human.

Dwayne passed down into the grave a sheet he'd taken from the trunk of his car and told Calvin to wrap it under his brother's body. Slowly Calvin worked Carol's feet then his legs then his torso and arms until the thin cotton sheet was completely beneath the body, the fabric lit blue by moon like a puddle of water. When it was done, Calvin pulled the corners together and tied them into a knot, and lying on his stomach, Dwayne took this thing from him in his fist, with his other hand still clenching his pistol. He grunted above and the body rose. The ground was slopped and soft now and Calvin leaned against the grave's wall until Dwayne had his brother somewhere he could not see from where he stood.

His arms and shoulders were stiff as wrung cloth and the arches of his feet were sore from kicking down onto the shovel's step. All over he was slicked with mud and sweat. Taking the shovel in his hands, he tossed it out of the hole and readied himself to climb out. He kicked up the wall as he jumped and caught the edge at his chest and pushed up with all his might, his face kissing the ground. Something hammered into the back of his head at that moment, the sound of metal clanking against skull, and his eyes lit white as if by a camera's flash, a sweeping blackness thereafter.

Calvin crumbled into the grave, his arms spread wide, with one leg tucked beneath him. The ground was cold and wet against his back, but he did not feel it. He saw and heard nothing. It would be daylight before he woke frozen to the bone. For the first time in days, he slept.

TWELVE

DWAYNE BREWER CARRIED HIS BROTHER'S BODY IN A KNOTTED sheet over his shoulder as if he was toting a sack of potatoes. And though he was freakishly strong, the weight sanded him down so that as he traversed a small hill and dropped over the other side he had to stop and rest with his hands on his knees until he'd caught his breath.

The trail that wound a half-mile into the woods behind the shotgun shack where Sissy had lived could be seen more as a tunnel through the trees than any visible path scored into the ground. First light glowed behind a treed horizon, but Dwayne could have found his way whether night or day, whether the path was grown over or exactly how his grandfather'd left it.

Only an iron door with black paint peeling to ragged patches of rust and a small wall of river stone cobble showed against the hillside. Even that was camouflaged by briar and vine. The rest of the root cellar was buried into the mountain to keep the temperature low and constant. Red Brewer's father had built this place and it would remain long after their name was gone. The construction wasn't all that different from root cellars and canning sheds old-timers kept all over the mountains, but what was strange was that he'd built it so far from the house. His grandfather had always run a thumper keg still that required good water, so he set up along a shallow creek and built this place a few feet away to store runs of white liquor.

Those last few steps, Dwayne hefted his brother a few feet at a time. His shoulders burned and his tired mind retreated to a memory when a thin, red mud wheelbarrow track had marked the path he'd taken. Back then, he and Sissy would help their grandparents run mason jars of canned summer vegetables from the house to the shed in a blue bucket wheelbarrow lined with old quilts.

Dwayne set the bundle behind him and lifted a thick iron bar from its welded latch, the heavy door groaning open on a rusted hinge. A whisper of air came onto him and the smell of it, the coolness of it against his face, took him back to a moment when he'd stood right there only reaching his grandfather's waist. A dressed deer had hung from a hook on the ceiling to dry age. His grandfather had brought him to work the dark, sinewy meat into cuts. There was so much memory tied to this place, so many memories of kin and the closest things he'd ever known to love.

Gradually his eyes adjusted to the darkness inside and he entered. There was no electricity and the lanterns that swayed from rafters were empty of oil. The sliver of light that carved through the doorway lit the dusty dirt floor, the pitched wood eight-by-eight supports, the crate shelves lining the walls where forgotten jars still held canned beans and hominy in clouded solutions. A small crack ran jagged along the mortar on the back wall and glistened with a slow seep of water that left the room damp and dank with mildew.

Dwayne carried his brother into the far corner and propped him against the cobbled wall. He pulled Sissy's knife from his pocket and sliced the sheet open as if it were a cocoon. The smell of rotting flesh was growing, and Dwayne was caked with it—his white undershirt and brown pants were stained with mud and blood and sweat and something else, something that leached through the sheet. He worked the fabric away from Sissy's body, cutting shreds at a time until only a bunched mat rested beneath him. Sissy's body was rigid so that it took a great deal of effort for Dwayne to balance his brother upright, his arms at his sides, his legs out before him as if he were just sitting there perched against the wall.

Clay covered Sissy's camouflage clothes and painted his darkened skin a dry, dusty orange. A tin pail sat by the door and Dwayne carried it outside to fill it with creek water to wash his brother's face. The ground was soft and green, a thick mat of turkeyfoot spreading right up to where the water ran. There was no color or tinge, the creek clear as crystal as he dipped the bucket full, swirled the water around the rusted bottom, emptied and filled the bucket again until what he carried matched the clarity of what flowed over stone and sand.

Back in the cellar, Dwayne cupped his hands full and poured water over his brother's head like a baptism. Carol's hair was thick and curled, a sandy color like hay, but it lay flat as the water slicked it against his scalp, tiny droplets like glass beads catching in his eyelashes. Dwayne wet one hand and swiped it down his brother's cheek, the texture like brushing rain from a suede coat. Something about that feeling made him almost sick with guilt and he couldn't bear to touch his brother again. He stood and took the pail and pitched water against Carol's face, then poured what remained over his head and arms. Though Carol was soaking wet—his clothes drawing tight to his body, the dusty ground darkened around him—Dwayne could see his brother more clearly now. His skin was greenish in hue, his arms blistered and dark as if charred by fire. There were blisters on his lips, an amber-colored resin dried at his mouth and eyes, that dark birthmark the only proof at all that this was Sissy.

Dwayne stood over what was left of his family. Until then, it had all been work, and only now could he stop to think about the absolute consequence of it all.

All his life, he'd felt a responsibility to shield his younger brother from harm, to ensure that he took the brunt of whatever pain this world dealt because he was tough enough to bear it. Whether it was standing between Sissy and their father when Red Brewer grabbed a glass gallon jug or an iron firedog to swing, or shoving Sissy in the closet when one of Red's drinking buddies wandered into the boys' bedroom late at night to crawl in bed beside them, Dwayne Brewer had taken everything he could, out of the deepest love he'd ever known.

Guilt washed over him then, an immense shame that hit him with an intensity he'd never felt before. He crashed to his knees sobbing and toppled face-first into his brother's wetted chest. Dwayne wailed and screamed and pounded his fists against the ground until his knuckles crusted with dirt and blood. "I'm sorry," he stammered. "I'm sorry!" His words were muffled but loud. The tears would wane only when something greater found him. Only one feeling could mask that kind of sadness, only one emotion he knew more powerful than suffering. In time, it would fill him. Only in time would he find a place to aim that rage.

THIRTEEN

CALVIN HOOPER WOKE AT FIRST LIGHT FROZEN TO THE bone. He was naked all but boxers and boots, his skin slicked and wetted with mud. The sound of his teeth clacking roused him. He was curled in the fetal position, shivering, and as he opened his eyes, his vision tightened onto something shiny in front of his face. He reached for what he saw, rolled the brass casing between his fingers and studied the copper jacket: a single .45 ACP cartridge, left in the grave like a promise.

Calvin clenched the bullet in his fist, rolled onto his back, and stared into empty sky. A few dim stars had yet to retreat to darkness. He lay there for a few minutes thankful for having woken at all. With the tips of his fingers he traced the cut along his left eyebrow then felt the knot at the back of his head. His skull throbbed with the pace of his heart, and as he stood the pain strengthened, pounding as he crawled his way out of the grave.

His parents' house overlooked the middle field and he couldn't risk being seen, so he kept tight to the hillside on his way home, slinking along a sagging fence line with posts grayed and thin as gnawed bones. There were so many questions, so many things he didn't know right then. He could still hear Dwayne Brewer's voice echoing, five words as finite and certain as those carved in gravestone. "He paid what he owed," he'd said. Soon enough Calvin would know his debt. The bullet he now carried in his hand ensured it.

FIELDS GREW THICK on both sides of Darl Moody's driveway: tall, golden oat grass ready to be cut and baled. Pasture butted against a thick copse of pine, the gravel drive carried on into the trees to where the doublewide stood with its beige siding stained and sagging. The shingled roof was littered rust-brown with pine needles. The ground was strewn the same, so that as Calvin stepped out, the soles of his boots were silent against the yard. He fished his pack of cigarettes out of the pocket of his jeans and blew a line of smoke into the sky, the top of the pine above him dead and filled with widowmakers.

A small covered porch led to the front door; a white plastic chair was slung to the side, the door hanging crooked from its hinges. He made his way up the steps and went inside. The entrance opened to a large living area where clothes were piled on a black leather couch. The coffee table in front of the couch was cluttered with bills and remote controls, an entertainment center catty-cornered against the wall.

He walked around the couch into the dining room: a hallway off to the right, the kitchen to the left, another bedroom on around from there. The candlelight bulbs of a cheap brass chandelier were lit over the dining room table, only four of the five bulbs aglow. The table was crooked and there was blood on the floor, that dark red color raising the hackles on his neck. He knelt there and examined the pattern dotted about the carpet. Something under the table caught his eye, a small silver bullet casing.

Still crouching, Calvin surveyed the room searching for where the bullet hit. Above him, the fifth bulb in the fixture hadn't burned out. It was shattered. The metal chandelier arm was mangled and there was a hole in the tiled ceiling panel behind it. A single casing on the floor and a hole in the ceiling, but there was not enough blood for anyone to have been shot and killed there. He rose to his feet and made his way around the rest of the house, the place empty and silent.

When he walked outside onto the front steps, he could see the barn down the drive through the pines. Two Tennessee Walkers stood side by side in the pasture off to the left when he came down the gravel, the grass high around them, horses old and rib-slatted. Calvin watched them and they didn't turn. A breeze pushed across the field slicking the grass to one side like parted hair and there was a chill to the air when it reached him.

In his mind, he already knew what was inside. He could walk the place by memory, having been in that place hundreds of times before: a pile of rusted T-posts in the corner, dust-covered quarts of motor oil lining a shallow ledge, brown-glass Clorox bottles, lengths of rope wound and draped on bent nails, bolt cutters here, a set of Allen wrenches there, three cage traps beside a dented gasoline can in the loft. It was a scene not unlike a hundred other barns in the county, a place filled with nothing of great importance. But as his hand touched the cold metal handle of the barn door, he was overcome with an ominous sort of sadness, something coming through his body, assuring him of what he would find.

Pulling the heavy door back on its rollers, he heard a barn swallow fly from its cob nest in the rafters, the sound of its wings pattering overhead then silence. The air carried a mix of old hay and gasoline and the dull iron smell of rust. There were no lights inside, only daylight coming through the open door. From the mouth of the barn, he could see Darl Moody against the round hay bale, his arms stretched at his sides, his head hung to his chest, the neck of his shirt red with blood. The rest of him was hidden behind an old Massey Ferguson tractor. Calvin inched closer to where he could see the loader raised high with its bale spear driven into Darl's chest, and for a second he stood there in absolute disbelief. In all his life, he'd never seen this sort of wickedness, the spectacle of what lay before him unreal, unfathomable.

Blood covered the front of Darl so that he was highlighted dark with it, the puddle under his feet sitting thick as paint on dirt like what might've been left from gutting a deer. Calvin collapsed to his knees. He was staring at the dusty ground, pins and needles stinging the palms of his hands, his arms unable to support his weight. A ringing rose in his ears and the room closed in around him and he couldn't breathe and he turned and crawled out of the barn, clawing his way across the gravel till his hands found grass, dew seeping through the knees of his jeans, the coldness of the world waking him up with a white-hot intensity.

Mourning found him there, a sorrow so deep that it clenched him into a ball and he sobbed like the world had ended. Seconds were hours and minutes were days, years passing in the decades of tears, a thousand or more before the feeling waned enough for him to make the call.

"Jackson County 911, what is your emergency?"

"I need help," Calvin said.

"Okay, sir, I need you to tell me your emergency."

Those three words were all he could stomach. He tried so desperately to speak.

"Sir? Sir, are you there?"

There was not enough breath inside him to answer.

FOURTEEN

FOUR HOURS INTO SITTING AT THE SHERIFF'S OFFICE WAIT-
ing for detectives to return from the scene, Calvin Hooper was stir-
crazy. The room wasn't much bigger than a closet and he'd
memorized every detail: the slate-colored level loop carpet; the
blank white walls; a round-face clock centered above the door with
its red second hand ticking away the last of twelve o'clock; the
rough texture of the gray plastic tabletop where he sat in a metal
folding chair, staring at a small video camera mounted against the
ceiling in the corner of the room.

He was convinced they were watching him. He tried to stay
calm, but the truth was he was losing his mind. The fluorescents
overhead were blindingly white, their reflection against the walls
surrounding him with light. It was like being snow-blind sitting
there, the room so bright he could feel it physically touching him,

beating against his arms and his face. Four hours he'd been sitting there. Four hours and no one had come in to say a word. He couldn't take it any longer. He knew if he sat there one more minute he was going to lose his mind.

Calvin stood and peered through the small shatterproof window in the door. No one appeared to be standing guard outside. He expected the door to be locked, but to his surprise it opened to an empty hallway, not a soul outside to stop him. Pulling his pack of smokes from his pocket, he headed back the way they'd brought him in. The front lobby was around the corner to the left.

He passed an open doorway and peeked into an office where a woman wearing too much makeup sat behind a desk pecking away at a keyboard. She glanced up at him and he could see the line where her foundation ended along her jaw, her face a darker shade than her neck. Tight curls streamed over both shoulders, her dark hair teased in the front. She squinted hard and started to stand. "Sir?"

Calvin sped up and didn't answer.

"Sir," she said again, now behind him in the hall. "Sir, where are you going?"

He turned around and showed her the pack of cigarettes in his hand. "I'm going to go outside and grab a smoke."

"No, I need you to go back down the hall and have a seat in that room." She came toward him, the pants suit she wore shushing as she walked.

"I've been sitting in there four hours and there hasn't been a soul come in there and say one word to me. Ain't said boo to a goose." Calvin was getting angry. "Now, I'm going to go outside and smoke a cigarette and when I'm through I'll come back in here and sit down."

"No, sir. You're going to go back to that room like I said and you're going to sit there and wait patiently." When she reached him, she latched ahold of his arm and Calvin jerked away from her.

"Get your goddamn hands off of me."

She swiped for him again and he leaned back. The woman was yelling that he was going to go back and sit in the room and Calvin was telling her he was going outside to smoke a cigarette, and they were at each other's throats when Detective Michael Stillwell came around the corner and pulled them apart.

"Hey," Stillwell stammered. "Hey. What's going on?"

The woman started to speak and Calvin cut her off. He'd known Michael Stillwell all his life, the two of them having played baseball together in high school, and though they'd never really been friends, Calvin was glad to see a familiar face. "I've been sitting in that goddamn room for four hours, Michael, and nobody's come in there to say a word to me. Now all I'm wanting is to go outside and smoke a cigarette."

"Not right now," Stillwell said. He had gray eyes and dark hair same as he always had, but there were bags under his eyes now and he'd softened up in the middle. He wore a cheap navy blue suit, one of those buy-two-get-the-third-free Belk jobs that wasn't fit for shit but minimum-wage job interviews and caskets.

"What do you mean? All I want to do is go outside and smoke a goddamn cigarette. Am I under arrest?"

"No, you're not under arrest."

"Then why can't I go outside?"

"I was on my way in to see you," Stillwell said. "Come on. Let's go back here and talk." Stillwell put one hand on Calvin's shoulder and opened his other to gesture down the hall. He led Calvin back to the interrogation room, opened the door, and held it for Calvin to enter. "Have a seat right there and I'll be back in a second."

Calvin walked into the room and plopped into the folding chair. He rubbed at his eyes with the heels of his hands, opened his eyes wide to the brightness of the room, and clenched his teeth.

In a minute or two Stillwell came into the room carrying two styrofoam cups. "Brought you some coffee," he said, setting both cups on the table. He took off his jacket and hung it around the back of his chair.

"I don't want any coffee, Michael. I told you I want a cigarette."

"Go ahead and smoke."

"They told me I couldn't smoke in here. Said nobody's allowed to smoke inside the building."

"And that's about the least of my worries, Cal," Stillwell said. "Ash into that coffee cup if you don't want it." He slid a steaming cup a little closer toward Calvin.

Calvin leaned back in his chair and dug around in his pocket. He shook a cigarette out of his pack and struck his lighter, took a long drag and blew the smoke overhead. The cloud broke against the ceiling and came down around them as he set his pack on the table, then centered the lighter on top.

"I looked through the written statement you gave when you got here, but I'm going to ask you some questions and I need you to be completely honest with me, Cal."

The cigarette dangled from Calvin's lips and he squinted his eyes to block them from smoke. He leaned back in the chair and shoved his hands into the front pocket of a dirty black hoodie with the HOOPER EXCAVATING logo on the chest.

"This is an official statement just the same as the written one and that means what you tell me better not change from here on out, you understand?"

Calvin nodded and the cigarette glowed from his lips.

"This is being recorded." Stillwell flicked his eyes toward the camera in the corner of the room. "So I need you to answer everything I ask as honest as you can. Tell me everything you can think of even if it doesn't seem all that important."

Again, Calvin nodded. He took his hand out of his pocket to ash the cigarette, flecks of burning tobacco hissing as they hit the coffee.

"So what time did you get over there to Darl's this morning?"

"About seven," Calvin said. "Maybe a little before."

"And what were you doing there?"

"I'd come over to try and help him with his tractor. He busted the boom. Wanted me to see if it was something we could fix or if he needed to buy a new one."

"So why'd you get there so early?"

"Seven ain't early," Calvin said. "Me and Dad got a big job going right now. I'm busy as hell at work and so was Darl. That's the only time either one of us had. I was going to take a quick look at it and head on to work. He was going to do the same."

"He was expecting you to come by this morning?"

"Well, yeah." That question seemed stupid to him. "Darl had some work this weekend and he needed to get the tractor fixed."

"When's the last time you talked to him?"

"I don't know. A day or two ago." Calvin took a long drag and tapped a fingernail of ash into the coffee. "I guess a couple days ago. I told him I'd be by there this morning."

"And you talked on the phone?"

"No." Calvin closed his eyes and shook his head. "No, I ain't talked to him on the phone since sometime last weekend."

"Then how'd you talk to him?"

"I ran into him at Ingles. He was sitting in his truck eating Burger King and I stopped by Ingles to pick up some milk and happened to see his truck."

"Was anybody with you?"

"No."

"Anybody see you?"

"I don't reckon." Calvin was starting to get confused. The questions Stillwell was asking made it seem like he was a suspect. "What's it matter if somebody saw me talking to him or not?"

"I'm trying to help you, Cal. That's all. If somebody tells me they were at the Ingles, it's my job to figure out whether or not that's true. So if somebody can tell me they saw you there, that helps all of us."

"I told you I was there."

"I know you did."

"Then why else would I have said it?" Calvin dropped the cigarette into the cup, the yellowed filter spinning where it floated.

"Tell me about this morning."

"What about it?"

"What'd you find when you got there?"

"I pulled up to the house and the door was standing open so I figured he was awake. When I got on the porch, I hollered for him and didn't get a response and so I went on in. I saw some blood there by the dining room table, but I didn't really think much of it right then—"

"You didn't think much of it?"

"No. A man works with his hands, he busts something open every day."

"So . . ."

"So I went on around the house thinking he might've been in the shower and I hollered back there in the bedroom, and when I never could find him I walked down to the barn figuring he might already be working on the tractor and that's when I found him."

"What did you find?"

Calvin Hooper slammed his fists against the table. The coffee cup rattled, but neither toppled nor spilled. "What the fuck do you mean what did I find?" His green eyes were wide and his bottom jaw jutted out in anger.

"I need you to tell me what you saw."

"You know what I saw! I saw Darl tied to that goddamn hay bale." Calvin fought hard to keep from crying. He could feel his eyes frosting with tears. "And I saw the blood. I saw all of that blood and him hanging there."

"And what did you do then?"

"Are you dumb or something? I called you!" Calvin started to sob and he buried his face in his hands. Stillwell reached over and set his hand on Calvin's shoulder and Calvin jumped away startled before crying harder when Stillwell squeezed onto him. "He was my best friend," Calvin stuttered. "Darl was like a brother to me."

Calvin hadn't slept or eaten in days, and over the past few hours he'd reached his threshold, the place deep inside that no man can point a finger to until he buckles. The place where he could take no more had come and gone in the blink of an eye and now here he sat little more than a husk of what he was a week before. The only sound now was their breathing and the slow tick of the second hand working its way around the clock face. Neither moved, and finally, in a few minutes, Calvin Hooper lifted his head, reached for his pack of smokes on the table, and lit another cigarette. He spun the lighter around on the tabletop a half turn at a time, staring blank and emotionless.

"What I'm going to ask you now is probably the most important thing I'm going to ask, Calvin."

Calvin looked at Stillwell from the corners of his eyes. He bit at a hangnail on his thumb and then took a long drag from his Winston.

"Who hated Darl enough to do that?"

"Nobody," Calvin said.

"You sur—"

"I'm sure," Calvin interrupted. "Darl Moody never met a stranger in his life. He never had a cross word with anybody that wasn't settled right then and there."

"Had he gotten into drugs? He owe anybody any money that you can think of?"

"No," Calvin said. "Darl drank a few cold beer, but that was it. Look, I don't know what you want me to say. Darl Moody was the same kid we went to high school with. He worked his ass off all week, loved to get in the woods, and usually tied one on come Friday. About the worst thing I ever knew him to do was to put that raccoon in Donald Ray's little gay-ass Miata when we were in eleventh grade. Outside of that, he was about as good a man as I ever knew."

"What happened was personal," Stillwell said. "What happened in that barn ain't the kind of thing somebody just up and decides to do."

"I don't know what to tell you."

"What happened to your eye?" Stillwell leaned back in his chair and crossed his arms over his chest.

The question caught Calvin off guard and for a short second he looked puzzled. "What?"

"I said what happened to your eye right there?" Stillwell gestured with the back of his hand to the side of Calvin's face.

Calvin lifted his left hand and patted gently beside his eye almost having forgotten what was there. He took a few quick puffs from his cigarette to finish and twisted the cherry off the filter before dropping it into the coffee. "I was cutting wood."

"When did you do that?"

"Yesterday," Calvin said. "I was felling a few trees and a limb come out of the top of one of them and smacked me in the back of the head. I got knocked down and landed on a rock." He kept his hand at the side of his face.

"Where were you cutting trees?"

"Up behind the house."

"Let me see the back of your head." Stillwell leaned to the left to try and get a better view and Calvin tilted his head forward and showed the egg-shaped knot. Stillwell grunted. "That looks like it hurt."

Calvin patted tenderly around the wound, grabbed his pack of cigarettes from the table, and shoved them into his pocket. "The way you're asking all these questions seems like you're saying I might've had something to do with this."

Stillwell didn't answer.

"Is that what you're saying? Am I a suspect?"

Stillwell made a fist with his right hand and fit his left overtop of it. He stared at his hands and squeezed his knuckles. In a moment he looked up. "It'd be naive to think that you weren't."

"So do I need to talk to a lawyer?"

"I don't know," Stillwell said. "Do you think you need to get a lawyer?"

"Look, am I under arrest here, because I—"

"No, no, you ain't under arrest," Stillwell interrupted him.

"Well is there anything else?"

"You got your phone on you?"

"Yeah."

"Then pull it out and put my number in it."

Calvin slid his cell phone from his pocket and entered the number Stillwell gave.

"You think of anything else, you call me."

"I've told you everything I know," Calvin said. He stood and Stillwell looked up and nodded, not another word spoken as Calvin left the room.

In the front lobby, a wall was lined with brass plaques engraved with the portraits and names of past sheriffs. Calvin didn't know why, but he walked over and studied the portrait of Sheriff Griff Middleton, who was killed in a holler up Little Canada in 1953 while he was hunting down some Woods boy for assaulting Norvella McCall. Sixty-three years later, having happened three decades before he was born, Calvin knew the story the same as everyone else to ever come out of Jackson County. Things had a way of never leaving these mountains. Stories took root like everything else. He was a part of one now, part of a story that would never be forgotten, and that made bearing the truth all the more heavy. Just as Dwayne told him the night before, a man's mind is its own kind of hell.

FIFTEEN

WHAT THE GROUND HAD SLOWED HASTENED THOSE FIRST few days Sissy sulked against the wall. His shoulders fell and his body limbered, but he was swollen now, his face grotesque and disfigured. The smell of rotting meat washed over Dwayne Brewer the minute he opened the door. That hot, soured smell was similar to roadkill bloated by sun, but it was bigger, richer, so that you could sense the size of what decayed.

Dwayne came into the room and sat down in front of his brother. He looked at his face, how his cheeks were a greenish-blue. Large blisters covered his arms, marbled skin almost glossy. As Carol bloated to twice his size, he outgrew his clothes so that the fabric cut hard into his skin, the bottom of his shirt rising high on his stomach. His eyes were popping out of his head, his tongue bulging from his mouth, and it was hard for Dwayne to see this, but for whatever reason he couldn't help but look.

Over the past few days, he couldn't stop remembering. It was like his mind was suddenly flooded with all the years they'd spent together, memories boiling out of him without any trigger or control.

One fall when Dwayne was about twelve years old, he'd camped in the wreckage of a fort he'd built. When he woke, a rafter of turkeys were picking about the ground for acorns, coming out of a thick hedge of laurel where they'd bedded down while he slept. "It's strange of turkeys not to roost in the trees, but these slept on the ground," Dwayne told his brother when he went home. That night they decided they'd wake up early the next morning and try to kill one with a bow and arrow.

The sun had not broken the ridge when he and his brother climbed the leaf-littered hillside to the ruins of the fort. Walls constructed with busted tires and pieces of scrap two-by-fours and plywood collapsed in on themselves, and the long piece of rusted tin he'd salvaged from the stream for a roof was crumpled like a smashed beer can.

The turkeys were scattered about the ground, dark shadows crouching in laurel. One of the birds was closer than the rest, a clear uphill vantage from here to there, and Dwayne coaxed his brother to take the shot. He took an arrow from his quiver and nocked it onto the bowstring, then handed the weapon to Sissy.

Drawing back, Sissy settled his aim. There was the short, swift *thooot*, and that arrow was into that bird's side before Dwayne ever had a thought. He watched as the bird screeched in terror, all of those other turkeys waking up and tearing off over the ground in a deafening madness, and that bird beat furiously with one wing, its other run through and pinned to its body by the arrow.

Dwayne and his brother prowled closer and the bird flapped itself in circles as that one side tried desperately to get away while the other was as useless to its body now as a tumor. When the bird stopped, Dwayne could see the blood pumping over its mottled feathers, a red so bright that it seemed to glow against such a dark backdrop. The bird cocked its head to the side and opened its sharp beak toward him and Dwayne could see something familiar in its eyes, something so familiar in its suffering.

The turkey collapsed onto its side and they stood there for a minute watching, waiting for what would come. Dwayne tiptoed closer. He'd never seen a bird blink its eyes until right then, and something about that, something in the way its eyes opened and closed, made him feel a sentience in its existence. Like that turkey wasn't some bird but something else entirely, something exactly like him. There was so much blood, all of the feathers wetted with it, and the bird opened its beak, a wheezing sound coming then like it was out of breath. Dwayne knew the bird was dying and there was nothing he could do to stop it. He also knew that it was suffering, and all he could think was that they had to end that suffering, to hasten its death. This was what was meant by mercy.

"You have to finish it off," he said.

Carol had the bow in his hands and he was watching the bird vacantly, his eyes filled with tears.

"Kill it, Sissy," he said, but his brother neither moved nor spoke.

Dwayne looked around the ground for something, not knowing exactly what he was looking for, and his eyes settled on a rock about the size of a football, a large hunk of milk quartz muddied with red clay. He picked up the rock with both hands. Standing above the bird, he raised the stone over his head and readied himself to end it. When it came down he closed his eyes, and when he opened them he saw he had failed. The ground was soft beneath the bird's head so that the blow only mangled it further, its wing flapping wrathfully, its head in slow contortion. Within its black stare, the boy could see forever and he could hear his brother wailing behind him.

He hurried and grabbed the rock again, readied himself, and came down harder, and this time when he opened his eyes the deed was done. The only movement now was in the way the wind ruffled bronze feathers. Dwayne Brewer had killed plenty of small game—rabbits, squirrels, and doves. He'd even killed his first deer the fall before. But this was something different entirely. He wasn't bothered by it. It was just different. It had felt necessary. Absolutely necessary.

When he turned around he saw his brother on his knees, his face beet red, that dark birthmark glossed with tears. Dwayne understood that his brother was not meant for this place, that some people were born too soft to bear the teeth of this world. There was no place for weakness in a world like this. Survival was so often a matter of meanness.

"You never had a mean bone in your body," Dwayne said as he looked across the floor to where his brother rested against the cobbled wall. And true as it was, the world's cruelty had found him just the same.

SIXTEEN

THE CORONER HELD DARL MOODY'S BODY TILL TUESDAY SO that he was buried two days later, nearly a week after Calvin found him. Leading up to the funeral, Calvin didn't think that he could do it. He couldn't imagine being able to carry the casket from the front of the church to the hearse, from the back of the hearse to the grave, knowing what he knew. But when Darl's mother asked him to be a pallbearer, he couldn't say no.

Strangely, as he carried that shiny black casket up the hill, he hadn't felt what he'd expected. Truth was, he'd felt nothing at all, merely a sleepy sort of delusion like he'd woken out of a dream. Strange. Unreal. Like he'd woken into a new world having never stepped foot there before.

It had always seemed unnatural for the sun to shine on a funeral. It had always seemed strange to bury bodies on a hill. Graves here were uneven things, one end dug deeper than another. Headstones dotted the slope above Chastine Creek. Some of the markers were so old and worn that the names had been erased by time. Some of the oldest had never held names because those left to the mountains knew who lay beneath them.

Darl Moody's mother wore a black dress that fit her like a nightgown and a stoic expression that demanded she had no more tears to cry. The plot beside her husband's grave was dug, a mound of red clay hidden on the other side. It must've been so extraordinary to be staring at a piece of ground meant for her, a grave that in time would've held her casket. Mothers should not bury their children. That was all Calvin Hooper could think as he stood there in a pair of pleated khakis and the nicest shirt he owned.

Darl Moody's death ripped Jackson County apart. Things like that didn't happen here. There were two or three homicides a year, but rarely more than that, and the ones that did happen were usually tied to drugs. Plenty of folks were bad off on meth or gooned out on pills, and folks like that had a tendency of stumbling into dangerous places, but not men like Darl, not families like the Moodys. Everyone in the county knew their family and there wasn't a cross word to say about a one of them. What happened was a tragedy and the community rallied behind them with hotdog suppers and cakewalks and gun raffles and turkey shoots to help with expenses like any other time something unexpected struck one of their own.

While the preacher read from the book of Corinthians, Calvin stood to the side and watched a murder of crows strut through the churchyard below. Angie leaned against him, her parents standing behind her.

Calvin looked at the family gathered under the shade of the graveside tent. Darl's sister, Marla, sat beside her mother with mascara running down her cheeks like wetted ink. Her husband was beside her with one hand gripped around his wife's knee, the other stroking the back of their little girl, who balanced on his leg with her thumb in her mouth. Their three boys were in the seats beside them, their eyes emptied by sorrow and wonder. Marla looked like Darl, the same long face. They had sharp noses and thick eyebrows like their mother, thin lips that always seemed sunk by sadness or anger. Their father had been a short, spindly man with arms that seemed too long for his body. His eyes were the color of sky, and thinking about him right then—how none of his features found their way into his children—Calvin could still see the thick veins that rose from his forearms and ran along his biceps like vines. The old man had been tough as a pine knot, partly because he'd had to be, and maybe that was what carried down, that toughness. And maybe that was enough.

"Now this I say, brethren, that flesh and blood cannot inherit the kingdom of God; neither doth corruption inherit incorruption," the preacher read. "Behold, I shew you a mystery; we shall not all sleep, but we shall all be changed, in a moment, in the twinkling of an eye, at the last trump: for the trumpet shall sound, and the dead shall be raised incorruptible, and we shall be changed."

Changed. That was as good a word as any. Nothing would ever be the same now. It couldn't be, and maybe that was the only certainty anymore.

A slight movement to his left caught his attention and Calvin turned to see his mother pressing a wadded tissue to the corners of her eyes. She wore black slacks and a dark silk blouse with shoulder pads, her flat silver hair brushed evenly to each side of her face so that it stretched to her stomach. He'd held it together until then, but there was something about looking at his own mother that hit him harder than the rest of it. He started to cry and before long he was weeping. His father turned to face him, his arm at the small of his wife's back, and Calvin saw his eyes melt with tears, though his old man would not let them fall, could not let them fall, because men didn't cry, and Calvin understood that. Seeing how close his father came was enough to justify his own tears; and when he felt Angie's father put a hand on his shoulder, Calvin fell apart. The most complex things said between men were often not spoken at all.

He did not move while the funeral went on and he did not move when it ended. Gradually those who gathered made their way down to their cars, and one by one, they left. In a few minutes, workers came up the narrow gravel road in a beaten cream-colored Ford with shovels loaded in the back. They studied him and Calvin thought he recognized the younger of the two as the brother of a Collins boy he'd worked with one winter at a tree farm in Tuckasegee.

The two men rolled back the fake-grass mat that had hidden the fill dirt from the family. They filled the grave a spade at a time, joking back and forth about something Calvin couldn't make out from where he stood. It took them a little more than an hour. The men were sticky with sweat, their khaki work shirts dark at their backs. The older one hoisted a jumping jack from the bed of the truck to compact the dirt on the grave. When the job was finished, they watched him as they drove away—incapable of understanding why he'd stayed. There was something inside that told him he had to see it through, that he couldn't leave until it was finished; but now that it was, he found it hard to walk away.

A hand grazing the back of his arm startled him and Calvin turned to find Angie with sunlight filling her eyes green as bottle glass. Her cheeks and nose were dotted with light orange freckles.

"Are you ready?" she asked.

"Yeah," Calvin said. "Yeah. I'll be there in a minute."

She leaned in to kiss him. "Okay."

Calvin watched her walk away, the wind blowing her sundress tight to her hip, her blond hair whipping about like licks of fire. A thinly knit navy sweater covered her arms, and her cowboy boots cut Vs on her calves. She was the reason he would bear this secret even if it haunted him the rest of his life. Angie was all he'd ever wanted and all he had now, and somehow he knew that could still be enough, that a man couldn't ask for anything more than that. *Maybe this is the only way the world is even,* he thought. *Maybe it takes this kind of suffering to have everything you always wanted.*

Across the road, a murmuration of starlings rose like a bruise from yellowed field. The birds twisted into the sky, flashed in blooms of black, then disappeared as quickly as they'd shown. Their path blinked against the mountainside and Calvin tried his best to follow them until they were too far away to see. A piece of scripture kept repeating in his mind, something the preacher had read minutes before. Four words played in his head over and over, but he could not remember what came before or after. There were only four words, and he knew not their meaning.

Death is swallowed up.

SEVENTEEN

DWAYNE GRABBED A BUCKED SECTION OF LOCUST AND STOOD it on a grayed poplar stump that had been used to bust wood for a decade. Holding the weight of the go-devil near the head with one hand, he gripped the bottom of the handle with his other, dropped the top hand as he came over his shoulder, and cracked the log in two with little effort at all. He tossed the wood aside, guzzled down what was left of a Busch heavy by his feet, crumpled the empty can in his fist, and reached for another log.

He was building a mountain of firewood and empty beer cans on a grassless patch of yard in front of the house. The sky was low and gray, but it hadn't rained. A strong breeze every now and again rattled rust-colored leaves on the ground around him. A faded and color-muddled tattoo of a skull wearing a cowboy hat with two pistols crossed over a Confederate flag swelled on the left side of his chest as he panted for air with a cigarette dangling from the corner of his mouth. Sweat rolled down his back and chest and soaked the waist of a navy pair of Dickies, so that the fabric darkened almost black.

The house had been built a room at a time from scrap wood salvaged and stolen. Nothing here was permanent and as each addition rotted away, a new one was hammered together from plywood and bent nails off another side so that slowly, through decades, the five-room shanty shifted around the property like a droplet of water following the path of least resistance. Red Brewer was no carpenter. Chicken coops were built better. So were doghouses. But this place had been the roof over their heads and had kept the rain off the Brewer clan's backs all Dwayne's miserable life.

Buzzards filled the trees around the house the same as they had for the past six months. Sometime early spring, wakes of birds came circling over the ridgeline in orbits of ten or twelve and lit on every limb there was to be had on the hill above the house. Since then, they'd never left. Every day the birds sat high in the oaks, glaring down on this tiny piece of land. Thick limbs bowed beneath their weight so that one's movement shifted the balance of them all and each had to flap a few strokes to regain its perch. As the sun rose each morning, one buzzard would spread its wings, hold them open and let the light burn the dew from its feathers. Another bird would join the first, and then another and another until the birds appeared like some black-winged crucifixion roosted in the trees.

At first, Dwayne was convinced they were a sign of wickedness to come, an omen. He'd never seen anything like it. Crows, sure, but not buzzards, not like that, not in all his life. After six months, though, they were something else in the background, something he wouldn't have paid attention to at all if not for the sound of their wings whipping about the air while he split the winter's cord.

Down the drive, he could hear a car coming toward him, and that sound caught him off guard because no one came here. At the bottom of the driveway, a dozen NO TRESPASSING and PRIVATE PROPERTY signs nailed to trees made the owner's intentions clear. A white tin sign rusted, and buckshot on the mailbox post was hand-painted to read TRESPASSERS MAKE FINE TROPHIES in uneven letters.

Holding the go-devil one-handed by his side, he took a long drag off his cigarette and waited for the car to show through the trees. The Crown Vic was unmarked, but a set of white strobes by the headlights pegged it for the law. Dwayne squeezed the neck of the maul handle until his fist was bloodless and white. He didn't wait for the car to reach him. He barreled straight toward it. And as he came to the driver's side, he bent down and peered in with a peculiar intensity. The window came down and Dwayne met the driver's eyes.

"Dwayne Brewer?"

"This is private property."

"I'm with the Jackson County Sheriff's Office."

"And like I said, this is private property."

"That doesn't matter, Mr. Brewer."

"How's that?"

"Because I don't need permission or a warrant to come up a driveway to the front of a house. Besides, I'm here to ask a couple questions about an active investigation. So you can call down to the office if you'd like, but they'll tell you exactly what I'm telling you."

"What investigation?"

"Why don't you let me pull on up and we'll talk."

Dwayne didn't answer, but the detective didn't wait for permission. He rolled up his window as he pulled forward, then parked behind Dwayne's Buick and stepped out.

"I'm Detective Michael Stillwell." He held out his hand and Dwayne glanced down at it then back up to his eyes.

"I don't much give a shit who you are," Dwayne said. "Tell me why you're here." The last of the cigarette burned down into the filter and he tossed the butt into the yard, then went for another beer from an opened case by the woodpile. He cracked the top and sucked the foam from the mouth of the can, traded hands and slung what spilled from his fingers. Setting the beer on the ground, he turned back to his work.

"I'm here investigating the death of Darl Moody."

"Who?" Dwayne asked with a puzzled look before splitting the log before him.

"Darl Moody," the detective said.

"Don't know him."

"So you don't know anything about what happened to him?"

"Why would I?" Dwayne bent and placed another log on the stump.

"Figured you might've read something about it in the paper."

"That liberal-ass rag ain't fit for shit but lining bird cages. I wouldn't even use it for kindling."

"Look," Stillwell chided. "I'll get right on with it, because I can tell you ain't much on me and I'm coming to that same feeling about you the longer I stand here."

Dwayne dropped the head of the maul to the ground and balanced himself against the butt of the handle like he was leaning against a cane.

"A man named Coon Coward told me you went by his house looking for your brother."

"What about it?"

"He said you and him looked at some pictures off a game camera he had in the woods, and that some of those pictures were of Darl Moody."

"I don't know if that's right or not."

"What do you mean? Either they were or they weren't."

"I don't know who was in them pictures, and like I told you, I don't give a shit. It might've been that old boy you're looking for or it might've been Randy fucking Travis. Either way, it wasn't what I come for and so it didn't make a bit of difference to me."

"And what had you come for, Mr. Brewer?"

"The old man told you." Dwayne picked up the go-devil and swung it hard into the next log, the split sections kicking off into the yard like shrapnel. "I come for my brother."

"Why would your brother have been there?"

"I'm sure the old man told you that, too."

"Just in case he didn't, why don't you tell me?"

"Ginseng." Dwayne grabbed the beer from the ground and took a long sip that spilled from the corners of his mouth and dribbled off his chin. "My brother was after that old man's ginseng."

"So'd you find him?"

"No," Dwayne said. "Ain't been home yet. I don't know where he's run off to."

"Whereabouts does your brother live?"

"Right up the road a ways. Head of Allens Branch. There's a whole bunch of mailboxes there at the bottom and one reads 'Brewer' and he's up at the very top there in my grandparents' old place."

"And you said you haven't seen him for how long?"

"You know, the longer I sit here answering your questions the more I'm coming to wonder just what in the fuck you're doing here." Dwayne dropped the maul to the ground and walked over close to the detective, trying to force a sign of weakness, but there was no visible change in emotion or stance.

"I told you why I'm here, Mr. Brewer."

"No, you told me you're investigating what happened to some old boy I ain't ever heard of, and what exactly that has to do with me or my brother ain't been said."

A low growl in the distance grew louder and louder as it came, until a heavy torrent of rain swept the trees and was on top of them. Neither moved from where he stood. They each squinted a bit as the rain washed over their brows, but for a few seconds they floated there scowling at one another like they were about to fistfight. The water was cold against Dwayne's bare skin, but he hardly felt anything at all.

"I'll be seeing you, Mr. Brewer," Stillwell said, extending his hand into the small gap between them, and again Dwayne only glanced down at his offering without a word.

The detective climbed into his car and backed unhurriedly into the yard. Dwayne shifted his stance as the car curved around the woodpile so that he faced him until the taillights disappeared into the haze of rain and descended cloud. The air was smoky and Dwayne shook the water from his face like a dog, then snatched the maul from the mud.

A heat rose in his chest till it boiled in his eyes, his ears humming with anger. On the stump, he set the next piece and came down hard, grunting as the locust splintered in two. He grabbed the next log and stood it on end, and imagined Stillwell's face on the sawn end of wood as he came down. The rain poured around him and steamed from his shoulders as he took another bucked section, imagined Darl Moody's face. Coon Coward came next and then Calvin Hooper and then he chopped them further into pieces, working until there was no more wood before him.

When the pile was split, he came down hard into the wood, the go-devil a dull thud scarring the rooted stump. The anger grew and Dwayne Brewer swung again and again until the wood was cross-hatched with marks from the maul's heavy edge. His muscles burned and he swung until his arms wore completely out, and when he could no longer lift the weight he laughed hysterically at how his body failed him. He collapsed to the ground and lay flat on his back. Harder and harder the rain came down, but he did not seek shelter.

EIGHTEEN

THE RAIN THAT HAD STARTED THE DAY BEFORE CONTINUED
through the night, so that by morning the jobsite was slopped.
Forecasts showed the weather breaking up by evening, but it would
be a day or two before they could get back to work. For once, Calvin Hooper didn't mind. There'd been so much going on that he'd
gotten behind on everything at home: the woodpile, sealing a mouse
hole in the cupboard, changing the oil in his rig.

An open outbuilding his grandfather'd built from warped pine
planks and rusted tin he salvaged from a derelict barn stood behind
the house. The old man had used the place to keep rain off his tractor, but nowadays Calvin used the cover to work on cars. He had
his white Ford Super Duty up on a set of rhino ramps. Lying flat on
the packed dirt floor, he pulled the pin on an oil drain valve he'd
installed on the pan after stripping the old plug with a cheap socket
set he bought from a man on the side of the highway. The valve

made the job easier and cut down on the mess fifteen quarts of 15W-40 could make. He opened the valve and the oil ran a black line into the container. While he waited, he stretched his hands and listened to the rain beat against the tin.

Someone came into the shed and as he rolled to look he could see two sets of feet: a pair of men's slacks covered the necks of black ankle-high boots that zipped up the sides, and two heavyset, liver-spotted legs, black leather flats scuffed and worn down to nothing. Calvin scooted out from under the truck, and Michael Stillwell offered his hand to help him from the ground. Sharon Moody stood behind Stillwell in a black T-shirt and a wool skirt with a plastic grocery bag tied over her head to shield her hair from the rain. Calvin stared at her, at how her face contorted into something halfway between smiling and crying. He pushed himself to his feet, dusted the dirt from his pants and his shoulders, then reached for a shop towel to wipe his hands.

Darl's mother came forward, and before Calvin could warn her he was dirty she had her arms wrapped around him and her face buried in his chest like he was the last thing in the world to hold on to. Only five days had passed since she laid her son in the ground, almost a week more since she'd gotten word of how Calvin found him. Calvin put his arms around her, careful not to get oil on the back of her shirt, and the two of them stood there for a long time tilting back and forth like they were slow dancing. Stillwell seemed like he was trying to read what was happening and that ate Calvin up. If Darl's mother weren't right there in his arms, he would've clobbered that boy right in his fucking nose.

Calvin felt her relax against him and Mrs. Moody pulled back and wiped the sides of her eyes with her fist. She grinned flatly and reached up with an open hand to pat the side of Calvin's face. The pain and loss was written in her eyes like words on a wall. Seeing it and knowing there was nothing to be said or done to change it twisted Calvin's heart and he had to look away to hold his composure. The light was gray outside and the rain made the house seem to shake behind it, and he watched the rain come down until the feeling passed.

"What are y'all doing here?"

"Michael came by the house this morning," Mrs. Moody said. "He mentioned he was on his way to drop something off at Coon Coward's and I told him I'd been meaning to get over there since his sister passed. Figured I might as well get out of the house for a bit. I need to get out of that house." She shook her head and squeezed at the bridge of her nose. "I keep going through all of Darl's stuff, going through pictures. I'm driving myself crazy, Calvin. I needed to get out of that house. So I told him if it was all right I'd like to ride with him."

Calvin waited on Stillwell to answer.

"I was planning on coming to see you afterward and Mrs. Moody said that it was all right to come by here first, to just go on and stop in."

"There's something about seeing you that makes it a little better," Mrs. Moody said. "Sitting in that house all day, all I keep thinking is how alone I am. Marla's come by with the kids and that's been nice, but I needed to get out of there. Seeing folks helps. And I haven't had a chance to thank you. I know how hard that was. What I asked." Her voice broke off. "I know how hard that must've been, but it's like it's always been here. You carry your own. Darl and you, the two of you might as well have been brothers."

Calvin wiped his hands on the shop towel again and tossed it onto a small shelf that ran the wall to the left, the wood scattered with tools and spent quarts of oil and a small black radio with its silver antenna stretched toward the rafters. The smell of rain filled the shed. He looked at Mrs. Moody and saw the same strength she'd always carried, a strength that hardened into something almost impenetrable after her husband passed. For as tough as the men were in these mountains, the women had always been stone. They were used to loss, accustomed to never having enough. They were fit for the harshness of this world. Calvin could feel all of that in her right then and he was almost jealous of her for that. He turned to Stillwell to focus. "So what brings you by?"

"The reason I've got to go by Mr. Coward's is that he brought me some pictures off a game camera he had out in the woods, and now that I've had the chance to look through them I needed to return the card."

"All right."

"Mr. Coward was out of town for a little over a week after his sister passed, and when he came back he checked the camera and there were some pictures on there of Darl going in and out every evening," Stillwell said. "He thought they might be helpful."

"I don't know how that'd be helpful, but okay."

"There were two pictures there at the end of someone going into the woods with Darl and helping him carry something out, and when I got to looking, it was you."

Calvin didn't know what to say, but he nodded his head in agreement.

"I thought you might be able to tell me what y'all were doing?"

Calvin glanced over at Mrs. Moody and she was looking at him the same way she'd done when he and Darl were kids, and he'd never been able to lie to her then and it was hard to imagine deceiving her now. He turned to the detective. "Darl was in there hunting."

"Okay."

"He knew Coon was out of town, I guess, and there's this buck he's seen going in and out of there for years and I reckon he figured it was as good a chance as he'd ever have. But like I said, I don't know how in the world that's helpful."

"So, is that what y'all were carrying out of there? That buck?"

"No," Calvin said. He shook his head. "I don't guess Darl ever did see that deer. But he shot a good doe way back in a cove at the far end of Coon's land, and he asked me to help him drag."

"That don't sound like Darl," Mrs. Moody said.

Calvin looked at her and could see the disappointment smeared across her face, and seeing that made him hate Stillwell for bringing her there, hate him for making her think one sour thing about her son. She'd had enough pain in her life already, and Darl had only been in the ground five days.

"Going in there while Coon was out of town. That don't sound like Darl."

"Yeah, it does," Calvin said. He looked at her and tried to smile to get her to realize that Darl going in there was perfectly in character. "You know as good as I do how much he loved hunting. Hell, that's all he ever thought about. Every winter it was playing around with those rabbit boxes and come spring it was turkeys. All summer it was chasing speckleds, and as soon as there came a bite in the air he wanted to be up in a treestand. God he loved hunting deer. I think he'd have lived in the woods like an Indian if he could've." Calvin chortled and watched her expression ease. "He'd been after that deer a long time, Mrs. Moody. Way he told it, it was the biggest thing he'd ever seen come out of Jackson County. And you know him, one way or another he was going to do his damnedest to get him. That's just how he was. Whatever he was after had to be the biggest and the baddest or it didn't interest him."

Mrs. Moody nodded her head and grinned solemnly. They all stood there for a few moments without saying a word and in time something seemed to change on her face, as if her question was answered.

"When you going to ask that girl in there to marry you?" she asked.

"I don't know," Calvin said. He looked at the ground and kicked at the dust with the toe of his boot before meeting her eyes.

"She's a keeper," Mrs. Moody said.

Calvin put his hands in the back pockets of his jeans and nodded.

"Was that her mama and daddy that was standing behind you at the service?"

"It was."

"That's what I thought," Mrs. Moody said. "Says an awful lot about how highly they think of you that they were there. That ought to mean something to you, Calvin. It means something to me."

She eyed him seriously and he found it hard to look at her right then.

"You know Marla's going to have another one," Mrs. Moody said. "Another little girl. Next April. That'll make five." She shook her head and came as close to smiling as her heart would allow. "Raising a brood, I'm telling you. It was bad enough with them three boys. Winking, Blinking, and Nod, that's what I call them, like those little birds Opie raised that time on *Andy Griffith*. Hellions is what they are. Don't know if they're keeping me young or killing me. A few more and I'll open up a daycare."

"You ought to go in there and see Angie before you leave." He looked through the rain at a small screened-in porch off the back of the house. Mrs. Moody came forward and pulled down on his shoulder and he lowered his head and let her kiss him on the cheek the way she had every time they said goodbye since he was five or six years old.

"You come by the house and see me," she said. "I've got some things I want to give you. Some things I think you might like to have."

"Yes, ma'am," Calvin said. "I will."

When she walked into the rain, there was no hurry in her step. She held her hands against her head to keep the plastic tight over her hair, and when she was up the back steps, Calvin turned to Stillwell.

"You got a lot of nerve bringing her over here."

"She told you. She wanted to ride over to Mr. Coward's with me. That's it."

"That's horse shit. They don't live two miles apart. You had to pass his house to get here. So don't tell me this is about giving her a lift over there."

"Then what is it, Calvin?"

"You brought her over here to see if you could get a rise out of me."

"And did I?"

"Fuck you, Michael." Calvin stepped face-to-face with him and prodded his finger into Stillwell's chest to punctuate his words. Calvin was a few inches shorter and he tilted his head up so they were eye to eye. "If you didn't have that badge on your belt right now, I'd whoop your ass. I'm telling you, if it wasn't for the badge, I'd bust your nose like when we was kids."

In their glory days at Smoky Mountain High, he and Stillwell had both asked Carla Mathis to prom and she said yes to Calvin. That afternoon on the baseball field, Stillwell beaned him once at batting practice and Calvin let it slide. But when Stillwell clipped his legs out from under him with a fastball as he dug back into the box, Calvin stormed the mound and beat him senseless, the coaches rushing out to pull them apart like dogs.

"Your eye's healed up," Stillwell said.

Calvin didn't answer.

"You know the blood came back from the house," Stillwell said. "It was Darl's."

"And who the hell else's would it have been?"

"Didn't know."

"Look, if you've got something you want to ask me, then come right out and ask it. That's the least you can do. Come over here and ask." Calvin backed away and snatched an oil filter wrench from the shelf. "But don't you put no more on that woman there than she's already got. Her son ain't been in the ground a week. You hear me?"

Stillwell didn't nod or speak.

"That woman's carried a lot more than her share in her lifetime and I be damned if I sit back and watch some son of a bitch like you shovel more on her. You do it again, and I'll go to the sheriff," Calvin said. "Him and my daddy's been friends a long time, and when I tell him you brought her over here like you did, you know that ain't going to sit well with him."

Silence held between them and Calvin widened his eyes to

demand an answer. Finally, Stillwell nodded. Calvin started to climb back under the truck to get back to work.

"You know Dwayne Brewer?"

"What?"

"Dwayne Brewer."

"No, I heard you," Calvin said. "I'm just trying to figure out why you're asking me if I know him."

"Well, do you?"

"Of course I do," Calvin said. "Most everybody in this county knows him, or knows of him. We went to school with his brother. You know that."

Calvin could tell Stillwell was trying to read his reaction, but he didn't say another word, didn't offer a hint of why he asked that question.

"What are you saying? You think Dwayne Brewer did it?"

"It was just a question." Stillwell scratched at the back of his head and took a can of dip from his pocket. He shoved his lip full of tobacco and brushed what fell from the front of his gray polo. "I don't have a whole lot to go on here. There's been a whole lot of crazy things happen in this county through the years, but the one thing that always seems to hold true is that the one who winds up guilty was usually close. Around here a man's a whole lot more likely to kill his cousin than he is to wander down the road and kill somebody he don't know."

"So what are you saying?" Calvin sat on the ground with arms draped over his knees.

"I'm saying if you think of anything, you give me a call, all right?"

"All right," Calvin said. He lay on his back and scooted under the truck.

"You got my number."

Stillwell walked out of the shed and into the rain. He splashed through puddles in the yard and up the back steps, the screen door slapping shut behind him. Calvin took a deep breath, closed his eyes, and exhaled against the undercarriage. Hearing that name had almost dropped him to his knees. He was scared to death knowing how close Stillwell was, but there was nothing he could do. What hung over his head could come crashing down any minute. There was no way to know when it all might fall to pieces.

NINETEEN

DWAYNE BREWER SWUNG THE IRON DOOR OPEN FOR LIGHT
so that he could see what was left of his brother. Standing there in
the mouth of the root cellar, he felt the darkened room breathe
against him, the smell a growing thing that had worsened since he
last came. He took shallow breaths to keep from gagging and staggered inside carrying a heavy bag of lime over one shoulder and a
tattered Bible in his hand. "You stink, brother," he said as he set the
bag by Sissy's feet.

Carol's skin was no longer bloated and tight. Over the course of
that past week it collapsed and liquefied into an almost creamy con-
sistency, the greenish-black of pond water. All of the fluids drained
from his body into a puddle around him. His skin seemed to be
ripping itself apart, splitting open and seeping black.

Kneeling beside Sissy's body, he dug their father's knife from
deep in his brother's pocket and opened the sodbuster. He sliced a

wide smile at the top of the heavy paper sack and tossed handfuls of lime onto the body like he was sowing seed. When a thin layer dusted Carol's clothes and flesh, Dwayne collapsed onto the dirt and leaned against a heavy pitched column with his legs hugged to his chest. Outside, leaves drifted about in a rust-colored clatter that rasped the ground as the wind came through the valley. Flies buzzed around his face and he swatted them away only to watch them light on his brother. Dwayne couldn't bear to look.

It was the fourth Sunday he'd spent without him, and that was the day that was hardest. Their grandparents had been greatly religious, and growing up he and Sissy spent most Sundays listening to their grandfather read scripture with a pair of wire-rimmed glasses propped on the edge of his nose in the front room of the shack where he lived. In summer, he'd take them on the road to tent revivals that sprang up in remote hollers, and when they were with him, they were safe. Maybe it was that being safe that made the words stick, but either way Dwayne Brewer had read the King James cover to cover a hundred times if he'd read it once.

Despite being believers, he and Sissy were never ones for church, for sanctuaries or the people who filled their pews. They'd tried once after their grandfather was gone. When the bell rang in that tiny white church along the stream, they walked right up to the front row so that they'd be close to the words. The preacher kept cutting eyes toward them through the opening prayer and they could hear folks whispering behind them. They didn't know any different, had never been before, so they didn't find it strange. The preacher was about to deliver his message when Dwayne felt someone tap him on the shoulder. He looked up and one of the ushers, a red-faced man with bloodshot cattle eyes, leaned down and whispered in his ear that he'd like them to come with him. Dwayne told his brother and Sissy whispered, "Why?" and Dwayne told him he didn't have the foggiest, but up they stood and down the aisle they went.

When they were at the back of the church, the usher opened his arm to a pew along the back wall. Dwayne told him he didn't understand and the man explained that he and his brother were making some of the people in the church nervous, that maybe it'd be best if they sat there at the back. That old familiar feeling found him right then and he latched on to that man's throat and squeezed till his eyes got buggy. People were turning around in the pews, men standing up and coming toward him, and Dwayne could see them out of the corners of his eyes, but he didn't care, he couldn't wait to explode when they were on him. All of a sudden he could feel someone patting him on the back, the nasally voice of his brother saying, "Maybe we ought to go, Dwayne. Maybe we ought to get out of here." Something about his brother's voice stopped him. He let go of that man right before the others reached him and he and his brother trudged out of there without so much as a word.

A few weeks later they were driving down the road and Dwayne saw on the church sign a message that read: GOD RECRUITS FROM THE PIT NOT THE PEDESTAL. He had guffawed at the thought, shaking his head as they passed, thinking, *You don't know a goddamn thing about it.*

He was staring at the soles of his brother's boots in a sort of illusory trance. "I was thinking yesterday morning about a passage in Isaiah," Dwayne said, as he opened his Bible across his knees. "Figured I'd read that this morning, if that's all right with you." He paused. "What it says is this. It says . . ."

Dwayne began to read the passage, the fifty-third chapter of Isaiah, which told of Christ being born not to kings, but to nothing, a tender plant rooted in dry ground. It was from there that He came to know suffering, the grieving and sorrow of sin.

"He was oppressed, and He was afflicted, yet He opened not His mouth: He is brought as a lamb to the slaughter, and as a sheep before her shearers is dumb, so He openeth not his mouth . . . And He made His grave with the wicked, and with the rich in His death; because He had done no violence, neither *was any* deceit in His mouth."

Dwayne thought of his brother and he thought of Christ and he could see no difference between. Both had been born at the bottom, their burden the weight of the wicked. Sin be the thorns in His head, the nails in His hands and feet, the spear in His side. Sin be the spit on Carol's face, the ridicule of poverty, the beatings, the torment of silence. It pleased the Lord to bruise them, to put their hearts to grief, for only through that suffering, through bearing the sin of many, could they make open the doors for those who had done them harm.

When he'd finished reading the chapter, Dwayne slapped the book closed. He tossed it into the dirt beside him, a poof of dust rising from the floor. He looked up with a tremendous smile and said, "Brother, you are like Jesus."

The room was still and in that stillness was a low static that sounded like crumpled newspaper. The noise came from his brother. Sissy whispered something Dwayne couldn't make out from where he sat and he turned his head to the side to listen closely. The sound was still too low to make out, barely audible but constant. He gaped wide-eyed at his brother's face, Sissy's lips seeming to quiver, and watched in amazement, as what he'd been praying seemed to be happening right before his eyes. When he was a boy, he had an aunt who could stop blood, who could read a verse from the Bible and stop blood from leaving a body. Her name was Opal and she could blow the thrush from a baby's throat by breathing into its mouth. There was a magic to this world. Dwayne had seen it. And right then he was sure he would see it again.

From where he sat, he couldn't make out the words and so he crawled closer and leaned his ear to his brother's lips. A whir of blowflies round as nickels circled their faces and lit on Dwayne's shoulders and back. He stared at his brother's arms where reddish-brown mites the size of pinheads scuttled over black skin, tiny eggs scattered over him like mustard seeds. The ground around him was pulsing with life, dull brown beetles, some iridescently green, centipedes spiraled like ammonites. The sound was low and constant, but he could not make out the words, and Dwayne leaned away so that he could read his brother's lips. That's when he saw it, a wriggling mass that moved as a cream-colored tongue, a single syllable broken into a thousand moving parts. The sight of it caught in Dwayne's throat and he ran his finger into his brother's mouth, scooping out all that he could. He slung his hand and the flies droned around him.

Amidst that horror, Dwayne Brewer was wrecked by a single heartbreaking thought. There was nothing he could do to stop what was happening. No matter what he did, the last thing in the world he loved was melting away like wax.

The smell he'd worked so hard to ignore turned his stomach then. He pushed to his feet and walked outside because there was no breath left in the room. Outside, a sharp wind stood the hairs of his arms on end and Dwayne closed his eyes and lifted his face to the sky. He could feel the sun warming his pale skin and he blinked awake to a golden light so piercingly yellow that it was as if he'd become a honeybee held in the palm of a dandelion. The air danced with the musk of dying leaves, an autumn crowded with oakmoss, oud, and leather. He breathed deeply and it filled his lungs with a calming sort of warmth.

How such wickedness survived amidst the beautiful had always baffled him. Why He would fill a world with this kind of suffering, a puzzle that carried no rhyme or answer and sat in Dwayne's heart like a stone. All he knew was that all his life he'd been asked to carry and he was tired. *Me and You been at each other for too long,* he thought. *The two of us, we've never seen eye to eye.*

TWENTY

CALVIN HOOPER PUSHED HIMSELF BACK IN A WEATHERED gray rocking chair with the toes of his leather brogans. Mrs. Moody sat next to him, the two slowly inching closer and closer together the longer they rocked. A speckled blue heeler named Prescott lay with his head resting flat on the porch planks between his front paws, smacking his lips with his tongue, panting, and looking back at the two of them when Calvin spoke.

"I don't think I could eat another bite if I tried."

"Something tells me when that pie comes out of the oven, you'll find room," Mrs. Moody said. "I bought that candy roaster off Lebern Dills. Went in there to see him about a church raffle and it looked about as pretty as a sunset sitting there on his floor."

They'd come for Sunday supper, Calvin and Angie, Marla, Rusty, and the kids, the whole house filled with smiling and laughing and fighting and bickering like it always had been. Mrs. Moody stretched three cans of salmon, a heap of pole beans, red potatoes, and vidalias, and two cakes of corn bread into a ten-dollar meal that fed them all.

Calvin could hear pots and pans clanking inside the house as Marla and Rusty split the dishes, her washing and him drying. Out in the yard Angie was carrying their littlest one, an amber-eyed little girl named Ruth, while the three boys showed her a lean-to they'd built at the edge of the woods.

"So, you bought that girl a ring yet?" Mrs. Moody looked over and raised her eyebrows.

"Not yet," Calvin said.

She reached across and placed her hand on top of his fingers. Liver spots dotted her hands, veins raised and blue, and she squeezed tight to his knuckles. "You know I'm giving you a hard time."

"I know it."

"But you ain't going to find one better than that," she said. "A woman like that doesn't come along every day."

"She's a good one," Calvin said, and that was it, because men here never said anything more than that, never let emotion show or opened their hearts with their tongues.

"Well, I'm going to run in the house right fast." Mrs. Moody leaned forward and pushed herself up from the rocking chair. "You need anything while I'm up?"

"No, ma'am."

The dog stood and raised his ears. He watched her with hopeful eyes and she scratched under his chin as she passed. When she was inside, Prescott plopped back down on the porch by Calvin's feet, curled himself into a ball, sighed, and closed his eyes.

The weather had turned warm the past two days. Seasons were

strange anymore, the world turning more peculiar as time passed. Nowadays, there might come two feet of snow that melted off by the next afternoon, then the day after that they were back to T-shirt weather in the middle of December. But it was nice to be sitting there right then. All Calvin could think was, *This is as nice as I've felt in a while.*

Over by an empty dogwood at the corner of the yard, Angie had the child hugged to her chest with one arm, her other wrapped around the youngest boy's waist as she boosted him into the tree. When he had ahold, she backed up and he swung his leg over the limb, hauled himself up, and climbed higher. The two older boys were already nearing the top and the little one was tearing up the tree like a monkey to catch them. Angie turned back toward the house with a big smile on her face. Calvin met her eyes and she shook her head.

He raised his hand cupped to his mouth and hollered, "They're going to break their necks!" And Angie nodded, but didn't say a word or turn around to stop them.

Seeing her standing there with that little girl on her hip, Calvin knew Mrs. Moody was right: Women like Angie Moss didn't come around often. He could see himself buying her a ring, something simple because that's what she'd always said, just something simple. He could see the two of them at the front of the church, all the folks who loved them smiling silently from the pews, see that little girl in her arms right then as their own. More than any of that, though, Calvin could see the two of them growing old together like everyone around them, like his own parents and like hers, sharing a quiet kind of love the same as Mrs. Moody and Darl's father. That kind of love wasn't for anyone outside the two of them. It was private and silent, sufficient as grace.

Something tapped against the porch planks beside his chair and Calvin looked over to find what had slipped from his pocket. There on those weathered slats as shiny as a coin lay the bullet he'd found in front of his face when he awoke in the grave. Calvin snatched it up, something so tiny filling him with a sense of exposure, like all that he carried was suddenly out on the table for anyone to see. He held that cartridge inside his fingers and scrubbed his thumb against the brass casing as if he were rubbing a worry stone. Ever since that day, he'd carried it. Ever since that day, it was impossible to forget even for a moment how quickly the hammer could come down.

The spring creaked open and slapped the screen door closed as Mrs. Moody came back onto the porch and the sound startled him. She had something wrapped in an old prairie queen quilt stitched from flour sacks and scraps of clothes. When she was standing in front of him, she held it out to him and Calvin took it from her hands.

"I wanted you to have this," she said.

What he held was heavy, and as he folded back the quilt he could see the stainless barrel and gray laminate stock, a short brush gun Darl had bought a few years back, for a hunting trip he took with a fellow named Goob to chase black bear in Maine.

"I can't take this," Calvin said.

"Yes, you can," Mrs. Moody insisted. "He'd want you to have that."

"You ought to give it to one of Marla's boys."

"Those boys will have plenty," she said. "He had a couple hunting rifles that belonged to his daddy and I figured I'd save those for the boys once they get old enough to have them. But this one I want you to have. He saved up for that rifle and that hunting trip for two years, and when him and that boy piled out of here I think that was about as happy as I ever saw him. They had one of those

GPS giving them directions and it routed them right through New York City. I can see the two of them in that pickup truck with dog boxes and a pile of walkers bawling in the back driving down Park Avenue." She laughed and shook her head. "He used to love when you'd go in the woods with him, running bear. I don't know that that was your cup of tea, chasing a bunch of dogs all over creation, but he loved it when you went with him."

Calvin ran his fingers over the receiver, shouldered the rifle, and ran the lever, its action smooth as silk. "I don't know what to say."

"Say you'll take those boys out in the woods when they're older and tell them stories about their uncle."

"I can do that," Calvin said.

"Then there's nothing else to say." Mrs. Moody reached across and patted him on his cheek the way she always did, squinted her eyes and clenched her jaw. No one had said a word about Darl that entire afternoon and there'd been something nice about that, something nice about life getting back to how it was even if that feeling was short-lived. The thing about this old world was that nothing had come along yet that could slow or stop its turning.

They sat for a long time without speaking, neither having words to say nor having any want to say them. Sometimes proximity was all that a person needed and that simple act of being close carried no need for sound. Tomorrow the sun would rise over the balsams the same as it had forever, but right then Calvin Hooper and Mrs. Moody watched its descent. The afternoon lowered dim as candlelight, a yellow pale but stunning. He watched Angie chasing the boys through the yard, all of them screaming and laughing, and all he could think was, *I have so much to lose.*

TWENTY-ONE

THE TEAL GRAND PRIX WAS PARKED IN FRONT OF THE CRUM-bling shack where Sissy Brewer lived. Dwayne had driven his brother's car home. The car's faded paint was a strangely bright juxtaposition to the whitewashed boards that curled away from the home's crudely framed bones. Dwayne was around back grabbing a can of mixed gas he'd let Carol borrow that summer. He could hear someone banging on the front door.

"Jackson County Sheriff's Office," they yelled. "Mr. Brewer, I need to speak with you. Jackson County Sherriff's Office. I need you to come to the door."

Dwayne Brewer peered around the side of the house, a dwelling on the verge of collapse. Stillwell stood on the porch with his right hand resting on the handle of his sidearm. Forest-green paint on the front door was aged to little more than stain, the grain of the wood raised on the surface like braille. He was beating the door with his fist till it shook loosely on bent hinges against the rotten jamb.

"Jackson County Sheriff's Office," Stillwell yelled. He stood there in a pair of olive drab 5.11 cargo pants and a black polo with a badge embroidered on the left breast. His hair was parted neatly. His face was clean-shaven.

A dried leaf scratched its way across the porch and a wood hen screeched somewhere off in the timbers. There was a window to the left of the door. A small bench sat in front of the windowsill with a chipped terra-cotta pot holding gray dirt and a gnarled dead plant. Stillwell knelt with his hand shading his eyes and leaned close to the glass to peer inside. The windowpanes were wavy glass clouded with grime, and as he rapped on the glass with his knuckle, the pane rattled against the grilles.

"Mr. Brewer. Jackson County Sheriff's Office. If you're inside, I need you to come to the door."

"He ain't here," Dwayne said as he stepped around the side of the house into the open.

Stillwell jumped at the sound of Dwayne Brewer's voice, his strong hand gripping his pistol. "Where is he?"

"Beats me," Dwayne said. He wore a pair of muddied blue jeans and a yellow-tinged wifebeater that hung loosely over his barrel chest. Dwayne Brewer looked almost simian, like something from a carnival that might make a living eating glass. "Ain't seen him."

"That's his car, ain't it?" Stillwell nodded to the Grand Prix.

"Yeah."

"So his car's here, but he ain't?"

"Looks that way."

"Well, where is he?"

"How the hell I'm supposed to know that?" Dwayne canted his head to the side and waited for an answer, a red can of gas in his right hand.

"You don't find it strange his car's here and he's not?"

"Of course it's strange, but Sissy's queer as a football bat. Besides, it's the tail end of ginseng season. He's got honey holes down in Oconee where the berries ain't even dropped. Hell, he might have run down there or on over into Georgia, for all I know. Wouldn't surprise me."

"And how would he have gotten there?"

"Might've hopped a goddamn train for all I know."

Stillwell came off the porch and walked to where the two of them were within arm's reach of one another. He was nothing standing next to a brute like Dwayne, Stillwell barely reaching his shoulders and Dwayne having him by a good hundred pounds. *I bet you I could stretch you out like a rabbit,* Dwayne thought. *I could take you by the legs, stretch you right fast, and break your neck like a rabbit's.*

Seeing Stillwell standing there lit Dwayne afire inside. While his brother rotted into nothing through those trees, the law was beating his door off the hinges. No one wanted to let a sleeping dog lie. No one wanted to give them a lick of peace.

"What you sniffing around here for anyways? Thought you was supposed to be figuring out what happened to that Moody boy?"

"I am."

"Then like I said, why you sniffing around here?"

"Trying to talk to your brother about anything he might've seen while he was stealing Mr. Coward's ginseng. That's what you said he was doing, right?"

"And what the hell's ginseng got to do with what happened to that Moody boy?"

"Nothing necessarily."

"So why's a homicide detective worried about an old man's ginseng patch?"

"We ain't lucky enough to have a homicide division," Stillwell said. "I've got a dozen open cases piled on my desk right now. Poaching ginseng lands on my plate the same as missing persons or murder."

"A man's got to prioritize."

"What you doing with that gas can?"

Dwayne Brewer looked down like he'd forgotten what was in his hand. "Needed mixed gas for the chainsaw. Forgot I'd let Sissy borrow it for a weed-eating job a couple months ago." He looked at Stillwell with an expression caught between boredom and disgust. "Think I'll be getting on to the house."

Stillwell held tight as Dwayne glided past him and headed across the yellowed yard. "Where's your car?"

"Down at the house," Dwayne shouted without turning.

"How you getting home?"

Finally, Dwayne stopped and spun back. "House is right through the woods a ways. Kitchens Branch is right over those hills." Dwayne nodded into the trees. The sunlight hit him just so, his eyes lit black as onyx.

"Want a ride?"

"No," Dwayne said, and turned.

"You see your brother, you tell him to call me," Stillwell shouted.

Dwayne lifted the gas can high as if to sign that he'd heard him, but he didn't turn back and he didn't answer, he merely wandered farther into the thicket of saplings and brush, the woods closing in around him.

TWENTY-TWO

DWAYNE HAD NOT BEEN BACK TO THE CELLAR, BUT AS HE made his way home through the woods he could not pass without speaking. Sitting the gas can by the door, he lifted the heavy bar and made his way inside.

"They've come looking for you, brother," Dwayne said. "And I don't see them dogs letting off any time soon."

In the month since Dwayne brought his brother into the root cellar, Carol Brewer's body had deflated like a forgotten balloon. All of the fluids had drained into an island around him, and now, nearly five weeks after he'd been killed, his skin was a dark grayish-brown and thin as tissue paper. Carol's face was no longer recognizable and Dwayne could not bring himself to look.

Sitting cross-legged on the floor, Dwayne leaned his head back against one of the pitched supports and closed his eyes, then let his chin fall to his chest. Setting his hands in the dust at his sides, he opened and closed his fingers, building tiny ridges of dirt between them, and then he traced shallow waves around his handprints. Suddenly he remembered a time when his back was striped and bruised from an extension cord his father swung like a bullwhip. He was only ten or eleven. Sissy might've been five or six. But glancing at a long shelf of rough-hewn pine along the wall to the right, he could see the mud pies lined up and hear Sissy saying, "You got to let them cool," like it was happening right there in front of his eyes.

The boy had an old bath towel tied around him like an apron and was playing house. Dwayne had scolded him for acting like a fag, but Sissy didn't care and before long his brother was playing right along and the two of them laughed and cut up and forgot for a short while what exactly they were hiding from. Sissy had a smile that could make a man forget he was dying. Crow's-feet spread at the corners of his eyes, his smile wide and his teeth unusually straight. That image stayed in Dwayne's mind like a photograph, and thinking of it, he chuckled under his breath and grinned.

The camouflage pants Sissy wore moved at his thigh like something was trying to come out of his pocket. Dwayne stared blank-faced and awestruck. The fabric jerked about again and something showed itself from beneath Sissy's leg, first a small, brown head swimming back and forth to free its body. Climbing to his feet, Dwayne watched as a young, rib-slatted rat crawled its way from underneath his brother's corpse and sprinted to the corner of the room. Fury and wrath grew within him and Dwayne held his arms wide as he loped forward.

The rat shot to the right, but Dwayne stomped his foot and cut off its path. It bolted back into the corner, stalled, then went left, but again there was nowhere to run and the rat curled tightly as if, by pulling its body in enough, it might disappear. He was almost on the rat now, and as he neared, the animal showed its small, yellowed teeth and hissed, but Dwayne's boot came down swiftly. He felt the tiny bones crack like matchsticks. Raising his foot, he saw the rat's body quivering, its movements now slow and dying. Dwayne braced his hands against cold cobblestones and came down again and again until all that was left was flesh flattened and bloodied in the dust.

Sissy sat there oblivious and rotting. Dwayne turned to his brother and an immense guilt settled in the well of his heart. *Some people never have much of nothing,* he thought. Some people have everything they love ripped from their hands as if God found humor in their suffering.

The sun burned white outside and Dwayne twisted away from the darkness and walked into the world. He made his way home with tears in his eyes the same as he had when he was a boy. When he reached the yard, he stood by the wood-splitting stump and studied the buzzards in the trees, just high-shouldered shadows scattered about the limbs. Dwayne yelled at the top of his lungs, no words, only a guttural cry from someplace deep inside that was absolutely on fire, and all of those other buzzards lifted to the air so that the limbs shook and the whole tree seemed to move.

To let a man like Calvin Hooper live after what he did was mercy, and there was no room for that in a world absent the slightest kindness. Dwayne's was a suffering that could only be soothed by knowing he was not alone. The only answer for that kind of loneliness was for others to endure the same.

TWENTY-THREE

HE STALKED HER FROM THE EDGE OF THE FIELD AS SHE unloaded groceries from the car, and he didn't move until he was sure. He'd been crouched there for a long time and his legs were tight and numb. Chickens scratched and pecked along the side of the house, one bronze and gray having spotted him a few minutes before now watching him suspiciously. When she went into the house, he rose and trotted over the open yard, the brood of hens dashing to the back of the house, his footsteps crunching dead grass.

Slinking onto the porch, he turned with his back against the clapboards. The doorway was open to his left. Adrenaline coursed through his veins now like it had the very first time. Ten years old, tucked in a ground blind with a rifle rested across his knees, Dwayne held his breath while a small doe came through a laurel thicket behind him. Footsteps tramped through dried leaves until the doe was close enough that he could've touched her, but he held his breath, his heart racing in his chest, his hair standing on end, amazed at how a man, if he's still enough, can completely disappear. It was that same feeling now, a hunter stalking prey, and he closed his eyes to listen to the slightest subtleties of sound.

Exhaling softly through his nose, he heard footsteps coming through the house. She was humming a song, her pace quick and unsuspecting. Closer she came. Closer still. She was almost there and he opened his eyes as she came through the door. Angie Moss did not turn as he took one long stride and hooked under her chin. One arm constricted into her throat, while the other forced the back of her head into the choke, him leaning back until her feet were off the ground and she kicked violently at his shins. Fingernails tore into his arms like hot irons, but he closed his eyes and let that feeling ease over him. It was easiest to embrace pain, to inhale deeply through his nose and lose himself for a short moment in the honeysuckle smell of her hair against his face. Angie reached up in a last-ditch effort to claw at his eyes, but Dwayne lifted his gaze to the tin awning and swayed his head slowly back and forth until her hands fell and her legs went limp and she at once melted against him.

This was not like the movies. This wasn't some chloroform-soaked-rag Hollywood bullshit. Dwayne Brewer understood this like he understood she would come to in a matter of seconds—ten seconds, maybe twelve—so he moved quickly. With short, hurried stutter steps he lowered her to the ground then rolled her onto her stomach, pulled a set of zip cuffs from the back pocket of his jeans, and married her wrists at the base of her spine. Counting in his mind, he turned her onto her side and waited for her to wake. Ten. Eleven. Her eyes opened and widened and she rocked her head back and forth trying to make sense of her surroundings, trying to decipher what was happening.

Dwayne watched her pupils dilate into focus, and when she saw him she tried to get up from the porch, but he straddled her chest and kept her there. Angie screamed and Dwayne slapped his hand over her lips and she bit at his fingers and thrashed her head, blond hair whipping about the dusty slats like threads of unraveled rope, the back of her skull thwacking against the boards. Some people gave up easy, and some fought like hell. Angie Moss bucked with a wildness he'd only seen in animals, but it was of little use. He knew to be patient. Her face flushed red and she huffed wet breaths from her nostrils over the back of his hand and he held her there until she slowed, her eyes filling with tears, her mascara running like watercolor, and in time she surrendered.

When she ceded, he leaned down and pressed his clean-shaven face against her cheek. Her skin was hot against him.

"I'm going to let you up now and you're not going to scream," he whispered. "You get to screaming and I'll rip the throat out of you like a goddamned speckled trout."

Leaning up, he held his grip tight over her mouth until her eyes widened and she nodded that she understood. He lifted his hand and that fast she took a gulp of air and kneed hard into his kidneys, letting out a cry that ripened her face tomato red.

"Suit yourself." Dwayne seethed as he stood and, with a fistful of her hair, yanked her to her feet.

Angie's legs whirled and she tore herself away from him. A tangle of thin corn-silk hair hung from Dwayne's fist. She made it to the edge of the porch and down the first step before her momentum got the better of her. Arms bound at her back shifted her weight forward and she slid out into the yard with the loose black skirt she wore spread over the ground like a blanket. She crashed not far from the porch and he made up that distance before she could right herself. Grabbing her by the hair again, he kept her hunched over and led her around the house to the shed out back where he'd hidden his car from the road.

With one arm holding her, he fought to get the key in the lock with his other hand, to pop the trunk, and as it opened, he reached inside for a roll of silver duct tape. That fast, and again she was gone. She wrestled free and sprinted for the front yard, but her feet got tangled in the loose flow of her skirt and she fell at the corner of the house. Hands bound, she writhed about on a grassless scab of red clay, trying to get to her feet, but again he was on top of her, his weight pinning her flat as he whipped the tape around her face and capped her cries inside.

Grabbing for her ankles, he ducked as her legs fired like pistons. A kick found its mark under his chin. A burst of white light flashed his eyes. As he swatted at the air trying to catch her feet, his vision returned and he managed to grab ahold of one leg then the other and finally bound her fully. Muffled screams stuttered against the tape over her mouth, her breaths loud huffs through her nose. He scooped his arm around her waist and carried her on his hip to the open trunk, tossed her inside, and glared down where her body bent over the spare tire, her skirt climbing her legs. She had beggar's eyes, an expression washed with terror, and he carried no pity for weakness. It sickened him the way she gave up, and he slammed the lid, satisfied to no longer have to look at her. There was only the pathetic sound of her now drumming about the inside of the trunk.

The sun descended and Dwayne looked toward the light to gauge the time. He'd figured she'd only be gone a few minutes, but it was hours he'd crouched in that field waiting, all that time making him more and more vulnerable. In the days after Calvin led him to the back pasture, Dwayne had set about to learn their schedules and knew them now down to the hour. Calvin came home around six.

He opened the driver's-side door, put his knee on the seat, and reached across the cab for his pistol. He shoved the 1911 into the back of his waistline and made his way to the house. The door was open, the front room filled with the smell of cheap cinnamon candles and cigarette smoke. Through a doorway to the right, he entered the kitchen, where bags of groceries lined Formica countertops and a small square table. Her cell phone lay at the edge of a woven beige place mat and he used it to check the time. It was four forty-five, and his mind eased knowing there was plenty of time to spare.

Dwayne rifled through the bags and spotted a tub of butter pecan ice cream and a can of sardines. He ripped the lid off the ice cream, scooped a bite along the crook of his finger, and shoveled it into his mouth. Starved to death, he worked his way through half the tub before he slowed enough to catch his breath. The fish he ate whole, and when he finished the last of the can, he licked the oil from his fingers and smoked a cigarette down to the filter before mashing it out on the linoleum under his boot.

It was a little after five when he stood from the table and slipped Angie's phone into his pocket. He gathered a few bags of groceries to take with him and headed out of the house through the back door, passing through a tiny screened-in porch floored with green outdoor carpet and down a few wooden steps to the backyard, where he loaded the groceries into the passenger-side floorboard. Climbing behind the wheel, he dug the 1911 from the base of his back and set the pistol on the dash. The exhaust sputtered as he backed into the yard and steered around the side of the house, passing Angie's car with its doors swung open and down the drive where field stretched to his right. He could hear her kicking at the sidewalls of the trunk and he closed his eyes and rubbed at his temples when he reached the edge of the road.

A pack of motorcycles roared around a curve, old men with Florida tags on tricked-out baggers chasing fall color as they barreled around switchbacks. Dwayne rolled down his window and threw a hand up as they passed. The bikes rumbled away and the sound of her grew deafening in their absence. He turned the radio on and cranked the volume as loud as it would go, the music scratching through busted speakers. Janis Joplin sang "Me and Bobby McGee," and he hummed along to a song he knew word for word as he whipped out onto the two-lane.

The sun continued down and the temperature fell with its light. Dwayne drove with his arm rested on the opened window, the cold air beating against the hairs of his arm. Dried blood painted his skin where Angie had clawed. He checked the rearview and when the chorus came he sang as loud as he could until all that existed was the road and the direction and the absolute truth of the words.

TWENTY-FOUR

CALVIN HAD SPENT THE DAY CLEARING A TANGLED THICKET of green briar, stickseed, and honeysuckle to make a tee box at the edge of a cliff so developers could bring potential buyers to see the view and slice golf balls into the valley. There was no cell service anywhere on the jobsite, so he'd been left to his mind all day to think about Darl and Dwayne and Angie while he worked. And as the sun sank low, he finally reached a point of certainty.

From the top of the cedar cliffs, the mountain dropped off one side toward Tilley Creek and the old Speedwell store, off the other side toward Lake Glenville and on south to Walhalla. At this elevation, the trees were bare, every contour and curve of the landscape finding definition in light and shadow, all of the mountains' secrets exposed by season. Spots of color broke apart the ridges only where cedars and balsams took root, tiny groves forest-green spread like patches of moss.

Hitting the kill switch, he climbed out of the glassed-in cab of the excavator and hopped down to the ground from the muddied steel tracks. The air smelled of turned dirt, and though that was something he'd smelled every day for a long time, the smell had a new meaning. Now the scent brought thoughts of Darl and Carol Brewer, of waking up shivering in the robbed bottom of a grave that could've easily become his own. The sun was nearly down, its yellow light tiger-striped by shreds of dark gray cloud. He stared off into the last of the day, dumb to everything but the bullet in his pocket.

On the way home, he stopped along the west fork of the Tucka-seigee where the Thorpe Powerhouse stood as it had since the early 1940s: an oddly tall, square building with cathedral-like windows stretching up its brick facade. A wide gravel lot spread at its side and Calvin slid in to check if she'd texted. This was the closest place to the jobsite for any sort of cell signal, but even here it was only enough for texts. He'd made a habit of stopping here each night on his way home. The phone dinged and Calvin opened his messages to a string of unanswered texts: The first said she was going grocery shopping and asked if he wanted anything, the next said she'd picked up some ice cream and was planning to make pork chops for dinner, and the last was a string of yellow-faced emojis blowing kisses and hearts. He texted back, "Headed your way. Pork chops sound great," hit send, and tossed the phone into the passenger seat of his truck before pulling back onto the road.

The two-lane hugged a silted stretch of river backed, sluggish and deep, behind a tall dam, then ran farther north past a trailer, a cabin, a few farms, and on through the Tuckasegee Straight. The truck was low on fuel, and when the warning light came on, Calvin realized he wouldn't get home without stopping, so he swung into Jimmy's Mini Mart to pump a few gallons of diesel.

When he climbed back into the cab, his cell phone was lit with a message that read, "Call me." He didn't think anything of it when he dialed, figured Angie might need him to run by the store. But when he heard the sound of Dwayne Brewer's voice, all of the feeling left his body.

"You know, I was starting to think you wasn't going to call."

That voice was unmistakable. Calvin's hands shook and his heart beat violently. He opened his mouth to speak, but there were no words. The air snagged in his throat like he'd had the wind knocked out.

"You hear me don't you? Calvin?"

He dropped the phone onto the floorboard and scrambled to pick it up. "I'm here," he said when he got the phone back to his ear. "I'm here."

"And where do we go from here?"

The question struck him. Calvin found it so strange the way Dwayne talked, always this self-righteous tone to what he said, like he was trying to teach you something. "If you lay a finger on her head I swear to God I will hunt you down and—"

"You might want to think about how you're talking to me."

"I swear to you, I'm going to—"

"Don't start talking stupid now," Dwayne cut him off. "I've got something I need you to do for me, and the way I figure, you owe it."

"What?" Calvin yelled. "What do you want?"

"I thought me and you might get together and talk about that."

"Tell me."

"No, I think it'd be best if we get together," Dwayne said. "I never was much on talking on the phone. I prefer to look a man in his eyes when I'm talking to him."

"I want to talk to her."

"What you're going to do is meet me up there where y'all are clearing all that land. You're going to meet me there at ten o'clock this evening and we're going to get all this straightened out. That's what you're going to do."

Calvin wondered how he knew about the jobsite, wondered how many days Dwayne Brewer had followed him.

"But you start talking crazy again, you go doing something crazy, Calvin, and I think you know how this is going to end. You know good and well what I'm capable of."

Calvin watched vacuous and unblinking through the windshield, thinking of how he'd woken curled beside her that morning. "Angie."

"Ten o'clock."

He could hear his own breaths as static on the line.

"Calvin, I want you to say it. I want you to tell me what you're going to do."

"Ten o'clock," he said. "I'll meet you there at ten o'clock."

"That's right," Dwayne said. "You meet me there and we'll get this squared away. We'll get this behind us and we'll get back to our lives."

"Okay," Calvin said, and the line went dead.

Up the road, a rail-thin coonhound crossed in front of a car. The driver slammed on brakes and blared the horn, but Calvin didn't hear a sound. He stared through the dusty glass and the world before him appeared as flat and unmoving as a painting. It wasn't like people said, it wasn't that time stood still, but rather that his mind raced at such an unfathomable pace that the world turned sluggish.

There was a ringing in Calvin's ears and his head felt like it was floating, like his body had up and vanished and left nothing outside his mind. Questions fell like pieces of a hillside breaking away. All of it came onto him at once until his mind was entirely taken. A landslide of thought gave way with nothing to slow it. There was no bottom to stop its fall.

TWENTY-FIVE

DWAYNE WIPED THE COBWEBS AND DUST FROM THE LAMP globes and filled the fonts with oil. The wicks were old and tattered, but when they were soaked with fuel they lit just fine. Low tongues of light tapped against the cobble walls and now he could see her. He watched the fire reflect in her eyes, then turned to his work.

Stepping over Angie's body as if she were little more than a log across his path, he unloaded the groceries he'd taken from the house onto a long pine shelf. When he'd finished, he came back and hooked his hands under her arms, hoisted her up, and propped her against the wall so that she sat with her arms at her back, her knees to her chest.

"I'm going to take that tape off and it's going to hurt," Dwayne said.

He stepped toward her and scratched at the tag end of tape and when he had it up he ripped the duct tape around her head, hair and skin coming with it as it freed. Angie winced and her eyes glassed over, but she neither screamed nor cried.

"You know who I am?" Dwayne asked.

She shook her head. "What is this place?" she asked. "What's that smell?"

"I want you to look across the room there." Dwayne nodded to the wall behind him and Angie leaned to peer around a pitched support.

The room was dark, but the lamplight reached the body enough to show Carol Brewer sitting there like some grotesque dummy. The skin was a dark gray in the yellow light, his face something from Halloween. Only the rough outline of his figure, the muddied clothes he wore, showed any sign that he'd ever been a living, breathing thing.

"What is that?"

"That's my brother," Dwayne said, and he turned to look where she stared. What was left of Carol filled him with great sadness.

"I'm going to be sick," she said, and no sooner had those words left her lips, Angie lunged to the side and threw up into the dirt beside her.

Dwayne pulled a yellow paisley handkerchief from his back pocket, unfolded it, and wiped the corners of her mouth. "You'll get used to the smell after a while."

"I don't understand," Angie said. "What happened to him?"

"What happened to him is why you're here."

"I don't . . ." she stuttered. "I don't understand."

"Darl Moody killed my brother," Dwayne said. "Darl Moody

killed him and Calvin helped cover it up. The two of them threw my brother off in a hole and buried him like trash. I wouldn't even have done a dog the way they did."

"That can't be true," Angie said. "Calvin couldn't have done that. There's no way. There's no way they could've done that."

"You can believe anything you'd like, but the truth's the truth just the same. The truth don't change because we don't want to believe it. God knows what the two of them did just like I do."

"What do you know about God?" Angie's face bled with anger.

Dwayne Brewer smiled and took a seat on the dirt floor. He crossed his legs and sat so they were looking eye to eye.

"Oh, a great deal, I imagine," he said. "I've read that book over and over again and I believe as much as any God-fearing man on this mountain that He's up there watching all this. The difference is that I know something they don't. What I know's He's got one sick, sick sense of humor." Dwayne shook his head and grinned. "Way I see it, the only thing He ever got right, the only thing He made absolutely perfect was these mountains. These trees. These creeks. Now, He got that part right," Dwayne explained. "But then He created man. He makes an animal so dumb that it destroys the very gift it was given and He sits back and watches. Now you tell me that ain't a sick sense of humor."

He traced his fingers through the dirt at his sides and continued.

"Take the story of Job. It was like He was sitting back and watching a kid pull the legs off a spider. The devil took everything Job had. On a bet, God let him murder Job's sons and daughters while they were sitting together at the supper table. Think about how that would eat your heart in two. If that wasn't enough, he covered that old boy's body in boils, let him get so sick that Job was begging

God to end it, and only then, only after all of that, does the Lord finally say, 'All right. I reckon that's enough.'"

Dwayne slapped the floor with both hands at his sides and laughed.

"No, I ain't that sick. I can see the humor in it, but I ain't that sick."

Angie was vacant and silent.

"So the thing is, I've read that book front to back a hundred times if I've read it once. I know what that book says more than most people. I just don't see it like they do. A God of mercy, they say. I look around this world and I don't see no mercy. They talk about a God of compassion. I want you to look around. You show me a place where compassion outweighs selfishness. The only thing we might agree on is forgiveness." Dwayne nodded his head. "I reckon He'd have to be forgiving when He's done plenty worse Himself. A God of forgiveness. Now that I can see."

Dwayne stood and walked a small circle around the room. He kicked at the dirt with the toe of his boot and when he was back near her he leaned against one of the support beams.

"You know, me and my brother used to play in here when we were kids. My grandfather built this place. Dug the whole thing out with a shovel and mattock. He carried the stone from the creek and cobbled these walls. He did every bit of it himself. Never asked nobody for nothing.

"When I was little, he used to use this place for a root cellar and canning shed. Sometimes he'd hang meat in here. Had a smoke shack he built up by the house, but he cured meat in here, salted it down on that plank right there." Dwayne nodded to where he'd set the supplies. "By the time I was growing up, though, he was old, and people didn't do a whole lot of stuff like that anymore, at least not like they used to. So me and my brother we kind of just took this place over as our own, used it like a sort of playhouse I guess you'd say."

"What was his name?" Angie asked.

"Who?"

"Your brother."

"Carol," Dwayne said. "His name was Carol, but we called him Sissy.

"I remember one time me and Sissy stayed here almost all summer. We'd sneak down to the house every couple days or so and steal enough food to get by, but other than that we stayed in the woods and did whatever we wanted."

Dwayne laughed at something that came into his mind, shook his head, and continued.

"One day we got bored of sitting up here and we decided we was going to walk all the way to town. So me and Sissy, we took off down Chipper Curve and on around by the paper mill and come into town, and there used to be this newsstand on Back Street and they used to sell candy bars and beer, magazines and what not. Sissy got the idea he was going to steal him a titty magazine. Well, right when he's shoving that magazine down the front of his pants that old boy that was running the register seen him and before I know it we were tearing out of there as hard as we could. We jumped the road and slid down into Scotts Creek and come up the other side and down the railroad tracks we went, now, by God we was gone."

Angie watched with a look on her face like she couldn't understand why he was telling her this.

"We get back here and we start looking through that magazine and old Sissy got all grossed out and I looked at him and I said, 'What's the matter with you?' And he said, 'I ain't know it looked like that.'" Dwayne laughed. "He said, 'I ain't know it looked like that, Dwayne.' And I told him, I said, 'I don't know what to tell you.' Old Sissy never was one for women," Dwayne said. "I think that first look ruined him or something. I don't know. He was different. I guess that's what I'm trying to say is my brother was just different. He wasn't cut out for the way this world is. But I loved him. Ain't make a bit of difference to me. I loved him."

"I'm sorry," Angie said. "I'm sorry for what happened to your brother, but there's no way Darl and Calvin could've done what you're saying. There's no way."

As soon as she said it, Dwayne jumped the gap between them and took ahold of her throat. "Don't you tell me they couldn't do it," Dwayne snarled. "I know what the two of them did! I know it because I heard Darl Moody say it right before I slit his throat! I know it because Calvin told me what they did when he dug my brother's body out of his pasture! So it don't make a goddamn bit of difference what you think happened or what you think the two of them are capable of because the truth's the truth just the same! I know what the two of them did just as God Himself knows it!"

Angie's face was flushed red and her eyes were wide and white. Dwayne squeezed Angie's neck as tight as he could before shoving her head against the stone behind her. When she was free, she took a gulp of air then another. Gradually she caught her breath and when her breathing eased Dwayne spoke with a strange calmness as if the rage that had filled him seconds before had never existed at all.

"The two of them took everything from me," he said. "They took the only thing I loved in this world." Dwayne glanced at his brother's body. "What's sitting right there is all that's left. A few more days and there won't be a thing. They took everything I loved, and that's why you're here."

"I'm sorry," Angie said. She was sobbing. "I'm sorry."

Dwayne reached into his pocket and came out with a knife that he flicked open effortlessly, its wide blade flashing white in the lamplight.

"No," Angie pleaded. "Please."

He stepped forward.

"I'm going to cut your wrists loose," Dwayne said. "And when I'm gone you can take that tape off your ankles."

"Please," Angie said. "Let me go."

"Each one of those lamps will burn close to a day," Dwayne said. "I'd burn one at a time if I was you. There's food and water there on that shelf."

"Just let me go."

"I'll be back in a day or so to check on you," Dwayne said. He stood before her with the knife held casually at his side. "Calvin does what he's told and all this'll be over." He knelt and reached for her hands at the small of her back, slid the knife under the zip cuffs and cut her free.

Dwayne closed the knife and slipped it back into his pocket as he rose. He crossed the room to the door, the rusted hinges groaning as he swung the door open. The world outside glowed blue with little more than half-moon. The night was cold and clear. He glanced up to stars that shined as steady and certain as they always had. Taking a deep breath, he felt the coldness of the air in his nose and when he lowered the heavy, iron bar across the door, he exhaled, not knowing when he'd return.

For so long, Dwayne Brewer had worked to keep everything

under his thumb. Control. That was the only way he'd ever felt at ease: when he was in complete control. *This world is about power,* he thought. *This world is about those born with it and those who take it for themselves.* As he came through the woods, he was filled with uncertainty, a feeling he hadn't known in a very long time. The world was completely out of his hands.

TWENTY-SIX

THE DEUCE AND A QUARTER HISSED ACROSS DAMP GRAVEL and rambled over rippled road so that Dwayne bounced around in the driver's seat like he was riding a horse. The road cut hard through a thicket of laurel that camouflaged the cliff face to the right, the left side dropping to a staircased creek that shaped the mountain now as it had for thousands of years before.

The gravel road hugged the hips of mountains, cutting back and forth along switchbacks to rise. In the years since the economy tanked and big money pulled out of the county, the private road had failed above a steep descent into the river. Erosion had bloodied the Tuckaseigee's west fork for weeks. The homesites once cleared for potential buyers were grown over with stickseed and saplings.

But now there was the promise of new money. Fix the roads, clear the lots, cut the golf course, slap up a billboard or two of some PGA star endorsing the place, and a drove of half-wits would pile north from Florida in Lexuses and Mercedes and Land Rovers to scope out second and third homes like a mass exodus of sun-stroked cattle. Those born here hated them. They cussed them at the grocery store and when their morning and evening commutes doubled because the leaf lookers drove twenty miles per hour up a mountain slated for forty-five. They cussed them under their breath and smiled to their faces because they had to, all the while wanting deep down to pull out a sodbuster and cut out their sunburned guts. But most of those born here made livings off of their fat pockets, and so in that way the relationship was symbiotic.

A sign showing off an architectural sketch of the future clubhouse framed with painted four-by-fours and an eve braided with cut laurel stood off the road to the right. Dwayne steered onto a gravel path that opened to an expansive clearing carved flat into the swale. The clouds were low so that the night's fog made it hard to see the trees at the edges. A plain of red clay stretched in all directions like a dried lake bottom.

Calvin Hooper stood there in dark slacks, a stained T-shirt, and a heavy duck canvas coat. He raised a lever-action rifle to his shoulder and came straight into the headlights, stepping sideways as the Buick neared until he was aimed at Dwayne's ear through the side glass. Dwayne rolled down the window like he was about to order food at a drive-thru, hung his arm casually down the door outside. He wore an olive-green thermal shirt, the box-weave tight on his chest and arms. His face was shaved close, but the hair was dark enough that even shaved it left a shadow that rose high on his cheeks.

"Get the fuck out of the car," Calvin snarled with his chin set out in anger and his brow low over his eyes.

Dwayne killed the engine and cut the lights. "This is probably the closest you've ever come to killing somebody, ain't it?"

"I said, get the fuck out of the car."

Dwayne smiled, paying no attention to the gun or the prospect of dying. He stared deep into Calvin's eyes because that's where the truth lay. "See, that's what most people never understand. You get deep enough and that feeling's buried inside everything that's ever had a heart that beats."

"Shut the fuck up, and get out of the car." Calvin kept lowering his aim just a hair and jerking it back up like he was scared to lose sight of Dwayne even for an instant.

"Take the Sylva Seven, or, shit, take what that Broom boy did to Doug Dietz a few years back. Cut the soles off a man's feet and made him walk to his own grave." Dwayne shook his head and examined the Buick emblem on the steering wheel. He rubbed his thumb over the raised vinyl. "Now, some folks couldn't imagine what'd bring a man to do something like that. But you tell them about Doug molesting that little girl, and that's all it took for plenty of folks, God-fearing Bible thumpers, to swear Doug Dietz got off easy. I heard an old lady say they should've run a pike pole right up his ass like a skewer. The crazy thing, she wasn't just saying it. She meant it. She'd have stood right there and watched them do it. And the thing they're all too blind to see is that one's no different than another."

"I'm not fucking around, Dwayne. Get out of the car."

"What I'm saying is that it's easy to take the high road so long as there aren't any stakes. But the minute you've got something to lose, a man'll do all sorts of things." Dwayne grabbed a pack of smokes off the passenger seat, slipped a filter between his lips, and mashed the car's lighter into the dash. In a moment, the lighter popped and Dwayne lifted the orange glow to his cigarette, took a drag, and exhaled a thin cloud of smoke into the space between them. "The only problem with what you're doing right now is that you ain't seen my cards."

"I'm the one with the gun, Dwayne."

"Life ain't the kind of thing you want to go all-in on one hand, Calvin." Dwayne opened the door and stepped out. Calvin backed away a few steps, the gun still high on his shoulder. He stared down the length of the barrel with both eyes open. "It's a whole lot smarter to bet a little at a time, see what a man's got in his hand before you go sliding all your chips into the middle." Dwayne strolled toward Calvin's truck.

"Don't go no farther, Dwayne! I mean it!"

Dwayne strutted unconcernedly toward Calvin's pickup.

"One more step and I'll blow your head off!"

"If you don't mind me asking, what'd this truck set you back?" He took a drag from his cigarette and blew the smoke down his chest.

"What'd you say?"

"I asked how much this truck cost. You look like you're doing pretty good for yourself, you know? Nice truck, big job, everything's lining up for you. I can see what a girl like her might see in a man like you. If a man's willing to sell his soul, he can have about anything in this world, can't he? I reckon that's what this is, ain't it? Selling your soul?" Dwayne opened his arms to the cleared land around him, at what used to be the top of a mountain.

"Shut the fuck up, Dwayne!" Calvin came forward until the gun was a foot from Dwayne Brewer's mouth. "Why don't you just shut—"

Those next words were cut off as Dwayne Brewer shoved the

barrel of the rifle toward the ground, pulled his pistol from his waistline, and jammed it into Calvin's temple. With his grip tight on the rifle, Dwayne turned Calvin like they were dancing and rammed him hard into the front bumper of the truck. Calvin's back arched with the weight of Dwayne pressing down on him, the pistol still crammed against the side of his head, and chest to chest Dwayne leaned forward till his lips were flush against Calvin's ear. "I was getting awful tired of you pointing that gun at me. So you're going to listen now, and I'm going to help you see things a little clearer than how you're seeing them." Dwayne eased away. "Let go of that gun and we'll talk like men instead of a couple kids playing cowboy and Indian."

Calvin nodded his head and let go. Pushing back, Dwayne held the lever action rifle down by his leg and holstered the pistol in the back of his pants.

The two men stood there catching their breaths in the fog.

"What this boils down to is what you've got to lose, Calvin, and that ought to be real clear right about now or else the two of us wouldn't be standing here. Stakes," Dwayne said. "When a man's got something to lose, that changes things. You find something a man loves more than himself and you can get him to do about anything in this world. Now you're going to do something for me. You do it and everything's going to be fine. But if you go any other route, Calvin, you do anything else at all, and I think you know how this is going to end. You know good and well what I'm capable of."

"What do you want me to do?"

"You're going to kill Michael Stillwell."

"Kill Stillwell? What are you talking about?"

"He's breathing down our necks. A man stares at something long enough and eventually he'll start to see it for what it is."

"I won't do that."

"Of course you will, Calvin." Dwayne smiled with great amusement. "You were going to kill me just a minute ago for what's at stake, and it's the same thing on the line now. You don't do it and I'll put a bullet in that woman of yours like I was shooting squirrels. What happened to Darl Moody ought to tell you that I'm nothing if not a man of my word."

"He's a goddamn detective. This county will be crawling with law if something happens to one of theirs. And even if I did, Dwayne. Even if I did kill him, what then? You think all this is going to go away? You think there won't be another comes in right after him?"

"For most the folks wearing that badge, it's a paycheck. You do what you can to keep from getting filled up with bullet holes. You put in your thirty years and you retire. There're crusaders and there're folks punching a time clock. I'd say it's about a fifty-fifty chance whether the next one cares like Stillwell does, and that's a chance I'm willing to take. Besides, this'll make that department forget all about what happened to Darl Moody, now won't it? They'll be so busy looking for you they won't even see me slip out of here."

"I won't do it."

"You call me when it's done."

"You're out of your mind."

"No, I'm seeing things quite clearly," Dwayne said. "I'm going to give you three days to get it done, and if it hasn't happened by then I'm coming and taking everything you love. I'll burn your whole goddamn world to the ground in the blink of an eye."

Calvin was silenced.

"That's what you took from me."

Dwayne slipped past Calvin and stood by the back tire. He worked the lever until all six rounds were scattered about the ground, then gently placed the rifle into the bed of the truck. When he returned to the front bumper he stood there and looked hard into Calvin Hooper's eyes.

"You know, what you've done to this mountain is worse than anything I've ever done in my life," he said. "Any given day any man can kill somebody, but this . . . this right here." He opened his arms and spun a circle to the cleared land surrounding them. "You've spit in the face of God." Dwayne stepped closer until there were only inches between them, him having to bow his head to meet Calvin's eyes. He raised his hand and patted Calvin on the cheek, then left his hand flat against his face so he could feel Calvin's beard prickly against his palm. "I don't see how you sleep at night."

Calvin swatted Dwayne's hand away. "You're out of your fucking mind!"

Dwayne smiled and strolled away. "Three days," he said without turning.

He climbed into the car and cranked the engine to life. The headlights flashed Calvin Hooper and he shaded his eyes, unwilling to face what was on him right then. Soon enough he would learn he was capable, and whether it was wickedness or love was no easy question. Deep enough down, every living thing was exactly the same. What will it took resided in every heart that beat.

TWENTY-SEVEN

JUST OVER MOODY BRIDGE, CALVIN PARKED IN A MUDDY pull-off along a freestone section of the Tuckaseigee where trout made meals of mayflies, and redhorse lined seams of current. A single-action Colt revolver that had belonged to his grandfather rested in his lap. The brass frame held a rainbow patina like oil on wet pavement, the blued barrel dark and dull. He'd only ever shot the pistol a handful of times. Never had cared much for guns aside from a few hunting rifles and a pump shotgun he kept for home protection.

Calvin opened the loading gate on the side of the revolver and shook a few tarnished shells from a ratty box of .45 long colts. He slid the cartridges into the cylinder a shell at a time, held the hammer half-cocked when he loaded the last. He remembered his grandfather shooting a pumpkin one fall, holding that revolver by his waist and fanning the hammer like a gunslinger in an old

Western. He remembered how the old man laughed when the gun was empty, how shattered pieces of pumpkin littered the yard.

On the passenger seat was a framed photograph he'd taken from the house. When Calvin pulled in and saw Angie's car sitting there in the driveway, the doors slung open, he knew that no matter the consequence he would do whatever Dwayne Brewer asked. Reaching across the cab for the picture, he flicked on the overhead light and looked at how happy they'd been. One of Angie's friends had started a photography business and told them she'd shoot them for free if they let her use the photos for her Facebook page. They dressed up nice one Sunday and took pictures around the farm— the same sitting in a field, standing by a barn, walking down a dirt road, leaning on a fence, watermarked photos as every other couple posted on Facebook. At the time, he'd thought it was stupid, but it had made Angie happy.

In the photo, the two of them walked through the field beside his house, golden light haloing the grass and their bodies. The thing he loved about that photograph was that it carried sound. She was laughing in the picture and just looking at it he could hear her, and that made the immediate decision easy. He didn't know what would come after, but as he watched the moonlight spark on the river's crests, what he had to do right then was as certain as any truth he'd ever known.

Up the road, Stillwell lived in a ranch-style home that had once belonged to a man named Ronald Brinkley. Michael had bought the place when the old man died of pneumonia one winter, the way Calvin heard it, scooping the place up for damn near nothing. Calvin set the picture back on the seat, took the pistol from his lap, and opened the door to the night. He stepped out and could hear the water running on the other side of the trees, the gravel scratching beneath his boots.

You do this and it'll all be over, he thought. He'd bury him at the jobsite where the ground was cleared and muddy. His heart raced and he stood there, body tingling, nearly out of breath. The unthinkable had suddenly become one more thing a man had to do to survive. He had everything in the world to lose, and only one way to keep it.

TWENTY-EIGHT

THERE WASN'T A SECOND SHE DIDN'T FEEL LIKE SHE WAS running out of breath. But as long as Angie didn't look at the body, she could keep from getting sick. There was the smell, sure—the putrid cross between rotting meat and sewage, this strange overwhelming sweetness almost like perfume—but it was the sight of him. Knowing the source of the smell made it unbearable. She was trapped in a room with a dead man. There was no way to couple with something like that other than to push it as far from her mind as she could. Force herself not to look. Believe it's not there.

As soon as she'd heard the bolt latch on the outside of the door, she knew she'd hear Dwayne Brewer coming when he returned. The thought of doing what she was told, trusting him that everything was going to be okay, never crossed her mind. If he was the man who killed Darl, if he was capable of something like that, then he was not someone to take at his word.

The room was dark and damp and as she made her way around the space with the lamp, she checked for anything she could use. Shelving lined all but the back wall, a freestanding set of shelves pieced together from apple crates in the center of the room. Ball jars loaded with vegetables—green beans, okra, corn and tomato succotash, pickled cucumbers and onions—sat dusty on all but the pine slab where Dwayne had set the groceries. Loose boards leaned against one corner of the room, a ripped bag of nails at the base of the wall, a bucket filled with old rags and a rusted section of chain.

Watching the flame waiver inside the lamp, an idea hit her and she took one of the jars off the shelf, popped the seal, and emptied a quart of beans onto the floor. The oil lamps were lined up on the pine shelf, their wicks extinguished to save oil. She took one of the lamps and slid the globe free. In a second, she had the burner out where she could empty the oil from the font into the jar. All she needed now was a torch, something she could light when she heard him at the door. A scrap section of two-by-twos rested with the boards in the corner of the room, and she wrapped its end with a piece of rag and soaked it with oil. Emptying one more lamp into the jar filled the glass to the brim. She'd keep these things together, and when she heard him, she'd light the torch. *Set him on fire like a brush pile.*

There was nothing to do now but wait, and that was the hard part. The unanswerable question. The waiting. How long would be trapped in that room? How long would the food and How long had she been there already? How long before started looking for her, and how long after her, and what if they didn't? What if this wa die? The questions and the unknowing boil fell against the wall and buried her face in push those questions from her mind because hope was the only thing to prevent breaking and she refused to break. Not with this child in her belly. Not as long as there was breath in her body.

It had surprised her how happy she was when that first pregnancy test she took in the Walgreens bathroom came back with that little plus sign, and when the next three came back the same, and when her doctor looked at her and said, "Yeah, you're pregnant," with a stoic expression because he wasn't sure how she'd take it because not everybody took it well. Despite how scared she was, she was happy.

She hadn't told Calvin, and wasn't sure how he'd react. She hoped he'd be happy, but how could she be sure? How could she be certain of anything anymore? If what Dwayne Brewer said was true, everything she thought she knew lay in a heap of ashes. How could the same man who opened his doors to her so that she could go back to school be capable of covering up a killing? How could he bury a secret like that inside himself? Again, she tried desperately to push all those questions away. She was going to be a mother. She kept telling herself that—*I'm going to be a mother.* Saying it aloud, "I'm going to be a mother." There was nothing else now. Nothing mattered but the child.

She was tired and it was hard to keep her eyes open, but she was scared to sleep. If she dozed off for a second, she might miss her chance. The thing about fighting sleep, though, is that the body has its own idea. Delirium starts to build and you tell yourself you'll close your eyes for a second and so you do. You open your eyes, and everything's fine and so you close them again, this time a little further. No one means to fall asleep behind the wheel. It just happens. And that's where Angie was headed, washing between dream, and soon she was almost there.

Suddenly she was roused by a sound moving across the floor on the far side of the room. With her eyes adjusted to how the dim lamplight pulsed against the cobble walls, she saw a shadow race across the floor. A rat ran the length of the wall, hopped onto the man's shoulder, and disappeared into a crack between the stones. For a second she wondered if she'd imagined it, if that animal was some sleep-deprived vision. But as she stared at the hole where the rat had vanished she could see the space was real. There was a dark gap cut between the stones where mortar should've been.

If he can get in, then I can get out.

Pushing herself up from the floor, she crossed the room and knelt to look at where the rat had burrowed into the wall. She pressed her hand flat against the stone and felt around in the hole, a space slightly bigger than a walnut, cold and wet against her fingers. Scratching with her fingernails, the mortar crumbled away into sand. She clawed at it then, raking her fingertips against the coarse concrete until her nails chipped, her skin rubbed raw and numb. When she couldn't use her hands, she used one of the nails from across the room. She gripped the nail like a knife and dug at the mortar, relentless and steadfast. Her knuckles were bloodied but eventually she chipped an inch or more deep all the way around the stone.

She scanned the room for something to pry the rock loose from the wall. All that she found was scrap wood, a long section of two-by-six split down the middle with bent nails. Bracing the corner of the board against a cobblestone edge, she kicked down hard and split the board in half. One end was full, the other a jagged shard that she stabbed as far back into the hole as sh͡ ͡ ͡ld to try and leverage the rock free. She worked the stone f͡ ͡ ͡ angles, but the wall was ungiving and as she straine͡ ͡ ͡ might the wood snapped in her hands and a splinte͡ through the ring finger of her left hand. Blood ran to her wrist, trickled down her forearm, and dripped from her elbow. She held her wrist in disbelief and fell to the ground with her legs tucked beneath her. Her eyes filled with tears and without control she cried out in pain.

There was something that settled in the pit of her stomach right then, something that said, *Quit crying and get up.* Grabbing the splinter by its base, she grit her teeth and ripped it free. She could feel her pulse throbbing in her hand, the blood puddling in her open palm, but she buried the pain deep and didn't make another sound. She wiped the blood against her skirt and turned back to the wall. *You're going to get out of here for this child,* she thought, the world having taken on a singular meaning. Nothing mattered outside of what she carried.

TWENTY-NINE

HALFWAY UP THE DIRT ROAD SOMETHING HELD CALVIN Hooper like chains. He couldn't take another step, couldn't will himself to move, even when he told himself, *It has to be this way.*

For the last hour, he'd stood on Moody Bridge mesmerized by the river. Moonlight made scales of the surface so that the water looked like a black snake basking in the valley's night. The revolver was tucked inside his coat and he tried to imagine what it would feel like to kill a man. It was one thing to end a life by accident, and not all that far a stretch to do the same in a moment of rage. Either could happen in the blink of an eye. But to do so knowingly, to roll it around in your mind and answer the questions of how you'd do it, when and where, now that was another matter altogether.

Calvin turned and looked toward the highway. Just south on 107 sat the Tuckasegee Trading Post, its red tin roof lit by a streetlamp at the corner of the narrow parking lot. Staring at something so familiar, he was struck by the ordinariness of it, how ordinary all of it had been. Five weeks ago he was no different from any other man in this county. Work, church, and family. That was it. Same as anyone else, just as plain as apple pie. But all it took was a phone call to rip the rug right out from under his whole life. One decision and now here he stood.

What was happening hadn't fully sunk in yet. Part of it was shock. It was that suddenly-staring-at-your-house-in-smoking-ashes kind of feeling that left Calvin in a sort of stupor. But the bigger part was that he wasn't ready to bear the blame. The devil drew the line between the selfless and the selfish so that often a man could not tell on which side he stood. Since the beginning, he'd told himself this was about Angie and how much he loved her. This was about a willingness to do whatever it took to keep her safe, to keep from losing her. There were some things worth dying for and some things worth killing for and some things that could make a man do all sorts of things he never knew he was capable of until the time came to do them. On the ride here, he'd been certain he loved her that much. But over the past few minutes he'd learned that killing a man was no easy thing.

There'd been so many nights standing by bonfires in empty pastures, empty beer cans littered at their feet, Calvin and Darl the only ones who hadn't turned in. During drunken conversations they swore they'd do anything for the other. One might be in a row with somebody, and the other might say, "I'll kill him," and they'd both get fired up and then they'd laugh. The thing was, they weren't just saying it. They meant it. They loved each other enough that they meant every word. But deep down no one ever really believes it's going to come to that. You say it like another way of saying *I love you.* You don't ever truly believe you're going to have to lay down your life.

Calvin walked to the other side of the bridge and gazed upriver. Off to the right he could see rolling hills in the distance, the moonlight teal against the grass. Along the road on the other side of the river, cut cornstalks stubbled a narrow strip of dirt. There was little doubt in his mind that Dwayne Brewer would do exactly what he said. *Like I was shooting squirrels.* That thoughtless. That easy.

"He's going to kill her," Calvin said under his breath. He said it again and those words spoken blew coals to flame and all of it came onto him then, a barrage of emotion—sadness and mourning and guilt and anger—and he leaned forward with his face afire and wept with an uncontrollable madness, his hands gripping the concrete parapet.

Right then, his mind was awash with memory. He thought about the first time he met Angie, how she'd laughed at him when he asked for her number, how she told him he needed to go home and take a shower, maybe think of cleaning himself up a little if he was going to come into a restaurant and hit on a waitress. She was working at O'Malley's then and he'd thought she was one of the college girls, thought she was older than she was, no clue aside from her accent that she was local. He remembered the first time he kissed her and how she'd been wearing something on her lips, how it left his mouth tingling and cool like peppermint. He remembered how hesitant she'd been to sleep with him, how long it had taken, and how he woke up early that next morning, the sun coming up outside, and he looked at her there asleep and he knew that she was the most beautiful thing he'd ever seen. He knew that there were some things on this earth that carried the fingerprints of God on their skin like clay carries the prints of the potter. Those eyes. Those gorgeous green eyes. He could see his entire life in them. He could hear her laugh. He could feel her body spooned against him while she slept, his arm wrapped over her and tucked between her breasts. He could smell her hair as he dipped his nose into it and inhaled and closed his eyes dancing between reality and dream, one no different from the other in that moment. All of that memory came onto him as he clenched tight to the bridge and he heaved forward and emptied himself into the river below. Staring down, the water disappeared under the bridge and that movement made him feel like he was swaying, a vertigo-type dizziness rocking his knees. He panted for air, spittle hanging from his bottom lip.

For so long Calvin had been terrified of what would happen if he told the truth. All he'd had to do was walk out of those woods. All he'd had to do was go to the sheriff and come clean. Thinking about what he'd covered up, he could see how selfish it all was, that none of it had a goddamn thing in the world to do with Angie or keeping her safe, that up until then every decision he'd made had been about himself. Every decision had been about keeping himself out of trouble. If he loved her, he would've done anything in the world to protect her, even if that meant giving his own life away.

That feeling in the pit of his stomach evolved into a sort of resolve. It was almost midnight when he marched off the bridge and he knew now what he had to do. He stopped at his pickup, opened the driver's-side door, and sat inside, looking at that photograph of Angie while he smoked a cigarette down to ashes. The revolver lay across his lap and he rubbed the blued cylinder with his thumb like he was polishing silverware. After he finished his cigarette, he slammed the door, and headed down the road to the brick house where Stillwell lived.

The light was on in the front room. The unmarked patrol car sat in the drive. Calvin stepped across a ditch and walked through the yard, dew on the grass slicking the soles of his boots. He came up the steps onto the porch and as he reached to knock on the door he understood that this was it, that there could be no turning back from here. In a moment, the porch light flicked on, the lock unlatched, and there he stood.

Stillwell was barefoot with a ratty Smoky Mountain High Booster Club T-shirt and a pair of dark basketball shorts with white stripes down the seams. There was a look of confusion in his eyes, his lips flat and his jaw clenched. Looking at him, Calvin could see the boy he'd grown up with, all those years having filled the saddlebags under his eyes. Still, it was the same man. The same kid he'd fought with on the practice field over a girl. The same kid who ran off gung ho after 9/11 their senior year in high school and joined the Marines. The same man who came home and took a job and went to work like all the rest of them because even when they left they always came back, these mountains always calling them home. They were all tied together in that way and Calvin hoped that was enough.

"Calvin?" he said.

"There's something I'm about to tell you and I need you to trust me, Michael. I need you to listen."

THIRTY

A SLOW TRAIL OF GRAY CURVED FROM THE CHIMNEY INTO a cloudless sky and filled the cove with the smell of wood smoke. They prowled beneath ragged jack pine following the gravel to where the yard opened to the house, the windows a yellow glow in a night dim and silent. Speaking with hand signals rather than words, they snuck around the Buick and stopped at the edge of the porch. Their eyes cut back and forth to one another, and each man nodded when he understood: There could be no hesitation from here.

Dwayne Brewer sat on the couch in the living room with a chainsaw in his lap and a round file in one hand sharpening teeth, oblivious to what was right outside. A single thunderous blow cracked the door back on its hinges, something rattling over the floor, a canister flipping end over end followed by a crack of light and sound. All he could see was white. A barrage of voices yelled, "Sheriff's Office! Search Warrant! Sheriff's Office! Search Warrant!" but Dwayne Brewer didn't hear a single syllable. An acrid phosphorus smell stung his nose and the smoke alarm beeped overhead. He opened his mouth wide trying to pop his ears, the ringing still loud as muffled voices began to break through. "Gun! Gun!" he heard someone yelling, and he knew they were clearing the 1911 from the coffee table in front of him. "Show me your hands, Dwayne. I want to see your hands."

Dwayne Brewer opened his hands and held them palms forward at the sides of his face like an idiot mime. A slight grin cut his cheeks. "I don't know why in the world you didn't just knock."

"Stand up," Stillwell ordered.

"I would've answered the door like a human being. I don't know why you don't just treat me like a human being."

"I said stand up."

"I can't see to stand up," Dwayne said. "All I see's white and I can barely hear a word you're saying."

He felt someone take the chainsaw from his lap, felt the thud on the floor by his foot. Someone had ahold of his arm. "Up!" the man yelled. "And go ahead and put your hands behind your back for me."

Dwayne stood, the front of his white undershirt and the thighs of his jeans painted with bar oil and grease. The man spun him around and cuffed his wrists.

"I hope you've got a search warrant," Dwayne said.

"We do."

"And what exactly are you looking for?"

"Right now this deputy's going to take you outside and you're going to hold tight."

"I want to see that search warrant," Dwayne said. His vision began to return. Everything was washed with white glare, streaked halos running from the edges of everything. Through the rest of the house he could hear the other deputies working to clear the rooms. "Need one, need one," someone yelled from the back of the house. "Clear," another yelled. Through the ringing, footsteps, and voices, a rerun of *Married with Children* was playing on the television behind him.

A young, baby-faced deputy in olive-drab cargo pants, a gray T-shirt, and a black bulletproof vest with the word SHERIFF centered in yellow led Dwayne onto the porch. The light from the house carried outside and Dwayne stood there feeling the rotten planks bow under his weight. The deputy backed him against a post and told him to hold still while he patted him down, asking him if there was anything sharp in his pockets.

"Just a pocketknife," Dwayne said, his mind immediately turning to the cell phones in his pockets, one belonging to Angie Moss. The deputy turned Dwayne's pockets inside out and set what he found on the warped railing. Dwayne could see a tribal tattoo wrapping the boy's bicep. He was solid up top, but looked to have skipped leg day, a pair of twigs holding him up, and Dwayne wanted desperately out of those cuffs, desperately to split that boy's head open like a cantaloupe. He took a deep breath and closed his eyes, tried to imagine the deputies working their way through each room.

A buck stove clanked in the corner of the living room, the metal popping and tinking as the heat built inside. Dark knots spotted the grain of pine-batten walls stained bronze. There was some furniture—a faux-suede couch, a coffee table, a side table, a lamp, and an ornate rocking chair by the stove. The living room opened to both sides, one side going into the kitchen, the other opening to a bedroom and hallway.

In the kitchen, white cabinets ran the length of the hardwood floor. The countertops were spotless. A cast-iron pan rested on the stove and a mudroom opened off the far side, a door there led into the backyard.

Down the hall, a bedroom cut off to the right. The walls were slatted together by old barn wood painted powder blue. Every room had a different construction like the place had been piecemealed together by a lunatic junkman. Nothing matched from one wall to the next. The floor in the bedroom to the right was uncovered flakeboard. A dozen or more chainsaws and flat-screen televisions he'd stolen were organized in rows. There was a conspicuous order to the room, to the entire house, for that matter. Everything was meticulously placed and clean, a place absent the slightest excess.

His bedroom was little more than a king-size mattress centered against the wall, no frame or box spring, no headboard, comforter, or sheets. A chest of drawers stood against the opposite wall, a tattered Bible centered on the walnut top. Other than that the room was empty, a dark burgundy carpet covered the floor, the drywall bright and blank as if it had been bleached.

There were a couple rifles in the closet, a lever-action Marlin .30-30 that belonged to his grandfather and a Remington 700 mountain rifle chambered in 7-08 with a Simmons Aetec scope he'd snatched up from Middleton Pawn for damn near nothing. The little Smith & Wesson Darl Moody had pulled on him that night in the doublewide was tucked under the pillow on his bed, and that was the only thing to worry about, though there was no way to really know to whom it belonged. What they had was circumstantial at best, and they sure as shit weren't about to stumble onto that root cellar off in the woods. Dwayne's mind eased at that thought, his shoulders falling, the fire sinking back into his chest. He opened his eyes and smiled.

In a few minutes, Stillwell came onto the porch. He wore the same olive-drab cargo pants and shirt as the rest of the twelve-man team, the cuffs of the pants tucked into the tops of Belleville boots, a black bulletproof vest strapped over his chest. He held the grip of his rifle casually with one hand, allowing the weight of the gun to hang on its sling.

"Found this in his pocket, boss man," the deputy who'd led Dwayne onto the porch said, holding up a broad-handled folding knife.

"Bag it."

"A couple of cell phones, too." The deputy nodded down to a pair of cell phones, one with a bright pink case and rhinestones.

Stillwell picked the phone up and hit the home button. A picture of Angie smiling filled the screen, her hands hung on Calvin's arm, his arm wrapped under her neck, his head down kissing her shoulder. "Where'd you get this?" Stillwell shook the cell phone in front of Dwayne's face.

"Found it," Dwayne said.

"Say you found it?"

"Sometimes I like to go walk around the college for exercise. There's a lot to look at over there. Well, I was strolling around this morning. Found that laying right out on the sidewalk like somebody might've set it there."

Stillwell stepped forward and pressed the corner of the phone hard into the center of Dwayne's forehead. "Where the fuck is she?"

"Who?" Dwayne raised his eyebrows like he hadn't the foggiest what in the world Stillwell was talking about.

"You better start thinking long and hard about what you're saying, Dwayne. Where the fuck is she?"

The rest of the deputies huddled around the porch waiting for a response.

"I don't have a clue what you're talking about," Dwayne said. "I told you. I found that phone sitting there on the sidewalk this morning."

Stillwell turned to the deputy.

"Take him down to the station . . ."

"For what?" Dwayne growled. "What in the hell am I being charged with?"

"Hold him in the interrogation room," Stillwell said. He stared hard into the deputy's eyes. "I don't want anybody talking to him till I get there. You understand?"

"Yes, sir," the deputy said.

"For what?" Dwayne yelled. "You need to tell me why I'm being arrested."

Stillwell turned to the deputies in the yard. "Rice, you're going to come with me. The rest of you go on home."

"We can all ride," one of the deputies standing in the yard said, looking around at the rest of the team with his arms crossed.

"No," Stillwell said. "Rice and Dills are on duty. Rice, you're going to come with me, and Dills is going to take Mr. Brewer. The rest of you get on back home to your families. I already dragged you out of bed."

"Somebody's going to tell me what in the hell this is all about. I want to see that warrant," Dwayne yelled. "I want to know what I'm being charged with."

"I'm not charging you with anything right now, Mr. Brewer." Stillwell spun and stepped toward him and Dwayne barreled forward. The deputy at his side clenched Dwayne's arm and was drug like he'd latched on to a pickup truck. A few other deputies rushed onto the porch to help, but Stillwell didn't move. They were chest to chest and Dwayne was snarling in his face.

"You can't tear somebody's house apart, throw them in handcuffs, and haul them off to jail without cause."

"That's where you're wrong," Stillwell said. "I can hold you forty-eight hours without giving you Miranda or charging you with anything, Mr. Brewer. You're a person of interest in an active investigation."

"What investigation?" Dwayne's face boiled. "Tell me what the hell this is about?"

"You know good and well what this is about, Mr. Brewer. You didn't find that phone on any goddamn sidewalk. You know that as much as I do."

"I don't know nothing more than what I've done told you, *boss man*," Dwayne said. He mocked that little baby-faced deputy, hocked a thick wad of crud from deep in his throat, and spit it right into Stillwell's face.

THIRTY-ONE

WHILE DWAYNE BREWER WAITED, HIS MIND WARPED WITH
rage. The cuffs on his wrists cut into his arms and his hands were
bloodless and numb. When Stillwell finally came into the room, he
carried a can of Coke and was wiping the mouth of the can clean
with the bottom of his shirt.

"You want something to drink?"

"I want out of these goddamn handcuffs."

Dwayne watched him lean to see where his hands stuck out between the chair back and seat. "Hell, those are mine," he said. "Glad
I saw that." He pulled out a chair at the table and scooted close.
"Booking desk's supposed to put you in a set of theirs when you
come in. Know how I know those ain't from the booking desk?"

Dwayne didn't know what the fuck he was yammering on about,
but he was growing tired of it fast.

"I know those didn't come from the booking desk, because they keep pink handcuffs." Stillwell shook his head and chuckled. "Pink handcuffs. No shitting you. When an officer brings in a prisoner, booking's supposed to take the prisoner out of the arresting officer's cuffs and put them in a set they keep at the desk. Thing was those dipshits kept losing them. I guess it's like anything else in an office. A stapler. Scotch tape. Don't realize you can't find it till you need it. So they bought a bunch of pink handcuffs to keep from losing them. Nowadays, a man can find anything on the Internet."

"That's a fine story there, boss man, but why don't you get these handcuffs off of me seeing as you said I wasn't being arrested. This sure doesn't feel like not being arrested."

"You're a big boy, Mr. Brewer." Stillwell stood up and shook a pair of keys loose from his front pocket. He still wore the olive-drab cargo pants, but had taken off his vest and T-shirt to a black compression shirt. "Some of these boys weren't sure they'd be able to handle you if you weren't cuffed up." He leaned down and fit the key into the cuffs, popped the ratchets loose. "But I ain't so worried about that." He folded the pair of hinged handcuffs with black cheek plates and stainless single-strands in half, slipped them into the woven leather holster on his belt, and took a seat at the table.

In such a tiny room, Dwayne Brewer seemed all that much bigger. His arms were massive, the white undershirt riding high on his biceps. Even his head was huge, a block of bone like he could take a baseball bat to the face and not even blink. White bracelets showed where the cuffs had cut off circulation and he stretched his fingers and rubbed his wrists.

"You going to tell me what this is all about?"

"You know what this is about."

"I've already told you—"

"You can keep right on with that I-don't-know-what-you're-talking-about bullshit, but that's not going to help either one of us," Stillwell interrupted.

Dwayne Brewer sneered at Stillwell coldly, a single thought rattling around his skull like a .22-caliber bullet. *I'll strangle the goddamn life out of you yet.*

"Why don't you start with the phone? Tell me where you got that cell phone?"

"I told you. I found it sitting on the sidewalk."

"Where?"

"Over there at the community college."

"You go there a lot?"

"Sometimes."

"You want me to believe you go over there and walk around that campus for exercise?"

"You saying a man like me can't walk around that place like anybody else?" Dwayne rocked himself back in the chair and laced his fingers behind his head. "I think that's pretty shitty of you."

"So you were walking around that campus and there that phone was?"

"Right there it was."

"You didn't think about taking it to security, maybe into the building where you found it and seeing if somebody might've dropped it on their way in? Seems like that'd be the civil thing to do. Don't you think?"

"Civility doesn't have much to do with anything anymore now, does it, boss man? You throw somebody in handcuffs because you don't like the way they look, don't like where they come from, and you hold them in here but say, 'Naw, we ain't arresting you,' and then you want to talk to me about civility." Dwayne leaned forward and slapped his hands flat against the table. "That's the pot and the kettle, ain't it?"

Stillwell grunted in a sort of half-assed agreement and nodded. "See, in my mind you picking up that cell phone and not having the decency to walk inside and see if it might've belonged to somebody, now, in my mind that's as bad as stealing. But that's just the way I see it."

Dwayne guffawed.

"Kind of like all those televisions and chainsaws you had stacked up in that room at your house. I imagine if we run the numbers, I'll wind up thinking the same thing about those. Probably even be a little more cut-and-dry."

"I run a legitimate business there, boss man."

"A legitimate business, huh?"

"That's right. I fix those up and sell them. You'd be surprised what folks throw away down there at the recycling center. I pick it up, I fix it, and I sell it."

"So when I run the serials on all those televisions and all those chainsaws not a one of them's going to come back stolen? Those two items seem to come up missing at B-and-E's a lot more often than toaster ovens."

"I don't know where any of it come from before it wound up at the dump, but you can certainly ride down there and ask the attendant and she'll tell you. Her name's Martha. She talks funny. Kind of harelip or a cleft palate or something. And the strangest thing, most them TVs don't got serial numbers when I find them."

"Here's the thing, Dwayne. I'll cut the bullshit." Stillwell cracked the top on his soda and took a long swig. "That phone you had, that phone belongs to a woman named Angie Moss, and the thing is, she's come up missing."

"Well, I told you where I found—"

"We can run the cell tower pings and see where that phone's been, and we'll get to that, but right now I want you to listen." Stillwell cut him off. "What makes that cell phone so damn interesting is that Angie Moss is Calvin Hooper's girlfriend, and Calvin Hooper, well, that's Darl Moody's best friend. So you see, you having that particular phone is awfully, awfully suspicious in that it has a direct line to why I came looking for you in the first place."

"I already told you that, too," Dwayne said. He reached across the table and grabbed Stillwell's drink, kept his eyes on Stillwell as he raised the can and took a sip. He sighed heavily with satisfaction, watched that son of a bitch's face turn. "I don't know anybody named Darl Moody, and I don't know anybody named Calvin Hooper." He slid the can back in front of Stillwell. Stillwell shook his head.

"You can have it," Stillwell said. "You enjoy that Coke and I'll enjoy getting the blood results off that knife we found in your pocket tonight."

"Blood." Dwayne laughed. "You ain't going to find any blood on that knife except maybe some squirrel blood or rabbit blood, something I cleaned and et."

"I kind of suspect I'm going to find Darl Moody's blood. I kind of suspect that might've been the knife you ran right straight across his neck."

"You know you keep talking about how you think I killed Darl Moody, but the one thing you still haven't ever mentioned is why. What reason would I have had to do a thing like that? I didn't even know him. So what, you think I just upped and decided to go kill some fellow I don't know for shits and giggles? I think we both know how that'll play out in a courtroom."

"What I think is that all of this, every bit of it, is tied to your brother."

That word *brother* came like a match tossed into a cup of gasoline. His fists tightened and he clenched his jaw, his eyes held open and unblinking.

"Let's talk a little bit about your brother," Stillwell said. He seemed to notice the change in Dwayne's demeanor and latched on. "You know I went to school with Carol. Sissy. Me and him were in the same grade." Stillwell stared into Dwayne Brewer's eyes. "He had a pretty rough time growing up, didn't he? I remember how everybody used to pick on him about that birthmark on his face. Used to make fun of him about his clothes, the fact his shoes wasn't any good.

"I remember one time we were in, I don't know, sixth grade, seventh grade, but Sissy was sitting there at his desk and he had this old book bag sitting on the floor, this old yellow satchel, and the top of it was open. Well one of the boys sitting next to him said he saw a roach come out of the top of his book bag and run across the floor. He started yelling and laughing and telling everybody what happened, and the teacher turned around and Sissy was red in the face, looked like he was about to cry. I don't know if there was really a bug came out of his bag or not. I didn't see it. That's just what that boy said he saw. I remember feeling bad about that. Kids can say a lot of horrible things."

"You don't know a goddamn thing about my brother," Dwayne said calmly. "You don't know a thing about how we came up or what we went through. Now, you can sit there and pretend that you do, pretend like you care, but you don't. Deep down, you know that. I've seen people like you all my life. You see somebody suffering and you don't do a thing in the world to help them. You sit there and you watch it and you keep quiet, don't say a word, just go on about your business. Maybe you laugh about it. Maybe you don't. But either way you go right on about your life without thinking twice. So don't talk to me about suffering. And don't you dare try to tell me you knew my brother or you understand how we came up. You don't know a goddamn thing about it."

"What I know is that your brother was back in there digging ginseng just like you said," Stillwell explained. "But here's what I also know. I know that Darl Moody was back in there hunting and that somehow or another he wound up accidentally killing Carol. I know that the same as you do. You went looking for your brother and the old man showed you those pictures off his game camera and that led you to Darl. That's the connection. So when you ask me what reason you would've had to kill Darl Moody, that's why. And that's what led you to Calvin Hooper and that's why Angie Moss up and vanished like smoke."

"That's a whole lot of fine storytelling, but I don't think you have a thing in this world to support any of that."

"What I've got is the end of the line, Dwayne. I've got the right thread and I might've hit a knot, but when I get this knot untied and pull that string this whole thing's going to come unraveled, and right there you'll be."

Dwayne's expression did not change. There was a strange calm over him now, that same feeling he'd had right before Angie Moss came onto the porch.

"You're in a position right now that I can still help you. You tell me where she is and I can still help you, Dwayne. I can tell the DA that you were cooperative and that it was because of you that Angie Moss is safe and sound. But if you let this play out, if you wait till I have everything I need to prove what I already know, then it's going to be too late. There's not going to be anything I can do to help you then. You know what they're going to do, Dwayne, they're going to kill you. A jury of your peers will convict you of murder and they will sentence you to die."

"I'm not interested in pretending you're here to help me," Dwayne said. "That good-guy, let-me-help-you bullshit's a waste of your time."

"They'll kill you, Dwayne. That is not an exaggeration."

Dwayne looked down at his hands and he opened his fingers against the tabletop. He focused there for a long time before lifting his eyes. "Let me put this in a way that maybe you'll understand," Dwayne said. "You ever been standing at a campfire and all of a sudden the wind shifts and there you are with all that smoke and ash and fire blowing on you, and you got to move from where you were standing to keep from getting burned up, to keep from choking on all that smoke?"

Stillwell nodded his head.

"All my life I've been walking around that fire and all my life that smoke's been following me. That's the only truth I know. That's how it's been for me and my brother since we came into this world. When you've lived a life like that and a man looks you square in the eye and tells you you might die, like dying is the biggest chip he could lay on the table, it's a goddamn joke. I ain't a bit more worried about dying than I am about skipping a meal. You can take that for whatever it's worth, boss man. It don't make a damn bit of difference to me."

THIRTY-TWO

CALVIN HOOPER SHARED A HOLDING CELL WITH THREE MEN he'd never seen before in his life. The cellblock smelled like sweat: four cells on each side, a narrow corridor straight down the center, locked steel doors at each end. A small rectangular window with crosshatched wire through the glass centered the top halves of the two doors, the fronts of the eight cells were open with bars.

All but Calvin wore the same orange-and-white-striped uniforms. Sharing his cell, a scrawny man with a receding hairline lay with hands interlaced behind his head on one of the two bottom bunks. He wore a thin beard along his jawline and no emotion on his face. A young Cherokee kid with jet-black hair and wide eyes couldn't sit still. He'd sit down on the bunk, scratch at his arms, stand up, pace the cell, sit back down, scratch his arms, his jaw working like he was chewing bubble gum. The third was an older man with salt-and-pepper hair cut close, had the slimy look of a pedophile. He smiled when they brought Calvin into the cell, and tried to make small talk. He said his name was Atkins and that he got picked up on an out-of-state warrant from Mississippi. "Headed back to the Velvet Ditch," he kept saying. "I hope they're holding my spot at City Grocery." He stood at the bars with his elbows resting on the cross support, his hands dangling outside.

Someone in another cell was beating on the bars, making a sort of two-tone rhythm and singing off-key. Another inmate kept yelling, "Shut the fuck up! For God's sake, shut the fuck up!" but the drummer kept drumming and his singing never ceased.

Calvin stood at the stainless-steel sink and cupped his hands under a running faucet. He brought the water to his face and wiped it over his eyes. The water was cold against his skin and he stood there letting it drip from his chin, his empty expression staring back in the smudged mirror glass. He had no clue what would come next. There was a short-lived moment standing there on Stillwell's front porch while Calvin let go of everything he'd held, laying all of it right there at Stillwell's feet, when he honestly believed that things were going to work out, that they'd bust down Dwayne Brewer's door and find Angie there in a backroom safe and sound. But happy endings weren't fit for shit but children's books and PG movies. Here he was, in a cell, with absolutely no idea what was happening on the outside, no idea whether or not Angie was safe, no idea what would come.

There on that porch Stillwell had explained how Darl covering up what had happened didn't change the crime, that either way he was guilty of manslaughter. He told Calvin in the state of North Carolina that accessory after the fact was punished two levels below the principal felony and that meant he was facing a year, two tops. There was a chance with a clean record he might even catch probation, though Stillwell doubted a judge would be that lenient. Either way, Calvin wasn't looking at much time at all for what he'd done to Sissy. Stillwell had told him this to try and ease his burden and convince him that everything was all right. But in truth, knowing that made it all the worse. A year of his life and he'd have been free. He'd risked everything he loved to keep from handing over a year of his life.

A loud buzzing came from the far end of the jail, the lock clacked open on the door. Rubber soles squeaked against the concrete floor followed by the clap of footsteps. He wasn't paying much attention to the noise until they passed in front of the cell.

Two deputies marched at the sides of Dwayne Brewer, each having one arm hooked at his elbow. One deputy was a medium-built man with his hair shaved high and tight, the other a skinny middle-aged woman with greasy curls draping her shoulders. As soon as Calvin saw him, his heart felt like it was going to explode. He watched silent and dumbstruck like he was witnessing a miracle.

Dwayne's head turned and their eyes met. He smiled and spun so that he was facing Calvin's cell and he lumbered toward the bars while the deputies tried their damnedest to turn him. When he was almost to the cell, he stopped. The deputies wrestled, but he was too big to be moved. Dwayne widened his stance and took root. He looked at the two bulls yanking his arms and nodded to the cell in front of him. "I'll take this one."

The female deputy slapped out a collapsible blackjack and hammered the backs of his knees. Dwayne collapsed, his face cringing with anger or agony and the place erupted with men shouting as the two officers dragged him away. In a few seconds, Calvin heard the lock click on a cell and the heavy barred door slammed closed soon after. The two deputies marched back through the center aisle, glancing into Calvin's cell as they passed. The inmates banged on their bars and yelled at the tops of their lungs. The door closed at the end of the hall. There was no one inside now but the prisoners, and they made their wildness known.

Calvin felt dizzy standing there and he braced himself against the sink.

The old man from Mississippi watched him curiously. "You all right?" he asked, but Calvin didn't have anything to say.

"Calvin Hooper," Dwayne roared, the rest of the inmates cowering at the sound.

There was a feeling in the air caught between fury and fear, a volatility like the room was filled with gasoline fumes and a single spark would burn them all alive. Calvin's hands trembled and his ears rang.

"You better pray you get out before I do," Dwayne yelled.

But praying wouldn't help a soul.

THIRTY-THREE

IN ONE WAY OR ANOTHER DWAYNE BREWER HAD BEEN THUMB-ing for a ride all his life. That afternoon was hot as hell for the last of October and as he followed the edge of the road, stumbling backward as cars approached, nobody slowed down and nobody stopped.

He'd walked out of the Justice Center without any boots and by the time he made it up Kitchens Branch the soles of his feet were black and raw. The front door of his childhood home was kicked in and he hobbled inside only long enough to grab a roll of duct tape and a bag of zip ties from a junk drawer in the kitchen, a butcher knife from a wooden block on the counter, and the Bible from his bedroom.

Smash-and-grab dipshits and frat boys fighting DUIs chose law-yers with billboards mimicking *Better Call Saul*, sleazebag attorneys with coffee-stained teeth who ran TV commercials with spaceships and cheesy special effects. But this wasn't Dwayne's first rodeo. Irving Queen was as filthy as they came in the courtroom, but the difference was, he usually won. Queen came from Caney Fork like the Moodys and the Hoopers, and most Queens were great people, one of the most talented bluegrass families to ever come out of Appalachia. Irving's side, though, was questionable at best, shady if you wanted to get right down to it. Starting with his great-grandfather, four generations had all run shine, so being a snaky-ass lawyer was an honest-to-God step in the right direction.

Before the guards even had time to get to lunch, that greasy little potato of a man waltzed into the Justice Center with sweat oozing from his bald head and he slapped a writ of habeas on Sheriff John Coggins's desk. Coggins wore a silver flattop and a jet-black *Magnum, P.I.*, 1970s porn 'stache that looked like absolute shit. His face turned sour at the sight of Queen, at the sight of what lay on his desk that morning. Knowing what his detective had pulled the night before was questionable at best, borderline illegal, he cut Dwayne loose rather than wait around for a judge to smack him in the back of the head.

Crossing the yard, the way the brittle grass crunched underfoot, the clay damp and cold, reminded Dwayne of childhood, the way they'd never worn shoes outside of winter. There was something strange about having been in a single place his entire life, growing up right there in that house and having never left. There was no telling how many times in his life he'd hiked this trail between his parents' and grandparents' houses. But yet there was no sentimentality tied to this place. There were no mixed feelings about leaving. In fact, he was surprised it had held together this long. He had always figured the time would come to run, and now that it was here it seemed like an overdue day of reckoning.

The buzzards no longer sat in the trees, and their absence made the world seem strangely empty. He wasn't sure what to make of it, why they'd come and where they'd gone. There was a sunken feeling in the pit of his stomach like he was nearing a moment of inevitability, like this hallowed hour was exactly what he'd always been headed toward.

All morning in that holding cell he'd racked his mind with where they'd go from here. There wasn't time to bury his brother and he wasn't ready for that anyways. Lying on that thin jail mattress, the wool blanket itching his bare back, he was almost thankful. If he'd been let out right then, turned loose after seeing Calvin Hooper pissing himself behind those bars, Dwayne would've acted in a moment absent of thought, and those types of decisions were almost always mistakes. The morning had given him time to think and now he had a plan. He'd take Carol's body with him and disappear to a place their grandfather had taken them when they were kids.

Dwayne was eleven or twelve when they paddled across Fontana in a fiberglass canoe with a hole crudely patched in the hull. It was late summer, something he had always remembered because there was jewelweed flowering all over the banks. Orange horn-shaped flowers spotted bloodred on the petals dangled like ornaments from stems fine as thread. As a kid, Dwayne believed the plant was magic, the way the seedpods exploded like fireworks if you brushed them with your fingertips, the way the backsides of their leaves lit silver when his grandfather held one underwater, a leaf turned to metal by some sort of Appalachian alchemy.

They followed the creek from where it emptied into the lake, catching horny heads and speckled trout on Little Cleo silver spoons for supper, wandering settlements long since abandoned, with names like Proctor and Cable Branch, Bone Valley and Medlin.

Nearly a week in the woods away from home and their father, that trip might've been one time in their lives when they actually felt completely safe. When they were grown, he and Sissy ventured back to that place many times to walk in the footsteps of their past. *Steal one of them boats at the Fontana Village marina*, he thought, *and that's where we'll go.*

The land between Kitchens Branch and Allens Branch rose to a crooked spine of ridgeline that continued north through hard timber toward Indian Camp Gap. The trail to his grandparents' shack wasn't so much worn into the land as a path carved by memory. The terrain steepened and the wet leaves felt like leather under his feet. A laurel thicket dropped off one side. Dwayne hugged an outcrop of lichen-covered granite and when he came around the bend a young cane-legged deer lifted its nose from the ground and stared with wide, unblinking eyes black as his own. Sunlight shone through the deer's raised ears, turning flesh to soft pink stained glass, his tall vertical antlers still in velvet.

Dwayne stood there for a minute mesmerized. The deer was still aside a slight flare of his nose. When Dwayne came toward him, the young buck dipped his head to the ground and sauntered out of the way for him to pass. Dwayne crept almost close enough to touch him, to trace his fingertips along buckskin flank, and as he glanced out of the corner of his eye he had this overwhelming sense that he was looking at his brother. The thought made him woozy and he stumbled until there were twenty or thirty yards stretched between them.

When he turned back, the deer stood on the path and examined him with that same glass-eyed stare. The buck took a few steps forward, stopped and craned his neck, then a few more. Dwayne knew what the old-timers said of such things and he wasn't ready to accept that fate, to allow that soul to usher him to his end. He scanned the ground and picked up a small white stone and chucked it as hard as he could.

"Get!" he yelled as the rock whizzed over the deer's back.

The buck took a few startled steps, but did not run.

"Get out of here!" Dwayne yelled again, stomping against the ground, and this time the deer turned, leapt, and in the blink of an eye was gone.

THIRTY-FOUR

THE FIRST LAMP HAD BURNED OUT SOME TIME AGO, THE flame pulling back and then gone. Angie'd slapped around the pine plank to find the box of kitchen matches, struck a match against the side of the box, and lit the next wick in line. The air was so still there was no need for glass chimneys, so she left them off to make things easier when the time came, the torch and jar of oil still sitting right there waiting.

Her thin black skirt was spread over the dirt floor like a beach towel and she sat on it with her legs hugged to her chest, her chin rested on her knees. Her skin was covered with goosebumps and she was shivering cold, having stripped down to her underwear so that she'd be ready to run. She wouldn't take the chance of getting tangled up again, tripping and falling because of her own stupid clothes.

All her life she'd been fast. She'd never had a long stride, but that hadn't stopped her from embarrassing every boy in her class at a footrace all the way up into high school. There was something about that place her mind went after the first mile or two, how thoughts gave way to an empty space governed solely by body and breath. She could run for days through these mountains, and as soon as she had her chance, she would.

Suddenly a sound at the door stole her breath. Her eyes opened terrified and she listened with an instinct-driven alertness because she wasn't sure if she'd really heard a noise or was starting to lose her mind. There was a heavy bang outside the door like metal breaking free and she jumped to her feet, snatching up the torch she'd made and lighting the end from the oil lamp's flame into a tall fire that whipped about the rafters and filled the room in amber light.

Her hands were shaking when she grabbed the Ball jar she'd filled with lamp oil, and the oil spilled over the rim and greased her fingers. The door started to open and the light outside was blindingly white. Dwayne Brewer manifested out of sunlight as her eyes adjusted to the brightness. Rushing forward, hissing through her teeth, she saw this look of absolute confusion spread over his face as she threw the oil onto him like she was pitching a cup of water into the yard. The lamp oil splashed his chest and soaked his shirt and Angie jabbed the torch at his stomach trying to light him on fire.

There was too much distance between them. Dwayne drove into the room, loping furiously forward. The smell of fuel drenched him like cologne and Angie swung the torch back and forth frenziedly, finally flinging the fire in a last-ditch effort before he reached her. The flames caught the top of his jeans and the fire roared up his chest and arm. He was engulfed, whirling his arm in violent circles and wrestling his shirt over his head. Angie shot for the opened doorway and he traced her arm as she passed. Tearing outside, she ran as fast as her legs would take her.

The air was unseasonably warm and birdsong filled the leafless trees. She glanced around, flustered, not recognizing where she was or having any idea which direction to go. Hillsides rose steeply to each side with outcrops of stone mounting jagged from dark soil, moss and bracken breaking the gray-brown deadness with evergreen. Trees towered high overhead and crosshatched a cloudless sky. There was no obvious trail to discern. Everything looked the same. She ran straight ahead with thin vines snaring her arms and legs like jute twine, briars clawing deep into her skin as she searched for an opening but found none.

Up ahead, she heard water and soon she was upon it, plodding downstream using the creek bed for her path. The stream was shockingly cold and the free stone bottom shifted beneath her steps. Her right ankle rolled hard and a bolt of pain fired up her leg. The water was so clear that judging the depth of her next step became impossible. She plunged into a pool where current wrapped her knees, then stumbled forward, bashing her legs on the rocks. Angie could hear something coming fast behind her, but she didn't look back. She picked herself up and kept going forward, stumbling now, her shins and knees hot with pain. The banks steepened at the sides into a deep gulley and soon the creek was loud. Water poured over a staircase of blackened boulders slick as glass. There was no way into the valley from here.

Dirt crumbled under her feet as she tried to scale the bank and seized a handful of long-stemmed ferns, trying to claw herself out of the bottom, but their thin roots pulled free. Slipping onto her stomach, she fought with everything in her power to get up the side of that bank, but the land was too steep and the dirt was too soft and there was nothing to grab on to, and that fast he had her. She felt hands clamp on to her ankles like bear traps, and as she looked over her shoulder there he was, Dwayne Brewer shirtless and crazed with burns spread red over his chest, arms, and neck like rash.

He yanked Angie down the bank and scrambled over her body, straddling her chest as she felt something slam into the side of her head like a meteor. Her vision flashed silver and returned in a stupefied blur. Her legs were covered with dirt and the air smelled of loam and moss and it filled her nose with a jarring sort of sweetness when the next blow came. Her head felt empty and she went out for a moment, all of her movements sluggish so that the next fist came without any resistance at all, hammering into her cheekbone. A firework flash of color filled her eyes, ears ringing, a split second of hot-white pain followed by absolute darkness.

THIRTY-FIVE

WHEN HE HAD HER BACK IN THE CELLAR, HE LAID HER ON
the floor, pulling her arms behind her, and cinching her wrists with
a zip tie behind a pitched support worn smooth by time. He did not
bother to bind her feet or to tape her mouth.

As soon as Dwayne caught her, he'd wanted desperately to rip
that knife back and forth across her neck till he hit bone. There was
a feeling of betrayal, a feeling he couldn't reconcile because he'd
had no reason to trust her in the first place. What stopped him
from killing her was that she was the last chip he had and the final
hand had not been dealt. At any moment the law could show and
she'd be his ticket out of there. The time had come to run. This was
the hour to gather his brother and leave this place forever.

Standing over Sissy's body, Dwayne studied what was left of him.
Carol's eyes were empty sockets, his mouth open in a wide, peculiar
smile just as perfect as ever, white teeth so even and straight they

looked like they'd been filed and polished. Scarecrow clothes fit loosely over a body shriveled down into nothing. Lime-dusted skin almost black in such light, the hide of his arms draping his bones like wet fabric. Studying his brother's face, Dwayne felt a mourning and regret that filled him with a revelatory desolation. He reached down and traced his fingers against the side of Carol's head and his brother's hair floated away from his scalp like stirred dust. Leaning down, Dwayne closed his eyes and kissed his brother's forehead.

"We're going to get out of here, now," he said. "Me and you, Sissy. Just like it's always been. Just me and you."

Dwayne shoveled his arms under his brother's body, one arm under his legs and one arm under his back. There was no weight to him now, and as he lifted, Carol's skin ripped apart like paper, the stained yellow bones of his arms finding light as they dangled under him. There was something wet and waxy against Dwayne's skin and he glowered in deep contemplation at what he held and how it crumbled. Carol's head was rocked back at an unnatural angle. His mouth drooped open, teeth startling white against black skin. The weight of Carol's boots were too heavy for what was left of him and his right foot broke away from his body, the boot landing on its side in the dust. The sight of this was the straw that broke him.

Carefully, he lowered his brother back to the ground. There was no way to carry Carol's body from this place without loading the pieces of him into some other vessel. He knelt there with his hands on his thighs, rocking back and forth, his eyes wide and empty. All that he loved had dissolved in his arms and the world was now void.

"'Why art thou so far from helping me, and from the words of my roaring?'" Dwayne whispered, the words little more than breath. "All my life," he said. "All my life You have forsaken me."

THIRTY-SIX

WHEN SHE WOKE, ANGIE COULD BARELY OPEN HER LEFT eye, her vision a muddled streak of colors and light blurred like frosted glass. Her head throbbed, every heartbeat a sledgehammer against her temples. She could tell that the side of her face was swollen and bruised.

The ground was cold against her bare legs. The heavy iron door was open and she could see outside into the woods. A strip of sunlight crossed the dirt floor and warmed her feet. She heard footsteps and in a second there he was standing over her like a tombstone. His figure was a dark silhouette backlit by the open door and it took a second to see him in any sort of detail.

Dwayne Brewer wore a pair of dirtied blue jeans, the fronts heavily stained and the knees muddied with dirt. He was barefoot and shirtless, the burns stretching from his stomach to his chest, climbing his neck and wrapping over his jaw. A faded tattoo was inked on his left breast. She glanced down and saw that he was holding a butcher knife loosely in his right hand. Her reflection shone in the face of the steel.

"Please," she whimpered. "Please, just let me go."

Dwayne shuffled forward with his feet on either side of her body, and when he was standing directly over her, he dropped to his knees with his legs straddled over her thighs like a saddle. The two were face-to-face. He took the blade and poked the knifepoint straight into her forehead. Angie's head rocked back until her crown was flush against whatever stood behind. He held the knife there like a needle prick and she felt a drop of blood run cold the length of her nose then fall to her chest.

"All I wanted was my brother," Dwayne said. "That's all I wanted." He pulled the knife back and swiped its tip against his pants. "You couldn't let me have that. You couldn't let me have one thing."

"I'm sorry," she said. "Please, just let me go."

"You're exactly like the rest of them," he said. "I didn't think you were, but you are. You look at people like me, and think you're better than I am. Well, I've got news for you. You're no better. You, Calvin, and Darl, the whole lot of us. 'A worthless person, a wicked man, goes about with crooked speech, winks with his eyes, signals with his feet, points with his finger, with perverted heart devises evil, continually sowing discord; therefore calamity will come upon him suddenly; in a moment he will be broken beyond healing.' You know that verse?"

Angie shook her head. "I'm sorry," she said again. She kept repeating those two words with every breath she took.

"That's Proverbs," Dwayne said. He placed his hand flat on her thigh, ran his palm up her leg, and hooked one finger under the hip of her underwear. Angie flinched, disgusted he could touch her.

"Please, please," she said. "I'm with child."

Dwayne's face shriveled with repulsion.

"I'm carrying a child," Angie said. "Please, just let me go. I have a baby."

"I don't consider it any sort of blessing to bring a child into a world like this."

Angie wept. "But I have a child. I have a child." That one thing was all she knew now, the only truth she held. The child. There was nothing outside of that.

He rose and hovered over her. "I've got to run back to the house," he said. "But I want you to think about what that verse means, what the last part of that verse is saying. *'Broken beyond healing.'*"

Dwayne didn't say another word. He simply turned and walked into the light. In a moment, he was gone, and the only sounds were those of birds and of Angie whimpering softly on the floor.

THIRTY-SEVEN

IT TOOK CALVIN HOOPER ALL OF FIVE MINUTES TO FIND Dwayne Brewer's address using an online property finder provided on the county's website. In the age of the Internet, a man could find anybody he wanted with little effort at all.

When Sheriff John Coggins stomped into the jail that morning shaking his head, he said he had no idea what had gone on the night before aside from a chicken-brained clusterfuck left on his desk like a lunch sack stuffed with shit. Calvin rushed out of the Justice Center and called one of the men who worked for him, a Hispanic named Miguel who could skin a tomato with a trackhoe blade. Miguel didn't ask any questions. He gave Calvin a ride to his truck and Calvin went home only long enough to grab the .45-70, throw the brush gun in the cab, and head back to town.

A dozen NO TRESPASSING signs marked the head of Dwayne Brewer's driveway, but Calvin eased past and motored on around the next bend. The road was cut into a hillside strangled by kudzu on both sides. He parked the truck in a shallow pull-off carved where dead vines lay over the ground like mats of tangled gray hair. A groundhog stood tall and watched him from a mound of red clay that marked its burrow in the kudzu patch. Calvin grabbed the gun and headed back the way he'd come.

He didn't know if Dwayne Brewer had made it home or not. All he knew for certain was that Dwayne had tromped out of the cell-block a good hour before the sheriff cut him loose. Either way Dwayne had a head start and odds were he was already home, but if he wasn't and he came up the road and saw Calvin's truck sitting in the ditch, there'd be no chance for surprise and that's why Calvin had driven past and parked up the road.

Tall jack pines stood on both sides of the driveway, the gravel washed-out and rutted with deep red-clay veins. A deer skull was screwed into one of the pines at the mouth of the road, a young cowhorn with thin green moss staining patches of milk-white bone. Calvin pushed into the woods to follow the driveway. Thick under-growth strangled the forest floor the way it did everywhere in the mountains anymore, the hills no longer allowed to burn the way they would naturally so that briar and shrub grew almost impene-trable. He used the short barrel of the lever action to push his way through blackberry bramble and honeysuckle vine along the right side of the drive. Darl's rifle was made for country like this, for a quick swing in thick cover when black bear and hog decided to charge. Thorns scratched at Calvin's arms and beggar's lice specked his clothes, but soon enough he was close.

When he could see the house through the trees, Calvin knelt to the ground and peered through a veil of saplings and brushwood. The trees were loud with birds and the whipping sound of a pileated woodpecker flapping heavy through the forest on wide-set wings. The weather had turned funny, a cold front coming in and bringing on fall a month ahead of schedule and now an Indian summer the last of October when the leaves were already gone. The sun beat hot against his back, the dark camouflage shirt he'd thrown on soaking up the heat. He sat still and quiet waiting for any movement, any sound from the house, but nothing came. When he was sure no one was outside, he climbed the hillside for a better vantage.

The house sat in the bottom of a shallow bowl, the land rising on all sides but the front. Calvin crept up the slope in a wide arc above the home. A tall, craggy-barked locust had fallen downhill with its base ripping the ground into a vertical barricade of mud and gnarled white roots. He could see the house clearly from here and decided to use the deadfall as a sort of ground blind to scout the property. The front yard was open, no windows on this side of the house, and a brown painted tin shed stood at the back of the property along the edge of the yard.

For a long time, nothing stirred except small, gray juncos flicking around the bushes and boomer squirrels racing back and forth from the pines. Calvin was antsy to move, already fearing the worst, but then he heard the sound of something coming through the woods on the opposite hill. Leaning around the roots, he saw a man coming through the trees. The man looked naked from such distance but as he came into the yard, Calvin could see that Dwayne Brewer had no shirt or shoes, a light pair of denim jeans being the only thing he wore.

There were only seventy-five, maybe a hundred yards between them, Calvin never having been a good judge of distance. He shouldered the Marlin rifle, rested his cheek on its gray laminate stock, and used the roots to brace his aim, to center the target through ghost ring sights. Easing the lever forward and back, he chambered a 300-grain Beartooth with little more than a dull click. There was something in Dwayne's hand, maybe a knife or a machete, but from such distance he couldn't be certain. Calvin's heart raced, his palms sweaty. He followed Dwayne with the sights to where he disappeared behind the house. A few seconds later, Dwayne emerged in the backyard and headed to the shed at the back of the property.

The metal door clanked and banged as Dwayne wrestled his way inside. Calvin couldn't see him once he went into the building and at that moment he was overcome with how ill prepared he was for this, how there was no way to know what lay ahead. Dwayne came back out with a camouflage tarp folded under his arm, a coil of rope in one hand, the knife held with its point to the ground. He headed back the same way he'd come and Calvin knew he must've been holding Angie somewhere off in the woods, that that's why the deputies hadn't been able to find her when they raided the house. When Dwayne came into the front yard, Calvin had the rifle pointed at the sky, struggling with his free hand to get his cell phone out of his pocket. He found the number and dialed, keeping his eyes on Dwayne as he headed back into the trees. The phone rang and no one answered and in a second it cut to voicemail.

"Pick up the phone," he muttered under his breath as he hung up and dialed again. "Pick up your fucking phone."

The line kept ringing and then he heard someone answer.

"Hello."

"I know where he's got her," Calvin said. "She's in the woods. He has her back in the woods behind his house."

"Who is this?"

"Listen to me, Michael. He's got her off in the woods somewhere behind his house. He's going there right now."

"Calvin?"

"Yes, goddamn it. You need to listen to me. Dwayne Brewer has her in the woods. I just watched him come out of there and now he's going back and I'm going after him. You need to get up here right now. Get up here to his house right now."

"Calvin, you need to slow down and tell me what you're talking about. Tell—"

"Get up here, Michael. He's got her in the woods behind his house. Do you hear me? I don't have time to keep saying it. Get up here now. She's in the woods and I'm going after them. When I find her, I'm going to do what I should've done in the beginning, Michael. I'm going to blow his fucking brains out."

Calvin hung up the phone without waiting for a response. Dwayne was already almost out of sight. He knew if he waited any longer he wouldn't catch up, that a man could lose track of what he was chasing in a hurry in these mountains and never see it again. Things had a tendency to disappear like ghosts in this place, into the trees, over the ridge, then gone.

He stumbled down the hill and hunched low as he crossed the yard trying to move fast but stealthily. The leaves crackled under his steps and he weaved through a maze of saplings standing thin as river cane. The hillside rose steep ahead and Dwayne had already crossed the horizon. *This is the end,* Calvin thought. *This is where it all ends. Right on the other side of those trees. Just over that hill.*

THIRTY-EIGHT

HALFWAY BACK TO HIS GRANDFATHER'S CELLAR, DWAYNE Brewer knew he was being followed. At first it was a gut feeling, a sort of paranoia that stopped him in his tracks and he knelt and waited and listened.

The mountains had a way of concealing sound so that something right over the ridge might as well be in another world. But the opposite was true as well. Inside a cove, every sound was cupped and amplified like it was being held inside a jar. That's how he knew someone was coming. Soon as they topped the ridge and started down the other side, the sound of footsteps rushing through leaves came to him like a voice.

He hid behind a giant tulip poplar and when he saw who trailed him he felt all of the blood in his body flush his face. His head was on fire, a fury spinning his mind thoughtless. The brown canvas pants and camouflage T-shirt Calvin Hooper wore blended into the hillside, but Dwayne could see him just fine, just as he could see the rifle Calvin carried. The 1911 would've felt so good in his hand right then, but the law had taken everything so that now he was left with only the knife he carried.

There was no way he could get his brother's body out of here now, and that thought packed dynamite inside him, knowing he'd have to leave Carol behind. He'd gone back to the house for a tarp and rope to gather the pieces. Every choice held consequence. Every step he'd ever taken in his entire life had led right to this.

Fate's a funny thing, he thought, the way things might seem meaningless at the time, but wind up being what brought down a man's whole life. There was so much hatred in his heart, so much disgust for how he'd never had the cards to play out a single hand. There had always been two choices: a man could lie there and take it, or he could grab whoever was closest and squeeze the life out of them so that he wasn't alone in his suffering. That choice had always been easy and his decision was no different now.

Dwayne set the rope and tarp at his feet, because he would no longer need them. Turning back to his path, he ran through the woods like an animal, barefoot and wild, the knife he carried gutting the air before him. Jagged sticks and stone shards stabbed the soles of his feet as he ran and he hobbled through the pain until he found the place his grandfather'd built.

He stood there out of breath for a moment, his chest heaving for air. Inside, he hovered over his brother's body, fully aware that he would likely never see him again. He was fixated on Carol's teeth, that smile so perfect and straight, his mouth open so that Dwayne could see every groove and ridge of his top molars, a sound accompanying that image as it settled inside him, the sound of his brother laughing. Carol had always had this goofy sort of laugh, the kind that made others join whether they were in on the joke or not. Dwayne's mind was consumed by that smile. He could see his brother on the other side of the room, that dish towel tied around his waist like an apron, hear him saying, "You got to let them cool," those mud pies lined out, those teeth spread wide and white. The thought of never seeing that again was too much to bear and he reached down and pinched one of Sissy's front teeth between his fingers. He wiggled the tooth back and forth and it slid free with little effort at all, its long yellow root like a fang cupped in the palm of his hand. He slipped that first tooth into his jeans and reached for the next. Those that pulled easily were taken, those that hung were left, and with his hand in his pocket he rattled the teeth like dice as he turned away.

The sun was on its descent and now found an angle that shined directly through the open door so that Angie's face was lit by blinding spotlight. She was crying, her breath stuttering from her lips. Her legs twisted and kicked at the dirt floor. Her body wove back and forth and her head rocked, all of her movements slowed and beaten, and she muttered the same few words in different order as if repeating them over and over might will them to be so. "Just let me go. Let me go. Please. I have a child. Let me go. I have a child. Please. Just let me go."

Kneeling behind her, he clenched a fistful of her hair and yanked the crown of her head into the post at her back. He nosed forward and whispered in her ear. "You remember what I told you. 'In a moment he will be broken beyond healing,'" Dwayne said. "Well, that time has come. He's coming, darling. Calvin's right out there in those woods, and the two of us are going to meet him."

Dwayne twisted her hair around his hand as if he were winding cordage, and when it was coiled he clamped as tight as he could.

Her skull tapped against the post and he glanced down to where her wrists were bound and slipped the knife into the crease between her arms. When she was free, he stood slowly. Her head remained flush against the post, her shoulders and back arching there, too, as she tiptoed upright. He eased the blade to her throat, serrated teeth gumming at her neck, then pulled her into him, letting go of her hair, and wrapping one arm tight around her chest.

"If you try to run, if you try anything at all, I'll yank this knife back and forth across your throat like a goddamned ripsaw. You understand me? I won't stop till I hit bone. You understand?"

He felt Angie's head nodding against his chest. "Yes," she said. "I understand."

"You think about that baby in your belly. Don't you think about nothing else. You hear me? Nothing else. Now, walk."

Dwayne took a step forward and Angie's feet faltered beneath her. They tripped those first few steps, each struggling to learn the other's timing, an awkward waltz where neither led nor followed. The world was blindingly white outside, a light shining with an intensity he'd never seen in all his life, and for a moment Dwayne held there in the open mouth of the cellar, not quite sure what to make of it. He hugged her tight to his chest and Angie's hands clasped on to his forearm, as if she would fall from some tremendous height if she let go.

All his life the world had seemed so exposed, like anything could be had if a man were willing to take it, the gate open and the road broad. But suddenly he had a strange feeling like it had closed in, like it had narrowed down into a cavernous place he could barely squeeze through and there was only one way out.

"Calvin," she whispered. "Calvin."

Dwayne glanced up and there he stood with his rifle shouldered, his eyes glaring down the length of the barrel. Calvin's teeth showed and there was a strange sound coming out of him, his teeth clacking, as Dwayne and Angie walked straight toward him. The woods were filled with a luminous sort of gleaming, jewel-like in the way the trees and branches shone, a light casting them glass.

"I'm leaving now, Calvin," Dwayne said as he turned and backed into afternoon sun. "You do something stupid and you'll lose the last of it. Think about that. Look at what you've lost and look right here in my arms at what you'll lose."

Calvin floated there in front of the root cellar, his knees half bent, his shoulders sagging like he was on the verge of collapse. Stumbling backward, Dwayne could feel the air opening around him and he knew where he had to go. *Just a little ways farther,* he thought. *I'm almost there.*

THIRTY-NINE

CALVIN COULDN'T LOOK AWAY FROM ANGIE'S EYES, THE WAY those eyes were begging him to save her, begging him to make everything okay. Her cheeks were red from weeping, her blond hair silken in the light. Bare legs streaked with mud, her knees were bruised and bloodied, but those emerald eyes seemed almost prayerful, like she was praying to him, like everything rested solely in his hands.

Angie braced tightly to Dwayne's arm and he held the knife's edge against her throat, her head tilted up like she was trying to keep her nose above water. Sweat streamed down Calvin's face and he kept opening his hands and clenching them tight on the rifle. His fingers were dead, sweat stinging his eyes as he glared down the sights. A voice in the back of his head kept saying, *Just shoot him. Shoot him, Calvin.* The top of her head didn't reach Dwayne's collarbones, but he'd never been a good shot and all he could think was how he'd fuck it up like everything else, how he'd pull the trigger and miss.

"How long you think you can follow me?" Dwayne said. He was taking long strides backward through the woods, the two of them no more than twenty feet apart.

"I'm not going anywhere."

"But I am, my friend. I am going somewhere. And we're getting close to the point where we part ways. Pretty soon you're going to have a decision to make."

The dirtied jeans Dwayne wore hooked under his heels as he back-stepped barefoot through the trees. His pale skin was dark with hair except a bright red stain over part of his chest and covering the arm he used to hold her. The mark was raised and blistered like he might've been burned. His face was this clean-shaven juxtaposition to the rest of his body, with eyes that seemed to hold the very end of the world. Reaching back into those hollowed eyes, Calvin could see there was nothing inside him. It was foolish to follow, to take a man like Dwayne Brewer on his word.

They ascended a gradual slope broken with post oak and poplar. Rusted leaves crackled under their steps and a flurry of tulip poplar seeds whirled down around them as wind bowed the treetops. It was one of those days where warm air rolled up from the gulf, the wind carrying the smell of saltwater six hundred miles from ocean to mountain. Off to the right, Calvin spotted an outcrop of boulders and he thought, *If I can back him into those rocks, I can force his hand.*

Calvin quickened his pace and rounded Dwayne to push him, and Dwayne seemed confused for a second as he turned, staring at Calvin like he was trying to read his tell. Dwayne trod carefully so that he never gave angle to his back. He kept Angie hugged to his chest, that knife pressed so hard into her neck that her skin lapped the edge. Peeking over his shoulder, he seemed to see where Calvin was forcing him and he sidestepped quickly, Angie's feet dragging the ground, but Calvin cut him off.

Soon Dwayne was backed against the boulders. Fallen leaves had blown against the outcrop in knee-high drifts, dark stone splotched with olive-gray patches of lichen. Dwayne tried to rush to his right but she was a burden to him now, and Calvin headed him off with the rifle, pulling the trigger, that .45-70 blew apart the mountains like a stick of dynamite.

His ears wailed and he racked the lever. Smoking brass ejected to his right as another cartridge rode forward. A wide circle was blown into the rock to the left of Dwayne's head, the stone opened white to quartz and feldspar.

"You're going to force me to do something I didn't want to do, Calvin," Dwayne yelled, all of their heads ringing. "When I cut her throat, that's on your hands."

"You're not leaving here with her."

"That's where you're mistaken." Dwayne shook his head and smiled. "You're getting awfully brave staring down the barrel of that rifle, but you're not thinking clearly. God be the man with the gun, but not today. Not this time. Not when you know what I'll do just to see the shattered look on your face."

"Calvin, please," Angie stuttered. "Please, just put the gun down."

"She's making good sense, Calvin. You put that gun down."

"Let her go."

"I let her go and you'll shoot me where I stand."

"No, he won't," she said. "He won't shoot you. Will you? Put the gun down, Calvin. Put it down."

"You ever think the three of us were meant to be right here, that all our lives we've been headed right here to this place, that it's fate? It's fate that brought us here."

"Shut your mouth, Dwayne."

"What if I told you I was a prophet?"

"I said shut your fucking—"

"What if I told you I was sent to teach you something, Calvin, that that's all the meaning my life ever had?"

Angie was sobbing, her eyes like glass, her breath sputtering from her lips.

"This is exactly how it was supposed to end," Dwayne said. "Every one of us fighting to hold on to what we love most, one no better than the other."

Calvin watched him but didn't speak.

"This is the only way it could have ended, ain't it? We've all been headed right here all along. All our lives. Every step we ever took brought us right here. Can you see that? Can you see that, Calvin?"

"You're out of your fucking mind."

"I'm no more out of my mind than you are, friend." He stretched his eyes wide and stared long into him, a look Calvin Hooper could feel boring through him.

"We're nothing alike," he said.

"You can't see it yet," Dwayne said.

"I can see fine."

"What I've taught you is all that there is, friend. It's everything."

"You haven't taught me a goddamn thing." His cheek was hot against the buttstock of the rifle and he could see his breath fogging and fading from the stainless receiver.

"That's where you're wrong," Dwayne said. "I think I've taught you the most valuable lesson in the entire world. For whom are you willing to lay down your life? Till a man knows that, he doesn't know anything. 'For men shall be lovers of their own selves, covetous, boasters, proud, blasphemers, disobedient, unthankful, unholy, without natural affection, trucebreakers, false accusers, incontinent, fierce, despisers of those that are good, traitors, heady, high-minded, lovers of pleasures more than lovers of God.' For whom are you willing to lay down your life, friend? Outside of that there is nothing."

"Shut the fuck up, Dwayne!"

"That's the reason all of us are here. That's the reason, but the difference is you took mine. You took everything I love. I watched it slip away like water through my fingers. You stole the only thing I loved in this world." Dwayne looked for a second like he was about to break, but then his brow lowered and he showed his teeth like an angered dog. He growled loudly as if in pain. "But that's okay. I can see that now. It's okay," he said. "Maybe it all had to be piled on me. Maybe I'm the only one on this goddamned earth could take it. And maybe that's what had to happen for your eyes to be opened. We're exactly the same, me and you."

"I'm nothing like you. Now, let her go. It's over."

Dwayne took a single step backward, his bare back pressed against the stone. He watched the sky and closed his eyes, took a few deep breaths, and a smile spread over his face. "You still can't see it," he said. "You still can't see it and it's right in front of your eyes. It's the reason we're gathered here. The only reason we're here is because of the ones we loved. That's the line that held us. I would've done anything in this world to keep my brother from en-during the slightest suffering. I would've given my life if I were asked. The reason you're here, Calvin Hooper, is because of this woman in my arms, and the reason she fought like hell is because of that little baby inside her. Are you so blind you can't see?"

Calvin didn't think he'd heard Dwayne clearly. He thought he'd misunderstood. But those words settled into him like he was being filled full of sand, weighing him down and holding him motionless. Confusion bent his face and he twisted his cheek against the rifle, staring hard into Angie's eyes. "Is it true?" he tried to say, but those three words fell silent, no air to breathe them over his tongue, so that she had to read what he was trying to say on his lips.

"Yes," she whispered. She was crying and there seemed to be little else inside her but that word. Her head rocked against Dwayne's chest. "Yes," she said.

Dwayne Brewer lowered his face to the side of her head and spoke as if he were telling her a secret. "He didn't know?"

"No," she said. Her head was shaking and she was blubbering hysterically. "No."

"What a strange, strange world, how a man ends up where he does," Dwayne said. "Sometimes it's his own doing, but most the time, most the time, it's like we're led along like starved dogs."

"Let her go." Calvin's voice was weak now, absolutely broken. He could feel his knees buckling beneath him, his legs about to dissolve. "I've already called the law, Dwayne. I called and they're on their way. They'll be here in a matter of minutes." He hesitated, his brain flooded with emotion. "You're not leaving here with her."

"I wish you hadn't done that," Dwayne said. "There was never any need for anyone outside of me and you. This was between us, friend. Just us. And I really wish you wouldn't have made me do this."

"Put the gun down, Calvin," Angie squealed. He could see Dwayne's arm tightening around her, the knife pressing harder into her throat. "For God's sake, put the gun down."

"I never wanted to hurt her," Dwayne said. "I never wanted anything to do with the lot of you. All I wanted was what you took." There was a deep and furious anger kindling on his words. "All I wanted was one thing, one thing, and I could've gotten by, but even that *you* took."

"Let her go," Calvin pleaded. "Just let her go."

There was something inexplicable in what Dwayne Brewer said next. It was as if he weren't talking to anyone there.

"All my life I've been begging You for mercy and not a day has it come. Not one day. Now I'm asking once more, and after this I'm done. I'll never ask You again," Dwayne said. "Now this is how it's going to play out if you want this baby to live, Calvin. I want you to walk right over there by that dogwood and sit that rifle down."

"Let her go." Calvin could tell that Dwayne was coming apart at the seams, and that instability scared him to death.

"Please, Calvin." Angie wept. "Just do what he says."

"I've asked you twice and that only leaves once more," Dwayne said. "You need to think about what you stand to lose, friend. Your load is heavy and my burden light. I cut her throat and everything you love is gone."

"You hurt her and I'll shoot you dead you son of a bitch."

"And I'll welcome that moment like company, friend," Dwayne said. His words were soft and calm.

"Put the gun down," Angie whispered. Calvin looked at her eyes, those eyes begging for salvation, begging him for something man was not meant to provide.

"I told you all along your time would come," Dwayne said.

"Do it, Calvin. For God's sake, just do what—"

"Are you willing to lay down your life for the ones you love?" Dwayne cut Angie's words short. "Are you willing to lay that rifle down and let me kill you to save her, to save the child she carries?"

"What?" Calvin's mind was whirling.

"It's simple," Dwayne said. "Are you willing to die for the ones you love?"

Calvin watched Angie's face flush white. Off from where they'd come, he could hear voices echoing in the distance and he knew the law would soon be upon them.

"Make up your mind, friend. One of you is not leaving this place today and only you can decide. If they reach us, it's over. You're the only one who can decide whether it's you or her."

Calvin had the rifle aimed at the bridge of Dwayne's nose, but he lowered his eyes to the ground. From her feet, he followed her legs upward settling on her stomach, imagining an entire life stretched before him. The swimming of his thoughts stifled the sounds around him. In that moment, his mind cut from madness to absolute certainty. There was no balancing between what it would be like to live without her and what it would be like to die. It was as easy a decision as he'd ever made in his life.

Without a word, he dropped his left hand from the foregrip, his right still bearing the rifle as he lifted the barrel to the sky. Backing toward the crooked dogwood, its bark scaled like snakeskin, he laid the rifle on the ground, held his hands at his chest with his palms open before him.

"Now get back over there where you were," Dwayne said. He neither lowered the knife nor lessened its pressure.

"Okay," Calvin said. "Okay." He sidestepped and Dwayne moved toward the rifle.

When he reached the dogwood, Dwayne shoved Angie forward and she crumbled loosely to the ground. There was no breath in

Calvin's lungs as Dwayne shouldered the rifle, settled his cheek against the stock, and took his aim. He came forward and soon enough the muzzle was within feet. Calvin lowered his head and stared at the ground, the place he would fall. *This is it*, he thought. *This is where it ends.* He gritted his teeth and closed his eyes trying to imagine what would come, death the greatest question of all.

"Raise your head," Dwayne said.

Calvin lifted his eyes to Angie. She was curled on the ground wailing and beating her fists bloody against the earth. She screamed his name at the top of her lungs but he heard nothing. He met Dwayne's eyes only for a moment, looking upward until there was only sky, cloudless and blue, the last of light filtering in from somewhere off to his left.

"Now can you see it?" Dwayne asked.

"Yes," Calvin said, and he could. He could see that there was a single, magnificent truth holding this world together. "Yes, I can see it."

"And isn't it beautiful," Dwayne said. "Isn't it the most beautiful thing you've ever seen?"

Calvin closed his eyes. He waited for the hammer to fall, the explosion of sound and light, the everything and the empty. Years passed in that waiting. Lifetimes. And though he was certain he was near, he would wait like all the rest for that great question to be answered, for when he opened his eyes and followed the sky down to where Dwayne had stood, he was gone, the woods empty, the devil having disappeared as if he'd never existed at all. Over the western horizon, the sun rode low on the ridge, a dull sunset so ordinary and unspectacular he would likely never remember. The voices neared, footsteps now loud in the cove.

Calvin fell to his knees and crawled to her. He wrapped his arms around her and held on to Angie as tight as he could, their bodies melding into a singular beating thing. His mind spun too fast for thought, his heart as wild as a panther's. He knew what it was to need and what it was to have plenty.

She was all there ever was.

FORTY

THAT LAST DAY OF OCTOBER, DWAYNE BREWER DROVE
through town at sunset, blue lights screaming past like meteors.
Steam bellowed from the smokestacks of the paper mill, white roiling into dull yellow sky, and he watched that place disappear in his
rearview like everything else before.

Passing Harold's Grocery headed into Dillsboro, he saw hundreds of birds filling the sky, a cloud of buzzards shifting on thermals, their wings tilting back and forth to steady their wide-set
whirling. He leaned low against the steering wheel to watch them
as he crossed the bridge over Scotts Creek. He wondered if they
would follow him, if they would always follow, and his heart knew
the answer, that their work lies all where and their wings tire not.

Through the windshield, empty flea markets and dimly lit filling
stations blurred by in his periphery. He rode past fields separated

from the highway only by thin tree lines, yellowed fields of oat grass and sedge where old barns crumbled in on themselves like gray ash. The highway was empty once he passed Bryson City, the dark shadows of mountains closing in, the night now fully upon him.

Fontana Lake opened over a bridge that crossed the Little Tennessee where it slowed through the narrows into stilled slack water. A few miles farther, the highway split one way into the gorge, the other toward Almond, and he followed the northwest fork along Fingerlake and over the mouth of the Nantahala.

He wasn't sure what to do with the car. His instinct said siphon the gas and douse the Grand Prix with fuel, plug the tank with a gasoline-soaked rag, and burn Carol's car to the ground. In such darkness, the fire would be seen for miles, drawing the law like moths, tall flames whipping at the sky, black smoke only serving to veil the starlight. He thought then of sinking the car in the water, the stilled surface gurgling a story until it stilled again. There were so many things buried here, entire towns, like Judson, flooded and forgotten, that he could not bear the thought of adding a single ghost. In the end, he simply pulled into a ditch near Fontana Village, rolled the window up on a white rag to make it seem as if he'd broken down and traveled on.

Dwayne backtracked two miles to the marina, slinking along the edge of the woods with Darl Moody's rifle stretched across his shoulders, his arms draped over the gun like a scarecrow. When he reached the water, a green tin roof covered the rental complex, the red glow of a Coke machine all that offered light. The dock stretched forth lined on both sides by pontoon boats, and from the shadows, he watched the place for a long time before he moved. The marina had been abandoned for season. The tourists and part-timers willing to fork over hundreds of dollars to rent a boat for an afternoon had already left and gone.

Canoes lined the end of the dock with their gunwales resting on sun-bleached planks, their hulls facing the sky. Dwayne flipped one of the canoes and balanced the keel against the edge of the dock to ease the boat into water. He found a paddle stood against the wall by the snack bar, the rolling counter door pulled down and padlocked for winter, and when he loaded all that he had into the canoe, he pushed out from the dock and cast his eyes over the water.

That night, Dwayne Brewer paddled across the sky. Each stroke dipped into the heavens, the stars vibrating on the water's surface like the strings of an instrument strummed by his gentle passing. He paddled four miles over the next few hours, recognizing the cove by a long strip of land that cut into Fontana like a dagger. He paddled past Cable Branch and Laurel Branch, tiny trickles of water heard rather than seen, then farther back to Proctor, where he beached the canoe on a shoreline muddied with clay. There at the edge of the woods his mind finally caught him and he leaned against the trunk of a dying hemlock thinking about all that had brought him there.

All his life he'd only known one answer to suffering, but that long-held truth had given way to something new. There in those woods with that knife held to Angie Moss's neck, he'd thought of his brother, thought of all that he'd lost, and that pain festered into a familiar feeling, a rage he could feel at the backs of his eyes. He wanted so desperately to kill her. He wanted to see that horrified, broken look sink across Calvin Hooper's bloodless face. He wanted someone else to suffer so that he wasn't alone, so that for once they were all the same, one no better than the next. With that gun in his hand, he was certain it would be so satisfying to kill him. His finger was nearing the trigger's break and it was almost euphoric. Right at that moment of reckoning, there was a feeling that came into him like molten lead, like he was being poured full, his insides searing with heat. He felt hands clasp on to his shoulders and all thought escaped him and he could hear a voice, a voice that did not speak in any language he'd ever heard though he immediately knew the meaning of what was spoken and did not question.

Let it go, the voice said. *All of it. Let it go.*

Dwayne sat against that hemlock all night watching the water, his body shivering cold, his heart a burning fire. The night gave way to morning, the stars drawing back and drawing back as darkness surrendered to light. A tangerine sun blushed the sky with a hue so breathtakingly beautiful that he was moved to tears. All that he'd carried all of his life rained from his eyes and soaked into the ground. Sunrise singed trees crimson, lit the lake the color of blood. The word dwelled there amongst him and he wept until he was weightless as dust blown to air.

Right then he knew both everything and nothing.

His mind was wiped clean as a child's and the former was passed away.

A HARD FROST bit the beautiful that spring, yellowed the willows the color of mustard and robbed the redbuds their bloom. But soon enough the temperatures rose and Dwayne Brewer was thankful.

The winter had been trying and many nights he believed he would freeze. He made shelter inside an earthen cavern carved beneath great boulders by water and time. When he arrived, he had nothing aside from a pair of jeans and a rifle. No shoes. No shirt. No food. Those first few weeks he broke into nearby cabins to scavenge clothes, rummaging through the dressers and closets of retirees, seldom finding anything that fit. A small general store by the marina kept beer and groceries, brightly colored tourist T-shirts with black bears and sunsets covering the front, the words VISIT THE SMOKIES stitched across the chest.

This morning he wore a pair of thin, pleated dress pants that had belonged to a man who was wider than he was tall. Dwayne cinched the brown trousers tight at his waist with his belt, unstitched the cuffs to give an extra inch though they still hit him mid-shin. He'd cut the ends out of a grass-stained pair of white leather Stride Rites, his toes hanging over the fronts, the cotton tube socks he wore were black and damp where they touched the ground. Only the middle letters of the word FONTANA shone on the turquoise T-shirt, a woman's navy blue trench coat buttoned tight around him. The coat fit him crudely, only the bottom button finding room to close. He was far too broad, so that the shoulder pads made sharp ridges between his neck and arms, the fabric about to pop. All that he wore was dirtied with soil, the colors darkened to earthen tones that blended against the mountainside. His hair was long and hot beneath his toboggan, his beard hanging down to his chest.

Winters were hard to survive as plants died back to nothing and a man was left to hunt small game for meals. But now the world was blooming and soon he'd have plenty: ramps and branch lettuce, maypops and chicken of the woods, dandelion greens and pokeweed, wild strawberries, blackberries, blueberries, huckleberries, muscadine, purslane and chicory, fiddlehead ferns and yellowroot. He walked a hillside covered with white trillium and mayapple that had yet to flower, the lobed leaves circling the shoots like umbrellas. The trapline made an irregular oval through the cove, a series of simple deadfalls and squirrel poles, tiny snares strung from fisherman's string. Most often he found chipmunks crushed under the stones, though when he was lucky, squirrels and rabbits fell prey.

Up ahead, Dwayne could see a robin thrashing about the ground, its tiny leg snared, its wings beating madly beside a young poplar thin as a cane. He sped toward the bird in great loping strides because sometimes things didn't hold, sometimes what was right in front of a man's eyes got away from him. Setting Darl Moody's rifle on the ground, he closed his hands around the robin's body, only the head showing from the top of his fist. He looked at its eyes, those black seed eyes outlined by white, the dark gray feathers of its head and sharp goldenrod beak. In an instant, he plucked the bird's head off like he was pulling a grape from a vine and set the body on the ground, its wings flapping hard, legs pulled inward, movements slowing, slowing, then stilled. He plucked orange feathers from skin, tore the breast free, and ate the tiny gob of flesh raw in a single bite, his fingers stained red and sticky with blood.

At the stream, he balanced the rifle against a tangle of exposed roots, cupped handfuls of water to his mouth and drank, wiping his beard with the back of his hand. He held his hands in the water, the creek ice-cold and clear as crystal. A school of small, olive-backed minnows darted about his fingers. The water held in an eddy and he could see his reflection and he stared at himself for a long time, barely recognizing what had become of him. He scrubbed his hands in the water to wash the blood, and as the surface sloshed about, his reflection muddled into glare and light. A tiger swallowtail landed on his knee, its papery wings swaying softly open and closed. The butterfly sipped water from the wetted fabric of his trousers then lifted and fluttered downstream.

A fleck of color caught his eye and Dwayne turned. Rising from the black soil, a single pink lady's slipper had bloomed early, its thistle-colored flower hanging from a thin green stem like a human heart. He strolled over and knelt beside it, tracing a petal with the tip of his finger, something so delicate and soft his callused skin could not feel. *This world is awash with miracles,* he thought. *How marvelous to simply bear witness.*

Crouched at the top of a knoll overlooking Possum Hollow, he could see down into the cove where a trail followed the stream and continued on around to the lakeshore. A pair of hikers, a young man and woman, had made primitive camp at the edge of the trail beside a thick copse of laurel. Their pale gray dome tent rose from the ground like a boulder. Their packs were leaned against a log. Dwayne had heard them the night before, could hear them laughing, and see the glow of their fire haloing the top of the hill. He knelt behind a fallen tree. The bark was gone and the wood was stained a deep rotted brown. They were cooking breakfast and the smell of it traveled between them, the sweet smoky smell of streaked meat sizzling in cast iron on the coals.

He braced the rifle against the trunk of the fallen tree and watched them through the sights. The hammer was back, the safety thumbed away. The woman had her palms open to the fire as if begging heat from the flames. The man was on hands and knees by circled stones, jabbing a fork at their meal, flipping their breakfast so that it would not burn. With the barrel balanced on the tree, Dwayne bore the rifle's weight solely with his right hand. He scratched the ridges along the front of the trigger with his fingernail. He had his left hand in the pocket of his pants and he was rolling his brother's teeth through his palm, Sissy's smile ticking in his hand like a fistful of marbles.

Dwayne Brewer wanted desperately to go down that hillside and tell them the good news. He wanted them to hold out their hands and he'd gift them the grace of God. There was mercy in the passing of strangers, in what watched from hillsides like ghosts, in the savage running barefoot through the soil. But the hearts of men were hardened things, their eyes not meant for seeing. So few were ready to live forever.

Not yet, sweet Lord, not yet.

ACKNOWLEDGMENTS

To Ezra for letting me dig holes, build fence, chase chickens, and run from rams with Irish names. To his dog, Kephart, for riding in my pickup and smiling at the madness. To Leigh Ann Henion for hanging paper targets. To Ashley for letting me hole up in the farmhouse while the story took hold and loving me while I was in a world outside our own. To our dog, Charlie, for showing me squirrels and rabbits and field grass and groundhog holes and sunsets and moonlight and everything else that makes dogs like us lives worth living. To the man at Quail Ridge Books who asked about grace, and Ray McManus, the red-dirt Jesus. And, most important, to my agent, Julia Kenny, my editor, Sara Minnich, and the entire team at Putnam, without whom my work would remain in a drawer.

DAVID JOY

"Joy's love and respect for language is clear through beautiful, gritty prose."

—*The Huffington Post*

For a complete list of titles,
please visit prh.com/DavidJoy